The yellowbacks... classics of popular fiction

The yellowjackets or yellowbacks were a great series of bestselling adventure and crime thrillers that had its origins in the mid to late 19th century following on from the 'penny dreadfuls'. They virtually began the mass market revolution of the early 20th century with a clear standard format and imprint/series livery (what would today be called branding). Hodder & Stoughton published the yellowjackets in two main series with series run dates of: 1923-1939 and later 1949-1957.

As the tagline ('where thrillers really began') on the back cover implies, the imprint and series focused on thrillers that were the bestsellers of their time. This current reissue or retro revival if you will, brings back many of these masterpieces, now classics in their own way and extends it further by including key titles from that period that were either great crime or thriller or even general commercial fiction (including sub-genres of noir, horror, gothic, romance, westerns, etc.) influences of their time. There are some perennial favourites and many rarities either lost or not easily available being revived in the current series. Writers and characters ranged from adventure heroes like Bulldog Drummond, Allan Quatermain, Richard Hannay or the Saint through thriller grandmasters Edgar Wallace and E. Phillips Oppenheim, crime and mystery maestros like Patricia Wentworth, GK Chesterton, Agatha Christie and the Detection club, to western and swashbucklers like Zane Grey, Max Brand, Captain Blood and even romance or general fiction classics like Hermina Black, Denise Robins, Marie Corelli or Stella Morton. These were books that had storytelling at their heart and always entertained.

The yellowbacks had both hardback (with varying design elements) and paperback (which built the series look) versions with the latter still carrying the imprint 'yellowjacket'. The current reissues pay tribute to both and use an amalgam of elements from both editions while retaining the complete yellow (or 'mustard-plaster') livery with the author's name in blue beveled type with a 'simulated emboss' effect and a white outer 'outline', and the book title in black. These reissues retain the distinctive size of the original mass market paperback and follow the three main category variations—the thrillers (crime, westerns, mystery, adventure) had blue lettering for the author's name, while Romance and softer general fiction had red; and other categories like humour had green.

For more detail and a full list of titles visit https://www.hachetteindia.com/home/yellowbacks

THE GOLDEN TRIANGLE:
THE RETURN OF ARSÈNE LUPIN

THE GOLDEN TRIANGLE: THE RETURN OF ARSÈNE LUPIN

Maurice Marie Émile Leblanc was a French novelist and writer of short stories, known primarily as the creator of the gentleman burglar, adventurer and detective Arsène Lupin, often described as a French counterpart to Arthur Conan Doyle's Sherlock Holmes and E.W. Hornung's Raffles.

Refusing the career that his father had set up for him at a card factory, Leblanc instead went to Paris in 1888, to pursue writing as a journalist. But he soon turned novelist and storyteller. His first novel, *Une femme (A Woman),* published in 1893 was a success and was followed by other works, such as *Des couples (The Couples), Voici des ailes (Here are Wings)* and a play *La pitié,* released in 1902, which was a flop. In 1905, Pierre Lafitte, the director of the monthly *Je sais tout,* commissioned a short story from Leblanc, with the brief that he was to combine the appeal of A.J Raffles by Ernest William Hornung and Sherlock Holmes. The result was 'L'Arrestationd'Arsène Lupin' ('The Arrest of Arsène Lupin') which was a huge success. Two years later, *Arsène Lupin, Gentleman Burglar* was released, and the rest was history – with one of the most successful series being born.

THE GOLDEN TRIANGLE: THE RETURN OF ARSÈNE LUPIN

Maurice Leblanc

HODDER AND STOUGHTON
YELLOW JACKET
hachette

The Golden Triangle: The Return of Arsène Lupin
First published in 1918.

This Hodder Yellowback edition © Hachette India 2023
(Registered Name: Hachette Book Publishing India Pvt. Ltd.)
An Hachette UK Company www.hachetteindia.com

1

The texts in these editions in most cases have been reprinted as is, with minimal editorial changes and by and large no bowdlerizing for political correctness; though in some editions, a few words and phrases considered archaic, or those considered offensive now, along with archaic punctuation may have been modified in places to make the text more accessible to today's readers. The narratives, language, beliefs, social mores and/or cultural depictions, in these volumes are a reflection of their times and must be viewed as such. They may also contain certain cultural, racial and gender prejudices and stereotypes that may be outdated or clearly wrong then and wrong today; but their removal would be tantamount to claiming these prejudices never existed. The Publisher does not endorse or support those depictions or stereotypes; and these books have been made available for a discerning audience that will read it for entertainment value and a chronicle/record of popular fiction of past times.

Cover design by Priya Singh adapted from the original classic yellowjacket by Hodder & Stoughton.

Cover illustration by Ishan Trivedi.

Series note: Some of the books in the series (unless otherwise credited) may have cover or inside illustrations from the original yellowbacks or early editions, and while full restoration has been attempted, some images may be grainy or faded due to the condition of the original material. The end notes or bonus material or blurb details may have been sourced from the public domain or free use publications such as Wikipedia and attribution is hereby made also allowing similar free use reproduction from here. Sources requiring further specific attribution may write in and further detailing and/or corrections shall be made in subsequent printings/editions.

Reprint specifications may be subject to change including but not limited to finishes, paper, colour sections.

ISBN: 978-93-5731-217-2

Hachette Book Publishing India Pvt. Ltd.
4th & 5th Floors, Corporate Centre,
Plot No. 94, Sector 44, Gurugram - 122 003, India

Typeset in Electra LT STD 10/12.5 pt by Manipal Technologies Limited, Manipal

Printed and bound in India by Manipal Technologies Limited, Manipal

MIX
Paper from responsible sources
FSC™ C043100

CONTENTS

1

CORALIE

It was close upon half-past six and the evening shadows were growing denser when two soldiers reached the little space, planted with trees, opposite the Musée Galliéra, where the Rue de Chaillot and the Rue Pierre-Charron meet. One wore an infantryman's sky-blue great-coat; the other, a Senegalese, those clothes of undyed wool, with baggy breeches and a belted jacket, in which the Zouaves and the native African troops have been dressed since the war. One of them had lost his right leg, the other his left arm.

They walked round the open space, in the centre of which stands a fine group of Silenus figures, and stopped. The infantryman threw away his cigarette. The Senegalese picked it up, took a few quick puffs at it, put it out by squeezing it between his fore-finger and thumb and stuffed it into his pocket. All this without a word.

Almost at the same time two more soldiers came out of the Rue Galliéra. It would have been impossible to say to what branch they belonged, for their military attire was composed of the most incongruous civilian garments. However, one of them sported a Zouave's *chechia*, the other an artilleryman's *képi*. The first walked on crutches, the other on two sticks. These two kept near the newspaper-kiosk which stands at the edge of the pavement.

Three others came singly by the Rue Pierre-Charron, the Rue Brignoles and the Rue de Chaillot: a one-armed rifleman, a limping sapper and a marine with a hip that looked as if it was twisted. Each of them made straight for a tree and leant against it.

Not a word was uttered among them. None of the seven crippled soldiers seemed to know his companions or to trouble about or even perceive their presence. They stood behind their trees or behind the kiosk or behind the group of Silenus figures without stirring. And the few wayfarers who, on that evening of the 3rd of April, 1915, crossed this unfrequented square, which received hardly any light from the shrouded street-lamps, did not slacken pace to observe the men's motionless outlines.

A clock struck half-past six. At that moment the door of one of the houses overlooking the square opened. A man came out, closed the door behind him, crossed the Rue de Chaillot and walked round the open space in front of the museum. It was an officer in khaki. Under his red forage-cap, with its three lines of gold braid, his head was wrapped in a wide linen bandage, which hid his forehead and neck. He was tall and very slenderly built. His right leg ended in a wooden stump with a rubber foot to it. He leant on a stick.

Leaving the square, he stepped into the roadway of the Rue Pierre-Charron. Here he turned and gave a leisurely look to his surroundings on every side. This minute inspection brought him to one of the trees facing the museum. With the tip of his cane he gently tapped a protruding stomach. The stomach pulled itself in.

The officer moved off again. This time he went definitely down the Rue Pierre-Charron towards the centre of Paris. He thus came to the Avenue des Champs-Élysées, which he went up, taking the left pavement.

Two hundred yards further on was a large house, which had been transformed, as a flag proclaimed, into a hospital. The officer took up his position at some distance, so as not to be seen by those leaving, and waited.

It struck a quarter to seven and seven o'clock. A few more minutes passed. Five persons came out of the house, followed by two more. At last a lady appeared in the hall, a nurse wearing a wide blue cloak marked with the Red Cross.

"Here she comes," said the officer.

She took the road by which he had arrived and turned down the Rue Pierre-Charron, keeping to the right-hand pavement and thus making for the space where the street meets the Rue de Chaillot. Her walk was light, her step easy and well-balanced. The wind, buffeting against her as she moved quickly on her way, swelled out the long blue veil floating around her shoulders. Notwithstanding the width of the cloak, the rhythmical swing of her body and the youthfulness of her figure were revealed. The officer kept behind her and walked along with an absent-minded air, twirling his stick, like a man taking an aimless stroll.

At this moment there was nobody in sight, in that part of the street, except him and her. But, just after she had crossed the Avenue Marceau and some time before he reached it, a motor standing in the avenue started driving in the same direction as the nurse, at a fixed distance from her.

It was a taxi-cab. And the officer noticed two things: first, that there were two men inside it and, next, that one of them leant out of the window almost the whole time, talking to the driver. He was able to catch a momentary glimpse of this man's face, cut in half by a heavy moustache and surmounted by a grey felt hat.

Meanwhile, the nurse walked on without turning round. The officer had crossed the street and now hurried his pace, the more so as it struck him that the cab was also increasing its speed as the girl drew near the space in front of the museum.

From where he was the officer could take in almost the whole of the little square at a glance; and, however sharply he looked, he discerned nothing in the darkness that revealed the presence of the seven crippled men. No one, moreover, was passing on foot or driving. In the distance only, in the dusk of the wide crossing avenues, two tram-cars, with lowered blinds, disturbed the silence.

Nor did the girl, presuming that she was paying attention to the sights of the street, appear to see anything to alarm her. She gave not the least sign of hesitation. And the behaviour of the motor-cab following her did not seem to strike her either, for she did not look round once.

The cab, however, was gaining ground. When it neared the square, it was ten or fifteen yards, at most, from the nurse; and, by the time that she, still noticing nothing, had reached the first trees, it came closer yet and, leaving the middle of the road, began to hug the pavement, while, on the side opposite the pavement, the left-hand side, the man who kept leaning out had opened the door and was now standing on the step.

The officer crossed the street once more, briskly, without fear of being seen, so heedless did the two men now appear of anything but their immediate business. He raised a whistle to his lips. There was no doubt that the expected event was about to take place.

The cab, in fact, pulled up suddenly. The two men leapt from the doors on either side and rushed to the pavement of the square, a few yards from the kiosk. At the same moment there was a cry of terror from the girl and a shrill whistle from the officer. And, also at the same time, the two men caught up and seized their victim and dragged her towards the cab, while the seven wounded soldiers, seeming to spring from the very trunks of the trees that hid them, fell upon the two aggressors.

The battle did not last long. Or rather there was no battle. At the outset the driver of the taxi, perceiving that the attack was being countered, made off and drove away as fast as he could. As for the two men, realizing that their enterprise had failed and finding themselves faced with a threatening array of uplifted sticks and crutches, not to mention the barrel of a revolver which the officer pointed at them, they let go the girl, tacked from side to side, to prevent the officer from taking aim, and disappeared in the darkness of the Rue Brignoles.

"Run for all you're worth, Ya-Bon," said the officer to the one-armed Senegalese, "and bring me back one of them by the scruff" of the neck!"

He supported the girl with his arm. She was trembling all over and seemed ready to faint.

"Don't be frightened, Little Mother Coralie," he said, very anxiously. "It's I, Captain Belval, Patrice Belval."

"Ah, it's you, captain!" she stammered.

"Yes; all your friends have gathered round to defend you, all your old patients from the hospital, whom I found in the convalescent home."

"Thank you. Thank you." And she added, in a quivering voice, "The others? Those two men?"

"Run away. Ya-Bon's gone after them."

"But what did they want with me? And what miracle brought you all here?"

"We'll talk about that later, Little Mother Coralie. Let's speak of you first. Where am I to take you? Don't you think you'd better come in here with me, until you've recovered and taken a little rest?"

Assisted by one of the soldiers, he helped her gently to the house which he himself had left three-quarters of an hour before. The girl let him do as he pleased. They all entered an apartment on the ground-floor and went into the drawing-room, where a bright fire of logs was burning. He switched on the electric light:

"Sit down," he said.

She dropped into a chair; and the captain at once gave his orders:

"You, Poulard, go and fetch a glass in the dining-room. And you, Ribrac, draw a jug of cold water in the kitchen... Chatelain, you'll find a decanter of rum in the pantry... Or, stay, she doesn't like rum... Then..."

"Then," she said, smiling, "just a glass of water, please."

Her cheeks, which were naturally pale, recovered a little of their warmth. The blood flowed back to her lips; and the smile on her face was full of confidence. Her face, all charm and gentleness, had a pure outline, features almost too delicate, a fair complexion and the ingenuous expression of a wondering child that looks on life with eyes always wide open. And all this, which was dainty and exquisite, nevertheless at certain moments gave an impression of energy, due no doubt to her shining, dark eyes and to the line of smooth, black hair that came down on either side from under the white cap in which her forehead was imprisoned.

"Aha!" cried the captain, gaily, when she had drunk the water. "You're feeling better, I think, eh, Little Mother Coralie?"

"Much better."

"Capital. But that was a bad minute we went through just now! What an adventure! We shall have to talk it all over and get some light on it, sha'n't we? Meanwhile, my lads, pay your respects to Little Mother Coralie. Eh, my fine fellows, who would have thought, when she was coddling you and patting your pillows for your fat pates to sink into, that one day we should be taking care of her and that the children would be coddling their little mother?"

They all pressed round her, the one-armed and the one-legged, the crippled and the sick, all glad to see her. And she shook hands with them affectionately:

"Well, Ribrac, how's that leg of yours?"

"I don't feel it any longer, Little Mother Coralie."

"And you, Vatinel? That wound in your shoulder?"

"Not a sign of it, Little Mother Coralie."

"And you, Poulard? And you, Jorisse?"

Her emotion increased at seeing them again, the men whom she called her children. And Patrice Belval exclaimed:

"Ah, Little Mother Coralie, now you're crying! Little mother, little mother, that's how you captured all our hearts. When we were trying our hardest not to call out, on our bed of pain, we used to see your eyes filling with great tears. Little Mother Coralie was weeping over her children. Then we clenched our teeth still firmer."

"And I used to cry still more," she said, "just because you were afraid of hurting me."

"And today you're at it again. No, you are too soft-hearted! You love us. We love you. There's nothing to cry about in that. Come, Little Mother Coralie, a smile... And, I say, here's Ya-Bon coming; and Ya-Bon always laughs."

She rose suddenly:

"Do you think he can have overtaken one of the two men?"

"Do I think so? I told Ya-Bon to bring one back by the neck. He won't fail. I'm only afraid of one thing..."

They had gone towards the hall. The Senegalese was already on the steps. With his right hand he was clutching the neck of a man, of a limp rag, rather, which he seemed to be carrying at arm's length, like a dancing-doll.

"Drop him," said the captain.

Ya-Bon loosened his fingers. The man fell on the flags in the hall.

"That's what I feared," muttered the officer. "Ya-Bon has only his right hand; but, when that hand holds anyone by the throat, it's a miracle if it doesn't strangle him. The Boches know something about it."

Ya-Bon was a sort of colossus, the colour of gleaming coal, with a woolly head and a few curly hairs on his chin, with an empty sleeve fastened to his left shoulder and two medals pinned to his jacket. Ya-Bon had had one cheek, one side of his jaw, half his mouth and the whole of his palate smashed by a splinter of shell. The other half of that mouth was split to the ear in a laugh which never seemed to cease and which was all the more surprising because the wounded portion of the face, patched up as best it could be and covered with a grafted skin, remained impassive.

Moreover, Ya-Bon had lost his power of speech. The most that he could do was to emit a sequence of indistinct grunts in which his nickname of Ya-Bon was everlastingly repeated.

He uttered it once more with a satisfied air, glancing by turns at his master and his victim, like a good sporting-dog standing over the bird which he has retrieved.

"Good," said the officer. "But, next time, go to work more gently."

He bent over the man, felt his heart and, on seeing that he had only fainted, asked the nurse:

"Do you know him?"

"No," she said.

"Are you sure? Have you never seen that head anywhere?"

It was a very big head, with black hair, plastered down with grease, and a thick beard. The man's clothes, which were of darkblue serge and well-cut, showed him to be in easy circumstances.

"Never... never," the girl declared.

Captain Belval searched the man's pockets. They contained no papers.

"Very well," he said, rising to his feet, "we will wait till he wakes up and question him then. Ya-Bon, tie up his arms and legs and stay here, in the hall. The rest of you fellows, go back to the home: it's time you were indoors. I have my key. Say Goodbye to Little Mother Coralie and trot off."

And, when Goodbye had been said, he pushed them outside, came back to the nurse, led her into the drawing-room and said:

"Now let's talk, Little Mother Coralie. First of all, before we try to explain things, listen to me. It won't take long."

They were sitting before the merrily blazing fire. Patrice Belval slipped a hassock under Little Mother Coralie's feet, put out a light that seemed to worry her and, when he felt certain that she was comfortable, began:

"As you know, Little Mother Coralie, I left the hospital a week ago and am staying on the Boulevard Maillot, at Neuilly, in the home reserved for the convalescent patients of the hospital. I sleep there at night and have my wounds dressed in the morning. The rest of the time I spend in loafing: I stroll about, lunch and dine where the mood takes me and go and call on my friends. Well, this morning I was waiting for one of them in a big café-restaurant on the boulevard, when I overheard the end of a conversation... But I must tell you that the place is divided into two by a partition standing about six feet high, with the customers of the café on one side and those of the restaurant on the other. I was all by myself in the restaurant; and the two men, who had their backs turned to me and who in any case were out of sight, probably thought that there was no one there at all, for they were speaking rather louder than they need have done, considering the sentences which I overheard... and which I afterwards wrote down in my little notebook."

He took the notebook from his pocket and went on:

"These sentences, which caught my attention for reasons which you will understand presently, were preceded by some others in which there was a reference to sparks, to a shower of sparks that had already occurred twice before the war, a sort of night signal for the possible repetition of which they proposed to watch, so that they might act quickly as soon as it appeared. Does none of this tell you anything?"

"No. Why?"

"You shall see. By the way, I forgot to tell you that the two were talking English, quite correctly, but with an accent which assured me that neither of them was an Englishman. Here is what they said, faithfully translated: 'To finish up, therefore,' said one, 'everything is decided. You and he will be at the appointed place at a little before seven this evening.' 'We shall be there, colonel. We have engaged our taxi.' 'Good. Remember that the little woman leaves her hospital at seven o'clock.' 'Have no fear. There can't be any mistake, because she always goes the same way, down the Rue Pierre-Charron.' 'And your whole plan is settled?' 'In every particular. The thing will happen in the square at the end of the Rue de Chaillot. Even granting that there may be people about, they will have no time to rescue her, for we shall act too quickly.' 'Are you certain of your driver?' 'I' am certain that we shall pay him enough to secure his obedience. That's all we want.' 'Capital. I'll wait for you at the place you know of, in a motor-car. You'll hand the little woman over to me. From that moment, we shall be masters of the situation.' 'And you of the little woman, colonel, which isn't bad for you, for she's deucedly pretty.' 'Deucedly, as you say. I've known her a long time by sight; and, upon my word... 'The two began to laugh coarsely and called for their bill. I at once got up and went to the door on the boulevard, but only one of them came out by that door, a man with a big drooping moustache and a grey felt hat. The other had left by the door in the street round the corner. There was only one taxi in the road. The man took it and I had to give up all hope of following him. Only... only, as I knew that you left the hospital at seven o'clock every evening and that you went along the Rue Pierre-Charron, I was justified, wasn't I, in believing...?"

The captain stopped. The girl reflected, with a thoughtful air. Presently she asked:

"Why didn't you warn me?"

"Warn you!" he exclaimed. "And, if, after all, it wasn't you? Why alarm you? And, if, on the other hand, it was you, why put you on your guard? After the attempt had failed, your enemies would have laid another trap for you; and we, not knowing of it, would have been unable to prevent it. No, the best thing was to accept the fight. I enrolled a little band of your former patients who were being treated at the home; and, as the friend whom I was expecting to meet happened to live in the square, here, in this house, I asked him to place his rooms at my disposal from six to nine o'clock. That's what I did, Little Mother Coralie. And now that you know as much as I do, what do you think of it?"

She gave him her hand:

"I think you have saved me from an unknown danger that looks like a very great one; and I thank you."

"No, no," he said, "I can accept no thanks. I was so glad to have succeeded! What I want to know is your opinion of the business itself?"

Without a second's hesitation, she replied:

"I have none. Not a word, not an incident, in all that you have told me, suggests the least idea to me."

"You have no enemies, to your knowledge?"

"Personally, no."

"What about that man to whom your two assailants were to hand you over and who says that he knows you?"

"Doesn't every woman," she said, with a slight blush, "come across men who pursue her more or less openly? I can't tell who it is."

The captain was silent for a while and then went on:

"When all is said, our only hope of clearing up the matter lies in questioning our prisoner. If he refuses to answer, I shall hand him over to the police, who will know how to get to the bottom of the business."

The girl gave a start:

"The police?"

"Well, of course. What would you have me do with the fellow? He doesn't belong to me. He belongs to the police."

"No, no, no!" she exclaimed, excitedly. "Not on any account! What, have my life gone into?... Have to appear before the magistrate?... Have my name mixed up in all this?..."

"And yet, Little Mother Coralie, I can't..."

"Oh, I beg, I beseech you, as my friend, find some way out of it, but don't have me talked about! I don't want to be talked about!"

The captain looked at her, somewhat surprised to see her in such a state of agitation, and said:

"You sha'n't be talked about, Little Mother Coralie, I promise you."

"Then what will you do with that man?"

"Well," he said, with a laugh, "I shall begin by asking him politely if he will condescend to answer my questions; then thank him for his civil behaviour to you; and lastly beg him to be good enough to go away."

He rose:

"Do you wish to see him, Little Mother Coralie?"

"No," she said, "I am so tired! If you don't want me, question him by yourself. You can tell me about it afterwards..."

She seemed quite exhausted by all this fresh excitement and strain, added to all those which already rendered her life as a nurse so hard. The captain did not insist and went out, closing the door of the drawing-room after him.

She heard him saying:

"Well, Ya-Bon, have you kept a good watch! No news? And how's your prisoner?... Ah, there you are, my fine fellow! Have you got your breath back? Oh, I know Ya-Bon's hand is a bit heavy!... What's this? Won't you answer?... Hallo, what's happened? Hanged if I don't think..."

A cry escaped him. The girl ran to the hall. She met the captain, who tried to bar her way.

"Don't come," he said, in great agitation. "What's the use!"

"But you're hurt!" she exclaimed.

"I?"

"There's blood on your shirt-cuff."

"So there is, but it's nothing: it's the man's blood that must have stained me."

"Then he was wounded?"

"Yes, or at least his mouth was bleeding. Some blood-vessel..."

"Why, surely Ya-Bon didn't grip as hard as that?"

"It wasn't Ya-Bon."

"Then who was it?"

"His accomplices."

"Did they come back?"

"Yes; and they've strangled him."

"But it's not possible!"

She pushed by and went towards the prisoner. He did not move. His face had the pallor of death. Round his neck was a red-silk string, twisted very thin and with a buckle at either end.

2

RIGHT HAND AND LEFT LEG

"One rogue less in the world, Little Mother Coralie!" cried Patrice Belval, after he had led the girl back to the drawing-room and made a rapid investigation with Ya-Bon. "Remember his name—I found it engraved on his watch—Mustapha Rovalaïof, the name of a rogue!"

He spoke gaily, with no emotion in his voice, and continued, as he walked up and down the room:

"You and I, Little Mother Coralie, who have witnessed so many tragedies and seen so many good fellows die, need not waste tears over the death of Mustapha Rovalaïof or his murder by his accomplices. Not even a funeral oration, eh? Ya-Bon has taken him under his arm, waited until the square was clear and carried him to the Rue Brignoles, with orders to fling the gentleman over the railings into the garden of the Musée Galliéra. The railings are high. But Ya-Bon's right hand knows no obstacles. And so, Little Mother Coralie, the matter is buried. You won't be talked about; and, this time, I claim a word of thanks."

He stopped to laugh:

"A word of thanks, but no compliments. By Jove, I don't make much of a warder! It was clever the way those beggars snatched my prisoner. Why didn't I foresee that your other assailant, the man in the grey-felt hat, would go and tell the third, who was waiting in his motor, and that they would both come back together to rescue their companion? And they came back. And, while you and I were chatting, they must have forced the servants' entrance, passed through the kitchen, come to the little door between the pantry and the hall and pushed it open. There, close by them, lay their man, still unconscious and firmly bound, on his sofa. What were they to do? It was impossible to get him out of the hall without alarming Ya-Bon. And yet, if they didn't release him, he would speak, give away his accomplices and ruin a carefully prepared plan. So one of the two must have leant forward stealthily, put out his arm, thrown his string round that throat which Ya-Bon had already handled pretty roughly, gathered the buckles at the two ends and pulled, pulled, quietly, until death came. Not a sound. Not a sigh. The whole operation performed in silence. We come, we kill and we go away. Good-night. The trick is done and our friend won't talk."

Captain Belval's merriment increased:

"Our friend won't talk," he repeated, "and the police, when they find his body tomorrow morning inside a railed garden, won't understand a word of the business. Nor we either, Little Mother Coralie; and we shall never know why those men tried to kidnap you. It's only too true! I may not be up to much as a warder, but I'm beneath contempt as a detective!"

He continued to walk up and down the room. The fact that his leg or rather his calf had been amputated seemed hardly to inconvenience him; and, as the joints of the knee and thighbone had retained their mobility, there was at most a certain want of rhythm in the action of his hips and shoulders. Moreover, his tall figure tended to correct this lameness, which was reduced to insignificant proportions by the ease of his movements and the indifference with which he appeared to accept it.

He had an open countenance, rather dark in colour, burnt by the sun and tanned by the weather, with an expression that was frank, cheerful and often bantering. He must have been between twenty-eight and thirty. His manner suggested that of the officers of the First Empire, to whom their life in camp imparted a special air which they subsequently brought into the ladies' drawing-rooms.

He stopped to look at Coralie, whose shapely profile stood out against the gleams from the fireplace. Then he came and sat beside her:

"I know nothing about you," he said softly. "At the hospital the doctors and nurses call you Madame Coralie. Your patients prefer to say Little Mother. What is your married or your maiden name? Have you a husband or are you a widow? Where do you live? Nobody knows. You arrive every day at the same time and you go away by the same street. Sometimes an old serving-man, with long grey hair and a bristly beard, with a comforter round his neck and a pair of yellow spectacles on his nose, brings you or fetches you. Sometimes also he waits for you, always sitting on the same chair in the covered yard. He has been asked questions, but he never gives an answer. I know only one thing, therefore, about you, which is that you are adorably good and kind and that you are also—I may say it, may I not?—adorably beautiful. And it is perhaps, Little Mother Coralie, because I know nothing about your life that I imagine it so mysterious, and, in some way, so sad. You give the impression of living amid sorrow and anxiety; the feeling that you are all alone. There is no one who devotes himself to making you happy and taking care of you. So I thought—I have long thought and waited for an opportunity of telling you—I thought that you must need a friend, a brother, who would advise and protect you. Am I not right, Little Mother Coralie?"

As he went on, Coralie seemed to shrink into herself and to place a greater distance between them, as though she did not wish him to penetrate those secret regions of which he spoke.

"No," she murmured, "you are mistaken. My life is quite simple. I do not need to be defended."

"You do not need to be defended!" he cried, with increasing animation. "What about those men who tried to kidnap you? That plot hatched against you? That plot which your assailants are so afraid to see discovered that they go to the length of killing the one who allowed himself to be caught? Is that nothing? Is it mere delusion on my part when I say that you are surrounded by dangers, that you have enemies who stick at nothing, that you have to be defended against their attempts and that, if you decline the offer of my assistance, I... Well, I...?"

She persisted in her silence, showed herself more and more distant, almost hostile. The officer struck the marble mantelpiece with his fist, and, bending over her, finished his sentence in a determined tone :

"Well, if you decline the offer of my assistance, I shall force it on you."

She shook her head.

"I shall force it on you," he repeated, firmly. "It is my duty and my right."

"No," she said, in an undertone.

"My absolute right," said Captain Belval, "for a reason which outweighs all the others and makes it unnecessary for me even to consult you."

"What do you mean?"

"I love you."

He brought out the words plainly, not like a lover venturing on a timid declaration, but like a man proud of the sentiment that he feels and happy to proclaim it.

She lowered her eyes and blushed; and he cried, exultantly:

"You can take it, Little Mother, from me. No impassioned outbursts, no sighs, no waving of the arms, no clapping of the hands. Just three little words, which I tell you without going on my knees. And it's the easier for me because you know it.

Yes, Madame Coralie, it's all very well to look so shy, but you know my love for you and you've known it as long as I have. We saw it together take birth when your dear little hands touched my battered head. The others used to torture me. With you, it was nothing but caresses. So was the pity in your eyes and the tears that fell because I was in pain. But can anyone see you without loving you? Your seven patients who were here just now are all in love with you, Little Mother Coralie. Ya-Bon worships the ground you walk on. Only they are privates. They cannot speak. I am an officer; and I speak without hesitation or embarrassment, believe me."

Coralie had put her hands to her burning cheeks and sat silent, bending forward.

"You understand what I mean, don't you," he went on, in a voice that rang, "when I say that I speak without hesitation or embarrassment? If I had been before the war what I am now, a maimed man, I should not have had the same assurance and I should have declared my love for you humbly and begged your pardon for my boldness. But now!... Believe me, Little Mother Coralie, when I sit here face to face with the woman I adore, I do not think of my infirmity. Not for a moment do I feel the impression that I can appear ridiculous or presumptuous in your eyes."

He stopped, as though to take breath, and then, rising, went on:

"And it must needs be so. People will have to understand that those who have been maimed in this war do not look upon themselves as outcasts, lame ducks, or lepers, but as absolutely normal men. Yes, normal! One leg short? What about it? Does that rob a man of his brain or heart? Then, because the war has deprived me of a leg, or an arm, or even both legs or both arms, I have no longer the right to love a woman save at the risk of meeting with a rebuff or imagining that she pities me? Pity! But we don't want the woman to pity us, nor to make an effort to love us, nor even to think that she is doing a charity because she treats us kindly. What we demand, from women and from the world at large, from those whom we meet in the street and from those who belong to the same set as ourselves, is absolute equality with the rest, who have been saved from our fate by their lucky stars or their cowardice."

The captain once more struck the mantelpiece:

"Yes, absolute equality! We all of us, whether we have lost a leg or an arm, whether blind in one eye or two, whether crippled or deformed, claim to be just as good, physically and morally, as anyone you please; and perhaps better. What! Shall men who have used their legs to rush upon the enemy be outdistanced in life, because they no longer have those legs, by men who have sat and warmed their toes at an office-fire? What nonsense! We want our place in the sun as well as the others. It is our due; and we shall know how to get it and keep it. There is no happiness to which we are not entitled and no work for which we are not capable with a little exercise and training. Ya-Bon's right hand is already worth any pair of hands in the wide world; and Captain Belval's left leg allows him to do his five miles an hour if he pleases."

He began to laugh:

"Right hand and left leg; left hand and right leg: what does it matter which we have saved, if we know how to use it? In what respect have we fallen off? Whether it's a question of obtaining a position or perpetuating our race, are we not as good as we were? And perhaps even better. I venture to say that the children which we shall give to the country will be just as well-built as ever, with arms and legs and the rest... not to mention a mighty legacy of pluck and spirit. That's what we claim, Little Mother Coralie. We refuse to admit that our wooden legs keep us back or that we cannot stand as upright on our crutches as on legs of flesh and bone. We do not consider that devotion to us is any sacrifice or that it's necessary to talk of heroism when a girl has the honour to marry a blind soldier! Once more, we are not creatures outside the pale. We have not fallen off in any way whatever; and this is a truth before which everybody will bow for the next two or three generations. You can understand that, in a country like France, when maimed men are to be met by the hundred thousand, the conception of what makes a perfect man will no longer be as hard and fast as it was. In the new form of humanity which is preparing, there will be men with two arms and men with only one, just as there are fair men and dark, bearded men and clean-shaven. And it will all seem quite natural. And every one will lead the life he pleases, without needing to be complete in every limb. And, as my life is wrapped up in you, Little Mother Coralie, and as my happiness depends on you, I thought I would wait no longer before making you my little speech... Well! That's finished! I have plenty more to say on the subject, but it can't all be said in a day, can it?..."

He broke off, thrown out of his stride after all by Coralie's silence. She had not stirred since the first words of love that he uttered. Her hands had sought her forehead; and her shoulders were shaking slightly.

He stooped and, with infinite gentleness, drawing aside the slender fingers, uncovered her beautiful face:

"Why are you crying, Little Mother Coralie?"

He was calling her *tu* now, but she did not mind. Between a man and the woman who has bent over his wounds relations of a special kind arise; and Captain Belval in particular had those rather familiar, but still respectful, ways at which it seems impossible to take offence.

"Have *I* made you cry?" he asked.

"No," she said, in a low voice, "it's all of you who upset me. It's your cheerfulness, your pride, your way not of submitting to fate, but mastering it. The humblest of you raises himself above his nature without an effort; and I know nothing finer or more touching than that indifference."

He sat down beside her:

"Then you're not angry with me for saying... what I said?"

"Angry with you?" she replied, pretending to mistake his meaning. "Why, every woman thinks as you do. If women, in bestowing their affection, had to choose among the men returning from the war, the choice I am sure would be in favour of those who have suffered most cruelly."

He shook his head:

"You see, I am asking for something more than affection and a more definite answer to what I said. Shall I remind you of my words?"

"No."

"Then your answer...?"

"My answer, dear friend, is that you must not speak those words again."

He put on a solemn air:

"You forbid me?"

"I do."

"In that case, I swear to say nothing more until I see you again."

"You will not see me again," she murmured.

Captain Belval was greatly amused at this:

"I say, I say! And why sha'n't I see you again, Little Mother Coralie?"

"Because I don't wish it."

"And your reason, please?"

"My reason?"

She turned her eyes to him and said, slowly:

"I am married."

Belval seemed in no way disconcerted by this news. On the contrary, he said, in the calmest of tones:

"Well, you must marry again! No doubt your husband is an old man and you do not love him. He will therefore understand that, as you have someone in love with you..."

"Don't jest, please."

He caught hold of her hand, just as she was rising to go:

"You are right, Little Mother Coralie, and I apologize for not adopting a more serious manner to speak to you of very serious things. It's a question of our two lives. I am profoundly convinced that they are moving towards each other and that you are powerless to restrain them. That is why your answer is beside the point. I ask nothing of you. I expect everything from fate. It is fate that will bring us together."

"No," she said.

"Yes," he declared, "that is how things will happen."

"It is not. They will not and shall not happen like that. You must give me your word of honour not to try to see me again nor even to learn my name. I might have granted more if you had been content to remain friends. The confession which you have made sets a barrier between us. I want nobody in my life... nobody!"

She made this declaration with a certain vehemence and at the same time tried to release her arm from his grasp. Patrice Belval resisted her efforts and said:

"You are wrong... You have no right to expose yourself to danger like this... Please reflect..."

She pushed him away. As she did so, she knocked off the mantelpiece a little bag which she had placed there. It fell on the carpet and opened. Two or three things escaped, and she picked them up, while Patrice Belval knelt down on the floor to help her:

"Here," he said, "you've missed this."

It was a little case in plaited straw, which had also come open; the beads of a rosary protruded from it.

They both stood up in silence. Captain Belval examined the rosary.

"What a curious coincidence!" he muttered. "These amethyst beads! This old-fashioned gold filigree setting!... It's strange to find the same materials and the same workmanship..."

He gave a start, and it was so marked that Coralie asked:

"Why, what's the matter?"

He was holding in his fingers a bead larger than most of the others, forming a link between the string of tens and the shorter prayer-chain. And this bead was broken half-way across, almost level with the gold setting which held it.

"The coincidence," he said, "is so inconceivable that I hardly dare... And yet the fact can be verified at once. But first, one question: who gave you this rosary?"

"Nobody gave it to me. I've always had it."

"But it must have belonged to somebody before?"

"To my mother, I suppose."

"Your mother?"

"I expect so, in the same way as the different jewels which she left me."

"Is your mother dead?"

"Yes, she died when I was four years old. I have only the vaguest recollection of her. But what has all this to do with a rosary?"

"It's because of this," he said. "Because of this amethyst bead broken in two."

He undid his jacket and took his watch from his waistcoat-pocket. It had a number of trinkets fastened to it by a little leather and silver strap. One of these trinkets consisted of the half of an amethyst bead, also broken across, also held in a filigree setting. The original size of the two beads seemed to be identical. The two amethysts were of the same colour and contained in the same filigree.

Coralie and Belval looked at each other anxiously. She stammered:

"It's only an accident, nothing else..."

"I agree," he said. "But, supposing these two halves fit each other exactly..."

"It's impossible," she said, herself frightened at the thought of the simple little act needed for the indisputable proof.

The officer, however, decided upon that act. He brought his right hand, which held the rosary-bead, and his left, which held the trinket, together. The hands hesitated, felt about and stopped. The contact was made.

The projections and indentations of the broken stones corresponded precisely. Each protruding part found a space to fit it. The two half amethysts were the two halves of the same amethyst. When joined, they formed one and the same bead.

There was a long pause, laden with excitement and mystery. Then, speaking in a low voice:

"I do not know either exactly where this trinket comes from," Captain Belval said. "Ever since I was a child, I used to see it among other things of trifling value which I kept in a cardboard box: watch-keys, old rings, old-fashioned seals. I picked out these trinkets from among them two or three years ago. Where does this one come from? I don't know. But what I do know..."

He had separated the two pieces and, examining them carefully, concluded:

"What I do know, beyond a doubt, is that the largest bead in this rosary came off one day and broke; and that the other, with its setting, went to form the trinket which I now have. You and I therefore possess the two halves of a thing which somebody else possessed twenty years ago."

He went up to her and, in the same low and rather serious voice, said:

"You protested just now when I declared my faith in destiny and my certainty that events were leading us towards each other.

Do you still deny it? For, after all, this is either an accident so extraordinary that we have no right to admit it or an actual fact which proves that our two lives have already touched in the past at some mysterious point and that they will meet again in the future, never to part. And that is why, without waiting for the perhaps distant future, I offer you today, when danger hangs over you, the support of my friendship. Observe that I am no longer speaking of love but only of friendship. Do you accept?"

She was nonplussed and so much perturbed by that miracle of the two broken amethysts, fitting each other exactly, that she appeared not to hear Belval's voice.

"Do you accept?" he repeated.

After a moment she replied:

"No."

"Then the proof which destiny has given you of its wishes does not satisfy you?" he said, good-humouredly.

"We must not see each other again," she declared.

"Very well. I will leave it to chance. It will not be for long. Meanwhile, I promise to make no effort to see you."

"Nor to find out my name?"

"Yes, I promise you."

"Goodbye," she said, giving him her hand.

'Mm *revoir,*" he answered.

She moved away. When she reached the door, she seemed to hesitate. He was standing motionless by the chimney. Once more she said:

"Goodbye."

"*Au revoir,* Little Mother Coralie."

Then she went out.

Only when the street-door had closed behind her did Captain Belval go to one of the windows. He saw Coralie passing through the trees, looking quite small in the surrounding darkness. He felt a pang at his heart. Would he ever see her again?

"Shall I? Rather!" he exclaimed. "Why, tomorrow perhaps. Am I not the favourite of the gods?"

And, taking his stick, he set off, as he said, with his wooden leg foremost.

That evening, after dining at the nearest restaurant, Captain Belval went to Neuilly. The home run in connection with the hospital was a pleasant villa on the Boulevard Maillot, looking out on the Bois de Boulogne. Discipline was not too strictly enforced. The captain could come in at any hour of the night; and the man easily obtained leave from the matron.

"Is Ya-Bon there?" he asked this lady.

"Yes, he's playing cards with his sweetheart."

"He has the right to love and be loved," he said. "Any letters for me?"

"No, only a parcel."

"From whom?"

"A commissionaire brought it and just said that it was 'for Captain Belval.' I put it in your room."

The officer went up to his bedroom on the top floor and saw the parcel, done up in paper and string, on the table. He opened it and discovered a box. The box contained a key, a large, rusty key, of a shape and manufacture that were obviously old.

What could it all mean? There was no address on the box and no mark. He presumed that there was some mistake which would come to light of itself; and he slipped the key into his pocket.

"Enough riddles for one day," he thought. "Let's go to bed."

But when he went to the window to draw the curtains he saw, across the trees of the Bois, a cascade of sparks which spread to some distance in the dense blackness of the night. And he remembered the conversation which he had overheard in the restaurant and the rain of sparks mentioned by the men who were plotting to kidnap Little Mother Coralie...

3

THE RUSTY KEY

When Patrice Belval was eight years old he was sent from Paris, where he had lived till then, to a French boarding-school in London. Here he remained for ten years. At first he used to hear from his father weekly. Then, one day, the headmaster told him that he was an orphan, that provision had been made for the cost of his education and that, on his majority, he would receive through an English solicitor his paternal inheritance, amounting to some eight thousand pounds.

Two hundred thousand francs could never be enough for a young man who soon proved himself to possess expensive tastes and who, when sent to Algeria to perform his military service, found means to run up twenty thousand francs of debts before coming into his money. He therefore started by squandering his patrimony and, having done so, settled down to work. Endowed with an active temperament and an ingenious brain, possessing no special vocation, but capable of anything that calls for initiative and resolution, full of ideas, with both the will and the knowledge to carry out an enterprise, he inspired confidence in others, found capital as he needed it and started one venture after another, including electrical schemes, the purchase of rivers and waterfalls, the organization of motor services in the colonies, of steamship lines and of mining companies. In a few years he had floated a dozen of such enterprises, all of which succeeded.

The war came to him as a wonderful adventure. He flung himself into it with heart and soul. As a sergeant in a colonial regiment, he won his lieutenant's stripes on the Marne. He was wounded in the calf on the 15th of September and had it amputated the same day. Two months after, by some mysterious wire pulling, cripple though he was, he began to go up as observer in the aeroplane of one of our best pilots. A shrapnel-shell put an end to the exploits of both heroes on the 10th of January. This time, Captain Belval, suffering from a serious wound in the head, was discharged and sent to the hospital in the Avenue des Champs- Elysees. About the same period, the lady whom he was to call Little Mother Coralie also entered the hospital as a nurse.

There he was trepanned. The operation was successful, but complications remained. He suffered a good deal of pain, though he never uttered a complaint and, in fact, with his own good-humour kept up the spirits of his companions in misfortune, all of whom were devoted to him. He made them laugh, consoled them and stimulated them with his cheeriness and his constant happy manner of facing the worst positions.

Not one of them is ever likely to forget the way in which he received a manufacturer who called to sell him a mechanical leg:

"Aha, a mechanical leg! And what for, sir? To take in people, I suppose, so that they may not notice that I've lost a bit of mine? Then you consider, sir, that it's a blemish to have your leg amputated, and that I, a French officer, ought to hide it as a disgrace?"

"Not at all, captain. Still..."

"And what's the price of that apparatus of yours?"

"Five hundred francs."

"Five hundred francs! And you think me capable of spending five hundred francs on a mechanical leg, when there are a hundred thousand poor devils who have been wounded as I have and who will have to go on showing their wooden stumps?"

The men sitting within hearing revelled with delight. Little Mother Coralie herself listened with a smile. And what would Patrice Belval not have given for a smile from Little Mother Coralie?

As he told her, he had fallen in love with her from the first, touched by her appealing beauty, her artless grace, her soft eyes, her gentle soul, which seemed to bend over the patients and to fondle them like a soothing caress. From the very first, the charm of her stole into his being and at the same time compassed it about. Her voice gave him new life. She bewitched him with the glance of her eyes and with her fragrant presence. And yet, while yielding to the empire of this love, he had an immense craving to devote himself to and to place his strength at the service of this delicate little creature, whom he felt to be surrounded with danger.

And now events were proving that he was right, the danger was taking definite shape and he had had the happiness to snatch Coralie from the grasp of her enemies. He rejoiced at the result of the first battle, but could not look upon it as over. The attacks were bound to be repeated. And even now was he not entitled to ask himself if there was not some close connection between the plot prepared against Coralie that morning and the sort of signal given by the shower of sparks? Did the two facts announced by the speakers at the restaurant not form part of the same suspicious machination?

The sparks continued to glitter in the distance. So far as Patrice Belval could judge, they came from the riverside, at some spot between two extreme points which might be the Trocadéro on the left and the Gare de Passy on the right.

"A mile or two at most, as the crow flies," he said to himself. "Why not go there? We'll soon see."

A faint light filtered through the key-hole of a door on the second floor. It was Ya-Bon's room; and the matron had told him that Ya-Bon was playing cards with his sweetheart. He walked in.

Ya-Bon was no longer playing. He had fallen asleep in an armchair, in front of the outspread cards, and on the pinned-back sleeve hanging from his left shoulder lay the head of a woman, an appallingly common head, with lips as thick as Ya-Bon's, revealing a set of black teeth, and with a yellow, greasy skin that seemed soaked in oil. It was Angèle, the kitchen-maid, Ya-Bon's sweetheart. She snored aloud.

Patrice looked at them contentedly. The sight confirmed the truth of his theories. If Ya-Bon could find someone to care for him, might not the most sadly mutilated heroes aspire likewise to all the joys of love?

He touched the Senegalese on the shoulder. Ya-Bon woke up and smiled, or rather, divining the presence of his captain, smiled even before he woke.

"I want you, Ya-Bon."

Ya-Bon uttered a grunt of pleasure and gave a push to Angèle, who fell over on the table and went on snoring.

Coming out of the house, Patrice saw no more sparks. They were hidden behind the trees. He walked along the boulevard and, to save time, went by the Ceinture railway to the Avenue Henri-Martin. Here he turned down the Rue de la Tour, which runs to Passy.

On the way he kept talking to Ya-Bon about what he had in his mind, though he well knew that the negro did not understand much of what he said. But this was a habit with him. Ya-Bon, first his comrade-in-arms and then his orderly, was as devoted to him as a dog. He had lost a limb on the same day as his officer and was wounded in the head on the same day; he believed himself destined to undergo the same experiences throughout; and he rejoiced at having been twice wounded just as he would have rejoiced at dying at the same time as Captain Belval. On his side, the captain rewarded this humble, dumb devotion by unbending genially to his companion; he treated him with an ironical and sometimes impatient humour which heightened the negro's love for him. Ya-Bon played the part of the passive confidant who is consulted without being regarded and who is made to bear the brunt of his interlocutor's hasty temper.

"What do you think of all this, Master Ya-Bon?" asked the captain, walking arm-in-arm with him. "I have an idea that it's all part of the same business. Do you think so too?"

Ya-Bon had two grunts, one of which meant yes, the other no. He grunted out:

"Yes."

"So there's no doubt about it," the officer declared, "and we must admit that Little Mother Coralie is threatened with a fresh danger. Is that so?"

"Yes," grunted Ya-Bon, who always approved, on principle.

"Very well. It now remains to be seen what that shower of sparks means. I thought for a moment that, as we had our first visit from the Zeppelins a week ago... are you listening to me?"

"Yes."

"I thought that it was a treacherous signal with a view to a second Zeppelin visit..."

"Yes."

"No, you idiot, it's not yes. How could it be a Zeppelin signal when, according to the conversation which I overheard, the signal had already been given twice before the war. Besides, is it really a signal?"

"No."

"How do you mean, no? What else could it be, you silly ass? You'd do better to hold your tongue and listen to me, all the more as you don't even know what it's all about... No more do I, for that matter, and I confess that I'm at an utter loss. Lord, it's a complicated business, and I'm not much of a hand at solving these problems."

Patrice Belval was even more perplexed when he came to the bottom of the Rue de la Tour. There were several roads in front of him, and he did not know which to take. Moreover, though he was in the middle of Passy, not a spark shone in the dark sky.

"It's finished, I expect," he said, "and we've had our trouble for nothing. It's your fault, Ya-Bon. If you hadn't made me lose precious moments in snatching you from the arms of your beloved we should have arrived in time. I admit Angèle's charms, but, after all..."

He took his bearings, feeling more and more undecided. The expedition undertaken on chance and with insufficient information was certainly yielding no results; and he was thinking of abandoning it when a closed private car came out of the Rue Franklin, from the direction of the Trocadéro, and someone inside shouted through the speaking-tube:

"Bear to the left... and then straight on, till I stop you."

Now it appeared to Captain Belval that this voice had the same foreign inflection as one of those which he had heard that morning at the restaurant.

"Can it be the beggar in the grey hat," he muttered, "one of those who tried to carry off Little Mother Coralie?"

"Yes," grunted Ya-Bon.

"Yes. The signal of the sparks explains his presence in these parts. We mustn't lose sight of this track. Off with you, Ya-Bon."

But there was no need for Ya-Bon to hurry. The car had gone down the Rue Raynouard, and Belval himself arrived just as it was stopping three or four hundred yards from the turning, in front of a large carriage-entrance on the left-hand side.

Five men alighted. One of them rang. Thirty or forty seconds passed. Then Patrice heard the bell tinkle a second time. The five men waited, standing packed close together on the pavement. At last, after a third ring, a small wicket contrived in one of the folding-doors was opened.

There was a pause and some argument. Whoever had opened the wicket appeared to be asking for explanations. But suddenly two of the men bore heavily on the folding-door, which gave way before their thrust and let the whole gang through.

There was a loud noise as the door slammed to. Captain Belval at once studied his surroundings.

The Rue Raynouard is an old country-road which at one time used to wind among the houses and gardens of the village of Passy, on the side of the hills bathed by the Seine. In certain places, which unfortunately are becoming more and more rare, it has retained a provincial aspect. It is skirted by old properties. Old houses stand hidden amidst the trees: that in which Balzac lived has been piously preserved. It was in this street that the mysterious garden lay where Arsene Lupin discovered a farmer-general's diamonds hidden in a crack of an old sundial.

The car was still standing outside the house into which the five men had forced their way; and this prevented Patrice Belval from coming nearer. It was built in continuation of a wall and seemed to be one of the private mansions dating back to the First Empire. It had a very long front with two rows of round windows, protected by gratings on the ground-floor and solid shutters on the storey above. There was another building farther down, forming a separate wing.

"There's nothing to be done on this side," said the captain. "It's as impregnable as a feudal stronghold. Let's look elsewhere."

From the Rue Raynouard, narrow lanes, which used to divide the old properties, make their way down to the river.

One of them skirted the wall that preceded the house. Belval turned down it with Ya-Bon. It was constructed of ugly pointed pebbles, was broken into steps and faintly lighted by the gleam of a street-lamp.

"Lend me a hand, Ya-Bon. The wall is too high. But perhaps with the aid of the lamp-post..."

Assisted by the negro, he hoisted himself to the lamp and was stretching out one of his hands when he noticed that all this part of the wall bristled with broken glass, which made it absolutely impossible to grasp. He slid down again.

"Upon my word, Ya-Bon," he said, angrily, "you might have warned me! Another second and you would have made me cut my hands to pieces. What are you thinking of? In fact, I can't imagine what made you so anxious to come with me at all costs."

There was a turn in the lane, hiding the light, so that they were now in utter darkness, and Captain Belval had to grope his way along. He felt the negro's hand come down upon his shoulder.

"What do you want, Ya-Bon?"

The hand pushed him against the wall. At this spot there was a door in an embrasure.

"Well, yes," he said, "that's a door. Do you think I didn't see it? Oh, no one has eyes but Master Ya-Bon, I suppose."

Ya-Bon handed him a box of matches. He struck several, one after the other, and examined the door.

"What did I tell you?" he said between his teeth. "There's nothing to be done. Massive wood, barred and studded with iron... Look, there's no handle on this side, merely a key-hole... Ah, what we want is a key, made to measure and cut for the purpose!... For instance, a key like the one which the commissionaire left for me at the home just now..."

He stopped. An absurd idea flitted through his brain; and yet, absurd as it was, he felt that he was bound to perform the trifling action which it suggested to him. He therefore retraced his steps. He had the key on him. He took it from his pocket.

He struck a fresh light. The key-hole appeared. Belval inserted the key at the first attempt. He bore on it to the left: the key turned in the lock. He pushed the door: it opened.

"Come along in," he said.

The negro did not stir a foot. Patrice could understand his amazement. All said, he himself was equally amazed. By what unprecedented miracle was the key just the key of this very door? By what miracle was the unknown person who had sent it him able to guess that he would be in a position to use it without further instructions? A miracle indeed!

But Patrice had resolved to act without trying to solve the riddle which a mischievous chance seemed bent upon setting him.

"Come along in," he repeated, triumphantly.

Branches struck him in the face and he perceived that he was walking on grass and that there must be a garden lying in front of him. It was so dark that he could not see the paths against the blackness of the turf; and, after walking for a minute or two, he hit his foot against some rocks with a sheet of water on them.

"Oh, confound it!" he cursed. "I'm all wet. Damn you, Ya-Bon!"

He had not finished speaking when a furious barking was heard at the far end of the garden; and the sound at once came nearer, with extreme rapidity. Patrice realized that a watchdog, perceiving their presence, was rushing upon them, and, brave as he was, he shuddered, because of the impressiveness of this attack in complete darkness. How was he to defend himself? A shot would betray them; and yet he carried no weapon but his revolver.

The dog came dashing on, a powerful animal, to judge by the noise it made, suggesting the rush of a wild boar through the copsewood. It must have broken its chain, for it was accompanied by the clatter of iron. Patrice braced himself to meet it. But through the darkness he saw Ya-Bon pass before him to protect him, and the impact took place almost at once.

"Here, I say, Ya-Bon! Why did you get in front of me? It's all right, my lad, I'm coming!"

The two adversaries had rolled over on the grass. Patrice stooped down, seeking to rescue the negro. He touched the hair of an animal and then Ya-Bon's clothes. But the two were wriggling on the ground in so compact a mass and fighting so frantically that his interference was useless.

Moreover, the contest did not last long. In a few minutes the adversaries had ceased to move. A strangled death-rattle issued from the group.

"Is it all right, Ya-Bon?" whispered the captain, anxiously.

The negro stood up with a grunt. By the light of a match Patrice saw that he was holding at the end of his outstretched arm, of the one arm with which he had had to defend himself, a huge dog, which was gurgling, clutched round the throat by Ya-Bon's implacable fingers. A broken chain hung from its neck.

"Thank you, Ya-Bon. I've had a narrow escape. You can let him go now. He can't do us any harm, I think."

Ya-Bon obeyed. But he had no doubt squeezed too tight. The dog writhed for a moment on the grass, gave a few moans and then lay without moving.

"Poor brute!" said Patrice. "After all, he only did his duty in going for the burglars that we are. Let us do ours, Ya-Bon, which is nothing like as plain."

Something that shone like a window-pane guided his steps and led him, by a series of stairs cut in the rocks and of successive terraces, to the level ground on which the house was built. On this side also, all the windows were round and high up, like those in the streets, and barricaded with shutters. But one of them allowed the light which he had seen from below to filter through.

Telling Ya-Bon to hide in the shrubberies, he went up to the house, listened, caught an indistinct sound of voices, discovered that the shutters were too firmly closed to enable him either to see or to hear and, in this way, after the fourth window, reached a flight of steps. At the top of the steps was a door.

"Since they sent me the key of the garden," he said to himself, "there's no reason why this door, which leads from the house into the garden, should not be open."

It was open.

The voices indoors were now more clearly perceptible, and Belval observed that they reached him by the well of the staircase and that this staircase, which seemed to lead to an unoccupied part of the house, showed with an uncertain light above him.

He went up. A door stood ajar on the first floor. He slipped his head through the opening and went in. He found that he was on a narrow balcony which ran at mid-height around three sides of a large room, along book-shelves rising to the ceiling. Against the wall at either end of the room was an iron spiral staircase. Stacks of books were also piled against the bars of the railing which protected the gallery, thus hiding Patrice from the view of the people on the ground-floor, ten or twelve feet below.

He gently separated two of these stacks. At that moment the sound of voices suddenly increased to a great uproar and he saw five men, shouting like lunatics, hurl themselves upon a sixth and fling him to the ground before he had time to lift a finger in self-defence.

Belval's first impulse was to rush to the victim's rescue. With the aid of Ya-Bon, who would have hastened to his call, he would certainly have intimidated the five men. The reason why he did not act was that, at any rate, they were using no weapons and appeared to have no murderous intentions. After depriving their victim of all power of movement, they were content to hold him by the throat, shoulders and ankles. Belval wondered what would happen next.

One of the five drew himself up briskly and, in a tone of command, said:

"Bind him... Put a gag in his mouth... Or let him call out, if he wants to: there's no one to hear him."

Patrice at once recognized one of the voices which he had heard that morning in the restaurant. Its owner was a short, slim-built, well-dressed man, with an olive complexion and a cruel face.

"At last we've got him," he said, "the rascal! And I think we shall get him to speak this time. Are you prepared to go all lengths, friends?"

One of the other four growled, spitefully:

"Yes. And at once, whatever happens!"

The last speaker had a big black moustache; and Patrice recognized the other man whose conversation at the restaurant he had overheard, that is to say, one of Coralie's assailants, the one who had taken to flight. His grey felt hat lay on a chair.

"All lengths, Bournef, whatever happens, eh?" grinned the leader. "Well, let's get on with the work. So you refuse to give up your secret, Essarès, old man? We shall have some fun."

All their movements must have been prepared beforehand and the parts carefully arranged, for the actions which they carried out were performed in an incredibly prompt and methodical fashion.

After the man was tied up, they lifted him into an easy-chair with a very low back, to which they fastened him round the chest and waist with a rope. His legs, which were bound together, were placed on the seat of a heavy chair of the same height as the armchair, with the two feet projecting. Then the victim's shoes and socks were removed.

"Roll him along!" said the leader.

Between two of the four windows that overlooked the chimney was a large fire-place, in which burnt a red coal-fire, white in places with the intense heat of the hearth. The men pushed the two chairs bearing the victim until his bare feet were within twenty inches of the blazing coals.

In spite of his gag, the man uttered a hideous yell of pain, while his legs, in spite of their bonds, succeeded in contracting and curling upon themselves.

"Go on!" shouted the leader, passionately. "Go on! Nearer!"

Patrice Belval grasped his revolver.

"Oh, I'm going on too!" he said to himself. "I won't let that wretch be..."

But, at this very moment, when he was on the point of drawing himself up and acting, a chance movement made him behold the most extraordinary and unexpected sight. Opposite him, on the other side of the room, in a part of the balcony corresponding with that where he was, he saw a woman's head, a head glued to the rails, livid and terror-stricken, with eyes wide-open in horror gazing frenziedly at the awful scene that was being enacted below by the glowing fire.

Patrice had recognized Little Mother Coralie.

4

BEFORE THE FLAMES

Little Mother Coralie! Coralie concealed in this house into which her assailants had forced their way and in which she herself was hiding, through force of circumstances which were incapable of explanation.

His first idea, which would at least have solved one of the riddles, was that she also had entered from the lane, gone into the house by the steps and in this way opened a passage for him. But, in that case, how had she procured the means of carrying out this enterprise? And, above all, what brought her here?

All these questions occurred to Captain Belval's mind without his trying to reply to them. He was far too much impressed by the absorbed expression on Coralie's face. Moreover, a second cry, even wilder than the first, came from below; and he saw the victim's face writhing before the red curtain of fire from the hearth.

But, this time, Patrice, held back by Coralie's presence, had no inclination to go to the sufferer's assistance. He decided to model himself entirely upon her and not to move or do anything to attract her attention.

"Easy!" the leader commanded. "Pull him back. I expect he's had enough."

He went up to the victim:

"Well, my dear Essarès," he asked, "what do you think of it? Are you happy? And, you know, we're only beginning. If you don't speak, we shall go on to the end, as the real *chauffeurs* used to do in the days of the Revolution. So it's settled, I presume: you're going to speak?"

There was no answer. The leader rapped out an oath and went on:

"What do you mean? Do you refuse? But, you obstinate brute, don't you understand the situation? Or have you a glimmer of hope? Hope, indeed! You're mad. Who would rescue you? Your servants? The porter, the footman and the butler are in my pay. I gave them a week's notice. They're gone by now. The housemaid? The cook? They sleep at the other end of the house; and you yourself have told me, time after time, that one can't hear anything over there. Who else? Your wife? Her room also is far away; and she hasn't heard anything either? Siméon, your old secretary? We made him fast when he opened the front door to us just now. Besides, we may as well finish the job here. Bournef!"

The man with the big moustache, who was still holding the chair, drew himself up.

"Bournef, where did you lock up the secretary?"

"In the porter's lodge."

"You know where to find Mme. Essarès' bedroom?"

"Yes, you told me the way."

"Go, all four of you, and bring the lady and the secretary here!"

The four men went out by a door below the spot where Coralie was standing. They were hardly out of sight when the leader stooped eagerly over his victim and said:

"We're alone, Essarès. It's what I intended. Let's make the most of it."

He bent still lower and whispered so that Patrice found it difficult to hear what he said:

"Those men are fools. I twist them round my finger and tell them no more of my plans than I can help. You and I, on the other hand, Essarès, are the men to come to terms. That is what you refused to admit; and you see where it has landed you. Come, Essarès, don't be obstinate and don't shuffle. You are caught in a trap, you are helpless, you are absolutely in my power. Well, rather than allow yourself to be broken down by tortures which would certainly end by overcoming your resistance, strike a bargain with me. We'll go halves, shall we? Let's make peace and treat upon that basis. I'll give you a hand in my game and you'll give me one in yours. As allies, we are bound to win. As enemies, who knows whether the victor will surmount all the obstacles that will still stand in his path? That's why I say again, halves! Answer me. Yes or no."

He loosened the gag and listened. This time, Patrice did not hear the few words which the victim uttered. But the other, the leader, almost immediately burst into a rage:

"Eh? What's that you're proposing? Upon my word, but you're a cool hand! An offer of this kind to me! That's all very well for Bournef or his fellows. They'll understand, they will. But it won't do for me, it won't do for Colonel Fakhi. No, no, my friend, I open my mouth wider! I'll consent to go halves, but accept an alms, never!"

Patrice listened eagerly and, at the same time, kept his eyes on Coralie, whose face still contorted with anguish, wore an expression of the same rapt attention. And he looked back at the victim, part of whose body was reflected in the glass above the mantelpiece. The man was dressed in a braided brown-velvet smoking-suit and appeared to be about fifty years of age, quite bald, with a fleshy face, a large hooked nose, eyes deep set under a pair of thick eyebrows and puffy cheeks covered with a thick grizzled beard. Patrice was also able to examine his features more closely in a portrait of him which hung to the left of the fireplace, between the first and second windows, and which represented a strong, powerful countenance with an almost fierce expression.

"It's an Eastern face," said Patrice to himself. "I've seen heads like that in Egypt and Turkey."

The names of all these men too—Colonel Fakhi, Mustapha, Bournef, Essarès—their accent in talking, their way of holding themselves, their features, their figures, all recalled impressions which he had gathered in the Near East, in the hotels at Alexandria or on the banks of the Bosphorus, in the bazaars of Adrianople or in the Greek boats that plow the Ægean Sea. They were Levantine types, but of Levantines who had taken root in Paris. Essarès Bey was a name which Patrice recognized as well-known in the financial world, even as he knew that of Colonel Fakhi, whose speech and intonation marked him for a seasoned Parisian.

But a sound of voices came from outside the door. It was flung open violently and the four men appeared, dragging in a bound man, whom they dropped to the floor as they entered.

"Here's old Siméon," cried the one whom Fakhi had addressed as Bournef.

"And the wife?" asked the leader. "I hope you've got her too!"

"Well, no."

"What is that? Has she escaped?"

"Yes, through her window."

"But you must run after her. She can only be in the garden. Remember, the watch-dog was barking just now."

"And suppose she's got away?"

"How?"

"By the door on the lane?"

"Impossible!"

"Why?"

"The door hasn't been used for years. There's not even a key to it."

"That's as may be," Bournef re-joined. "All the same, we're surely not going to organize a battue with lanterns and rouse the whole district for the sake of finding a woman..."

"Yes, but that woman..."

Colonel Fakhi seemed exasperated. He turned to the prisoner:

"You're in luck, you old rascal! This is the second time today that minx of yours has slipped through my fingers! Did she tell you what happened this afternoon? Oh, if it hadn't been for an infernal officer who happened to be passing!... But I'll get hold of him yet and he shall pay dearly for his interference..."

Patrice clenched his fists with fury. He understood: Coralie was hiding in her own house. Surprised by the sudden arrival of the five men, she had managed to climb out of her window and, making her way along the terrace to the steps, had gone to the part of the house opposite the rooms that were in use and taken refuge in the gallery of the library, where she was able to witness the terrible assault levied at her husband.

"Her husband!" thought Patrice, with a shudder. "Her husband!"

And, if he still entertained any doubts on the subject, the hurried course of events soon removed them, for the leader began to chuckle:

"Yes, Essarès, old man, I confess that she attracts me more than I can tell you; and, as I failed to catch her earlier in the day, I did hope this evening, as soon as I had settled my business with you, to settle something infinitely more agreeable with your wife. Not to mention that, once in my power, the little woman would be serving me as a hostage and that I would only have restored her to you—oh, safe and sound, believe me!—after specific performance of our agreement. And you would have run straight, Essarès! For you love your Coralie passionately! And quite right too!"

He went to the right-hand side of the fireplace and, touching a switch, lit an electric lamp under a reflector between the third and fourth windows. There was a companion picture here to Essarès' portrait, but it was covered over. The leader drew the curtain, and Coralie appeared in the full light.

"The monarch of all she surveys! The idol! The witch! The pearl of pearls! The imperial diamond of Essarès Bey, banker! Isn't she beautiful? I ask you. Admire the delicate outline of her face, the purity of that oval; and the pretty neck; and those graceful shoulders. Essarès, there's not a favourite in the country we come from who can hold a candle to your Coralie! My Coralie, soon! For I shall know how to find her. Ah, Coralie, Coralie!..."

Patrice looked across at her, and it seemed to him that her face was reddened with a blush of shame. He himself was shaken by indignation and anger at each insulting word. It was a violent enough sorrow to him to know that Coralie was the wife of another; and added to this sorrow was his rage at seeing her thus exposed to these men's gaze and promised as a helpless prey to whosoever should prove himself the strongest.

At the same time, he wondered why Coralie remained in the room. Supposing that she could not leave the garden, nevertheless she was free to move about in that part of the house and might well have opened a window and called for help. What prevented her from doing so? Of course she did not love her husband. If she had loved him, she would have faced every danger to defend him. But how was it possible for her to allow that man to be tortured, worse still, to be present at his sufferings, to contemplate that most hideous of sights and to listen to his yells of pain?

"Enough of this nonsense!" cried the leader, pulling the curtain back into its place. "Coralie, you shall be my final reward; but I must first win you. Comrades, to work; let's finish our friend's job. First of all, twenty inches nearer, no more. Good! Does it burn, Essarès? All the same, it's not more than you can stand. Bear up, old fellow."

He unfastened the prisoner's right arm, put a little table by his side, laid a pencil and paper on it and continued:

"There's writing-materials for you. As your gag prevents you from speaking, write. You know what's wanted of you, don't you?

Scribble a few letters, and you're free. Do you consent? No? Comrades, three inches nearer."

He moved away and stooped over the secretary, whom Patrice, by the brighter light, had recognized as the old fellow who sometimes escorted Coralie to the hospital.

"As for you, Siméon," he said, "you shall come to no harm. I know that you are devoted to your master, but I also know that he tells you none of his private affairs. On the other hand, I am certain that you will keep silent as to all this, because a single word of betrayal would involve your master's ruin even more than ours. That's understood between us, isn't it? Well, why don't you answer? Have they squeezed your throat a bit too tight with their cords? Wait, I'll give you some air..."

Meanwhile the ugly work at the fireplace pursued its course. The two feet were reddened by the heat until it seemed almost as though the bright flames of the fire were glowing through them. The sufferer exerted all his strength in trying to bend his legs and to draw back; and a dull, continuous moan came through his gag.

"Oh, hang it all!" thought Patrice. "Are we going to let him roast like this, like a chicken on a spit?"

He looked at Coralie. She did not stir. Her face was distorted beyond recognition, and her eyes seemed fascinated by the terrifying sight.

"Couple of inches nearer!" cried the leader, from the other end of the room, as he unfastened Siméon's bonds.

The order was executed. The victim gave such a yell that Patrice's blood froze in his veins. But, at the same moment, he became aware of something that had not struck him so far, or at least he had attached no significance to it. The prisoner's hand, as the result of a sequence of little movements apparently due to nervous twitches, had seized the opposite edge of the table, while his arm rested on the marble top. And gradually, unseen by the torturers, all whose efforts were directed to keeping his legs in position, or by the leader, who was still engaged with Siméon, this hand opened a drawer which swung on a hinge, dipped into the drawer, took out a revolver and, resuming its original position with a jerk, hid the weapon in the chair.

The act, or rather the intention which it indicated, was foolhardy in the extreme, for, when all was said, reduced to his present state of helplessness, the man could not hope for victory against five adversaries, all free and all armed. Nevertheless, as Patrice looked at the glass in which he beheld him, he saw a fierce determination pictured in the man's face.

"Another two inches," said Colonel Fakhi, as he walked back to the fireplace.

He examined the condition of the flesh and said, with a laugh:

"The skin is blistering in places; the veins are ready to burst. Essarès Bey, you can't be enjoying yourself, and it strikes me that you mean to do the right thing at last. Have you started scribbling yet? No? And don't you mean to? Are you still hoping? Counting on your wife, perhaps? Come, come, you must see that, even if she has succeeded in escaping, she won't say anything! Well, then, are you humbugging me, or what?..."

He was seized with a sudden burst of rage and shouted:

"Shove his feet into the fire! And let's have a good smell of burning for once! Ah, you would defy me, would you? Well, wait a bit, old chap, and let me have a go at you! I'll cut you off an ear or two: you know, the way we have in our country!"

He drew from his waistcoat a dagger that gleamed in the firelight. His face was hideous with animal cruelty. He gave a fierce cry, raised his arm and stood over the other relentlessly.

But, swift as his movement was, Essarès was before him. The revolver, quickly aimed, was discharged with a loud report. The dagger dropped from the colonel's hand. For two or three seconds he maintained his threatening attitude, with one arm lifted on high and a haggard look in his eyes, as though he did not quite understand what had happened to him. And then, suddenly, he fell upon his victim in a huddled heap, paralyzing his arm with the full weight of his body, at the moment when Essarès was taking aim at one of the other confederates.

He was still breathing:

"Oh, the brute, the brute!" he panted. "He's killed me!... But you'll lose by it, Essarès... I was prepared for this. If I don't come home tonight, the Prefect of police will receive a letter... They'll know about your treason, Essarès... all your story... your plans... Oh, you devil!... And what a fool!... We could so easily have come to terms..."

He muttered a few inaudible words and rolled down to the floor. It was all over.

A moment of stupefaction was produced not so much by this unexpected tragedy as by the revelation which the leader had made before dying and by the thought of that letter, which no doubt implicated the aggressors as well as their victim. Bournef had disarmed Essarès. The latter, now that the chair was no longer held in position, had succeeded in bending his legs. No one moved.

Meanwhile, the sense of terror which the whole scene had produced seemed rather to increase with the silence. On the ground was the corpse, with the blood flowing on the carpet. Not far away lay Siméon's motionless form. Then there was the prisoner, still bound in front of the flames waiting to devour his flesh. And standing near him were the four butchers, hesitating perhaps what to do next, but showing in every feature an implacable resolution to defeat the enemy by all and every means.

His companions glanced at Bournef, who seemed the kind of man to go any length. He was a short, stout, powerfully-built man; his upper lip bristled with the moustache which had attracted Patrice Belval's attention. He was less cruel in appearance than his chief, less elegant in his manner and less masterful, but displayed far greater coolness and self-command. As for the colonel, his accomplices seemed not to trouble about him. The part which they were playing dispensed them from showing any empty compassion.

At last Bournef appeared to have made up his mind how to act. He went to his hat, the grey felt hat lying near the door, turned back the lining and took from it a tiny coil the sight of which made Patrice start. It was a slender red cord, exactly like that which he had found round the neck of Mustapha Rovalaïof, the first accomplice captured by Ya-Bon.

Bournef unrolled the cord, took it by the two buckles, tested its strength across his knee and then, going back to Essarès, slipped it over his neck after first removing his gag.

"Essarès," he said, with a calmness which was more impressive than the colonel's violence and sneers, "Essarès, I shall not put you to any pain. Torture is a revolting process; and I shall not have recourse to it. You know what to do; I know what to do. A word on your side, an action on my side; and the thing is done. The word is the yes or no which you will now speak. The action which I shall accomplish in reply to your yes or no will mean either your release or else..."

He stopped for a second or two. Then he declared:

"Or else your death."

The brief phrase was uttered very simply but with a firmness that gave it the full significance of an irrevocable sentence. It was clear that Essarès was faced with a catastrophe which he could no longer avoid save by submitting absolutely. In less than a minute, he would have spoken or he would be dead.

Once again Patrice fixed his eyes on Coralie, ready to interfere should he perceive in her any other feeling than one of passive terror. But her attitude did not change. She was therefore accepting the worst, it appeared, even though this meant her husband's death; and Patrice held his hand accordingly.

"Are we all agreed?" Bournef asked, turning to his accomplices.

"Quite," said one of them.

"Do you take your share of the responsibility?"

"We do."

Bournef brought his hands together and crossed them, which had the result of knotting the cord round Essarès' neck. Then he pulled slightly, so as to make the pressure felt, and asked, unemotionally:

"Yes or no?"

"Yes."

There was a murmur of satisfaction. The accomplices heaved a breath; and Bournef nodded his head with an air of approval:

"Ah, so you accept! It was high time: I doubt if anyone was ever nearer death than you were, Essarès." Retaining his hold of the cord, he continued, "Very well. You will speak. But I know you; and your answer surprises me, for I told the colonel that not even the certainty of death would make you confess your secret. Am I wrong?"

"No," replied Essarès. "Neither death nor torture."

"Then you have something different to propose?"

"Yes."

"Something worth our while?"

"Yes. I suggested it to the colonel just now, when you were out of the room. But, though he was willing to betray you and go halves with me in the secret, he refused the other thing."

"Why should I accept it?"

"Because you must take it or leave it and because you will understand what he did not."

"It's a compromise, I suppose?"

"Yes."

"Money?"

"Yes."

Bournef shrugged his shoulders:

"A few thousand-franc notes, I expect. And you imagine that Bournef and his friends will be such fools?... Come, Essarès, why do you want us to compromise? We know your secret almost entirely..."

"You know what it is, but not how to use it. You don't know how to get at it; and that's just the point."

"We shall discover it."

"Never."

"Yes, your death will make it easier for us."

"My death? Thanks to the information lodged by the colonel, in a few hours you will be tracked down and most likely caught: in any case, you will be unable to pursue your search. Therefore you have hardly any choice. It's the money which I'm offering you, or else... prison."

"And, if we accept," asked Bournef, to whom the argument seemed to appeal, "when shall we be paid?"

"At once."

"Then the money is here?"

"Yes."

"A contemptible sum, as I said before?"

"No, a much larger sum than you hope for; infinitely larger."

"How much?"

"Four millions."

5

HUSBAND AND WIFE

The accomplices started, as though they had received an electric shock. Bournef darted forward:

"What did you say?"

"I said four millions, which means a million for each of you."

"Look here!... Do you mean it?... Four millions?...

"Four millions is what I said."

The figure was so gigantic and the proposal so utterly unexpected that the accomplices had the same feeling which Patrice Belval on his side underwent. They suspected a trap; and Bournef could not help saying:

"The offer is more than we expected... And I am wondering what induced you to make it."

"Would you have been satisfied with less?"

"Yes," said Bournef, candidly.

"Unfortunately, I can't make it less. I have only one means of escaping death; and that is to open my safe for you. And my safe contains four bundles of a thousand bank-notes each."

Bournef could not get over his astonishment and became more and more suspicious.

"How do you know that, after taking the four millions, we shall not insist on more?"

"Insist on what? The secret of the site?"

"Yes."

"Because you know that I would as soon die as tell it you. The four millions are the maximum. Do you want them or don't you? I ask for no promise in return, no oath of any kind, for I am convinced that, when you have filled your pockets, you will have but one thought, to clear off, without handicapping yourselves with a murder which might prove your undoing."

The argument was so unanswerable that Bournef ceased discussing and asked:

"Is the safe in this room?"

"Yes, between the first and second windows, behind my portrait."

Bournef took down the picture and said:

"I see nothing."

"It's all right. The lines of the safe are marked by the mouldings of the central panel. In the middle you will see what looks like a rose, not of wood but of iron; and there are four others at the four corners of the panel. These four turn to the right, by successive notches, forming a word which is the key to the lock, the word Cora."

"The first four letters of Coralie?" asked Bournef, following Essarès' instructions as he spoke.

"No," said Essarès Bey, "the first four letters of the Coran. Have you done that?"

After a moment, Bournef answered:

"Yes, I've finished. And the key?"

"There's no key. The fifth letter of the word, the letter N, is the letter of the central rose."

Bournef turned this fifth rose; and presently a click was heard.

"Now pull," said Essarès. "That's it. The safe is not deep: it's dug in one of the stones of the front wall. Put in your hand. You'll find four pocket-books."

It must be admitted that Patrice Belval expected to see something startling interrupt Bournef's quest and hurl him into some pit suddenly opened by Essarès' trickery. And the three confederates seemed to share this unpleasant apprehension, for they were grey in the face, while Bournef himself appeared to be working very cautiously and suspiciously.

At last he turned round and came and sat beside Essarès. In his hands he held a bundle of four pocketbooks, short but extremely bulky and bound together with a canvas strap. He unfastened the buckle of the strap and opened one of the pocketbooks.

His knees shook under their precious burden, and, when he had taken a huge sheaf of notes from one of the compartments, his hands were like the hands of a very old man trembling with fever.

"Thousand-franc notes," he murmured. "Ten packets of thousand-franc notes."

Brutally, like men prepared to fight one another, each of the other three laid hold of a pocket-book, felt inside and mumbled:

"Ten packets... they're all there... Thousand-franc notes..."

And one of them forthwith cried, in a choking voice:

"Let's clear out!... Let's go!"

A sudden fear was sending them off their heads. They could not imagine that Essarès would hand over such a fortune to them unless he had some plan which would enable him to recover it before they had left the room. That was a certainty. The ceiling would come down on their heads. The walls would close up and crush them to death, while sparing their unfathomable adversary.

Nor had Patrice Belval any doubt of it. The disaster was preparing. Essarès' revenge was inevitably at hand. A man like him, a fighter as able as he appeared to be, does not so easily surrender four million francs if he has not some scheme at the back of his head. Patrice felt himself breathing heavily. His present excitement was more violent than any with which he had thrilled since the very beginning of the tragic scenes which he had been witnessing; and he saw that Coralie's face was as anxious as his own.

Meanwhile Bournef partially recovered his composure and, holding back his companions, said:

"Don't be such fools! He would be capable, with old Siméon, of releasing himself and running after us."

Using only one hand, for the other was clutching a pocketbook, all four fastened Essarès' arm to the chair, while he protested angrily:

"You idiots! You came here to rob me of a secret of immense importance, as you well knew, and you lose your heads over a trifle of four millions. Say what you like, the colonel had more backbone than that!"

They gagged him once more and Bournef gave him a smashing blow with his fist which laid him unconscious.

"That makes our retreat safe," said Bournef.

"What about the colonel?" asked one of the others. "Are we to leave him here?"

"Why not?"

But apparently he thought this unwise; for he added:

"On second thoughts, no. It's not to our interest to compromise Essarès any further. What we must do, Essarès as well as ourselves, is to make ourselves scarce as fast as we can, before that damned letter of the colonel's is delivered at headquarters, say before twelve o'clock in the day."

"Then what do you suggest?"

"We'll take the colonel with us in the motor and drop him anywhere. The police must make what they can of it."

"And his papers?"

"We'll look through his pockets as we go. Lend me a hand."

They bandaged the wound to stop the flow of blood, took up the body, each holding it by an arm or leg, and walked out without anyone of them letting go his pocketbook for a second.

Patrice Belval heard them pass through another room and then tramp heavily over the echoing flags of a hall.

"This is the moment," he said. "Essarès or Siméon will press a button and the rogues will be nabbed."

Essarès did not budge.

Siméon did not budge.

Patrice heard all the sounds accompanying their departure: the slamming of the carriage-gate, the starting-up of the engine and the drone of the car as it moved away. And that was all. Nothing had happened. The confederates were getting off with their four millions.

A long silence followed, during which Patrice remained on tenterhooks. He did not believe that the drama had reached its last phase; and he was so much afraid of the unexpected which might still occur that he determined to make Coralie aware of his presence.

A fresh incident prevented him. Coralie had risen to her feet.

Her face no longer wore its expression of horror and affright, but Patrice was perhaps more scared at seeing her suddenly animated with a sinister energy that gave an unwonted sparkle to her eyes and set her eyebrows and her lips twitching. He realized that Coralie was preparing to act.

In what way? Was this the end of the tragedy?

She walked to the corner on her side of the gallery where one of the two spiral staircases stood and went down slowly, without, however, trying to deaden the sound of her feet. Her husband could not help hearing her. Patrice, moreover, saw in the mirror that he had lifted his head and was following her with his eyes.

She stopped at the foot of the stairs. But there was no indecision in her attitude. Her plan was obviously quite clear; and she was only thinking out the best method of putting it into execution.

"Ah!" whispered Patrice to himself, quivering all over. "What are you doing, Little Mother Coralie?"

He gave a start. The direction in which Coralie's eyes were turned, together with the strange manner in which they stared, revealed her secret resolve to him. She had caught sight of the dagger, lying on the floor where it had slipped from the colonel's grasp.

Not for a second did Patrice believe that she meant to pick up that dagger with any other thought than to stab her husband. The intention of murder was so plainly written on her livid features that, even before she stirred a limb, Essarès was seized with a fit of terror and strained every muscle to break the bonds that hampered his movements.

She came forward, stopped once more and, suddenly bending, seized the dagger. Without waiting, she took two more steps. These brought her to the right of the chair in which Essarès lay. He had only to turn his head a little way to see her. And an awful minute passed, during which the husband and wife looked into each other's eyes.

The whirl of thoughts, of fear, of hatred, of vagrant and conflicting passions that passed through the brains of her who was about to kill and him who was about to die, was reproduced in Patrice Belval's mind and deep down in his inner consciousness. What was he to do? What part ought he to play in the tragedy that was being enacted before his eyes? Should he intervene? Was it his duty to prevent Coralie from committing the irreparable deed? Or should he commit it himself by breaking the man's head with a bullet from his revolver?

Yet, from the beginning, Patrice had really been swayed by a feeling which, mingling with all the others, gradually paralyzed him and rendered any inward struggle illusory: a feeling of curiosity driven to its utmost pitch. It was not the everyday curiosity of unearthing a squalid secret, but the higher curiosity of penetrating the mysterious soul of a woman whom he loved, who was carried away by the rush of events and who suddenly, becoming once more mistress of herself, was of her own accord and with impressive calmness taking the most fearful resolution. Thereupon other questions forced themselves upon him. What prompted her to take this resolution? Was it revenge? Was it punishment? Was it the gratification of hatred?

Patrice Belval remained where he was.

Coralie raised her arm. Her husband, in front of her, no longer even attempted to make those movements of despair which indicate a last effort. There was neither entreaty nor menace in his eyes. He waited in resignation.

Not far from them, old Siméon, still bound, half-lifted himself on his elbows and stared at them in dismay.

Coralie raised her arm again. Her whole frame seemed to grow larger and taller. An invisible force appeared to strengthen and stiffen her whole being, summoning all her energies to the service of her will. She was on the point of striking. Her eyes sought the place at which she should strike.

Yet her eyes became less hard and less dark. It even seemed to Patrice that there was a certain hesitation in her gaze and that she was recovering not her usual gentleness, but a little of her womanly grace.

"Ah, Little Mother Coralie," murmured Patrice, "you are yourself again! You are the woman I know. Whatever right you may think you have to kill that man, you will not kill him... and I prefer it so."

Slowly Coralie's arm dropped to her side. Her features relaxed. Patrice could guess the immense relief which she felt at escaping from the obsessing purpose that was driving her to murder. She looked at her dagger with astonishment, as though she were waking from a hideous nightmare. And, bending over her husband she began to cut his bonds.

She did so with visible repugnance, avoiding his touch, as it were, and shunning his eyes. The cords were severed one by one. Essarès was free.

What happened next was in the highest measure unexpected. With not a word of thanks to his wife, with not a word of anger either, this man who had just undergone the most cruel torture and whose body still throbbed with pain hurriedly tottered barefoot to a telephone standing on a table. He was like a hungry man who suddenly sees a piece of bread and snatches at it greedily as the means of saving himself and returning to life. Panting for breath, Essarès took down the receiver and called out:

"Central 40.39."

Then he turned abruptly to his wife:

"Go away," he said.

She seemed not to hear. She had knelt down beside old Siméon and was setting him free also.

Essarès at the telephone began to lose patience:

"Are you there?... Are you there?... I want that number today, please, not next week! It's urgent... 40.39... It's urgent, I tell you!"

And, turning to Coralie, he repeated, in an imperious tone:

"Go away!"

She made a sign that she would not go away and that, on the contrary, she meant to listen. He shook his fist at her and again said:

"Go away, go away!... I won't have you stay in the room. You go away too, Siméon."

Old Siméon got up and moved towards Essarès. It looked as though he wished to speak, no doubt to protest. But his action was undecided; and, after a moment's reflection, he turned to the door and went without uttering a word.

"Go away, will you, go away!" Essarès repeated, his whole body expressing menace.

But Coralie came nearer to him and crossed her arms obstinately and defiantly. At that moment, Essarès appeared to get his call, for he asked:

"Is that 40.39? Ah, yes..."

He hesitated. Coralie's presence obviously displeased him greatly, and he was about to say things which he did not wish her to know. But time, no doubt, was pressing. He suddenly made up his mind and, with both receivers glued to his ears, said, in English:

"Is that you, Gregoire?... Essarès speaking... Hullo!... Yes, I'm speaking from the Rue Raynouard... There's no time to lose... Listen..."

He sat down and went on:

"Look here. Mustapha's dead. So is the colonel... Damn it, don't interrupt, or we're done for!... Yes, done for; and you too... Listen, they all came, the colonel, Bournef, the whole gang, and robbed me by means of violence and threats... I finished the colonel, only he had written to the police, giving us all away. The letter will be delivered soon. So you understand, Bournef and his three ruffians are going to disappear. They'll just run home and pack up their papers; and I reckon they'll be with you in an hour, or two hours at most. It's the refuge they're sure to make for. They prepared it themselves, without suspecting that you and I know each other. So there's no doubt about it. They're sure to come..."

Essarès stopped. He thought for a moment and resumed:

"You still have a second key to each of the rooms which they use as bedrooms? Is that so?... Good. And you have duplicates of the keys that open the cupboards in the walls of those rooms, haven't you?... Capital. Well, as soon as they get to sleep, or rather as soon as you are certain that they are sound asleep, go in and search the cupboards. Each of them is bound to hide his share of the booty there. You'll find it quite easily. It's the four pocket-books which you know of. Put them in your bag, clear out as fast as you can and join me."

There was another pause. This time it was Essarès listening. He replied:

"What's that you say? Rue Raynouard? Here? Join me here? Why, you must be mad! Do you imagine that I can stay now, after the colonel's given me away? No, go and wait for me at the hotel, near the station. I shall be there by twelve o'clock or one in the afternoon, perhaps a little later. Don't be uneasy. Have your lunch quietly and we'll talk things over... Hullo! Did you hear?... Very well, I'll see that everything's all right. Goodbye for the present."

The conversation was finished; and it looked as if Essarès, having taken all his measures to recover possession of the four million francs, had no further cause for anxiety. He hung up the receiver, went back to the lounge-chair in which he had been tortured, wheeled it round with its back to the fire, sat down, turned down the bottoms of his trousers and pulled on his socks and shoes, all a little painfully and accompanied by a few grimaces, but calmly, in the manner of a man who has no need to hurry.

Coralie kept her eyes fixed on his face.

"I really ought to go," thought Captain Belval, who felt a trifle embarrassed at the thought of overhearing what the husband and wife were about to say.

Nevertheless he stayed. He was not comfortable in his mind on Coralie's account.

Essarès fired the first shot:

"Well," he asked, "what are you looking at me like that for?"

"So it's true?" she murmured, maintaining her attitude of defiance. "You leave me no possibility of doubt?"

"Why should I lie?" he snarled. "I should not have telephoned in your hearing if I hadn't been sure that you were here all the time."

"I was up there."

"Then you heard everything?"

"Yes."

"And saw everything?"

"Yes."

"And, seeing the torture which they inflicted on me and hearing my cries, you did nothing to defend me, to defend me against torture, against death!"

"No, for I knew the truth."

"What truth?"

"The truth which I suspected without daring to admit it."

"What truth?" he repeated, in a louder voice.

"The truth about your treason."

"You're mad. I've committed no treason."

"Oh, don't juggle with words! I confess that I don't know the whole truth: I did not understand all that those men said or what they were demanding of you. But the secret which they tried to force from you was a treasonable secret."

"A man can only commit treason against his country," he said, shrugging his shoulders. "I'm not a Frenchman."

"You were a Frenchman!" she cried. "You asked to be one and you became one. You married me, a Frenchwoman, and you live in France and you've made your fortune in France. It's France that you're betraying."

"Don't talk nonsense! And for whose benefit?"

"I don't know that, either. For months, for years indeed, the colonel, Bournef, all your former accomplices and yourself have been engaged on an enormous work—yes, enormous, it's their own word—and now it appears that you are fighting over the profits of the common enterprise and the others accuse you of pocketing those profits for yourself alone and of keeping a secret that doesn't belong to you. So that I seem to see something dirtier and more hateful even than treachery, something worthy of a common pickpocket..."

The man struck the arm of his chair with his fist:

"Enough!" he cried.

Coralie seemed in no way alarmed:

"Enough," she echoed, "you are right. Enough words between us. Besides, there is one fact that stands out above everything: your flight. That amounts to a confession. You're afraid of the police."

He shrugged his shoulders a second time:

"I'm afraid of nobody."

"Very well, but you're going."

"Yes."

"Then let's have it out. When are you going?"

"Presently, at twelve o'clock."

"And if you're arrested?"

"I sha'n't be arrested."

"If you are arrested, however?"

"I shall be let go."

"At least there will be an inquiry, a trial?"

"No, the matter will be hushed up."

"You hope so."

"I'm sure of it."

"God grant it! And you will leave France, of course?"

"As soon as I can."

"When will that be?"

"In a fortnight or three weeks."

"Send me word of the day, so that I may know when I can breathe again."

"I shall send you word, Coralie, but for another reason."

"What reason?"

"So that you may join me."

"Join you!"

He gave a cruel smile:

"You are my wife," he said. "Where the husband goes the wife goes; and you know that, in my religion, the husband has every right over his wife, including that of life and death. Well, you're my wife."

Coralie shook her head, and, in a tone of indescribable contempt, answered:

"I am not your wife. I feel nothing for you but loathing and horror. I don't wish to see you again, and, whatever happens, whatever you may threaten, I shall not see you again."

He rose, and, walking to her, bent in two, all trembling on his legs, he shouted, while again he shook his clenched fists at her:

"What's that you say? What's that you dare to say? I, I, your lord and master, order you to join me the moment that I send for you."

"I shall not join you. I swear it before God! I swear it as I hope to be saved."

He stamped his feet with rage. His face underwent a hideous contortion; and he roared:

"That means that you want to stay! Yes, you have reasons which I don't know, but which are easy to guess! An affair of the heart, I suppose. There's someone in your life, no doubt... Hold your tongue, will you?... Haven't you always detested me?... Your hatred does not date from today, it dates back to the first time you saw me, to a time even before our marriage... We have always lived like mortal enemies. I loved you. I worshipped you. A word from you would have brought me to your feet. The mere sound of your steps thrilled me to the marrow... But your feeling for me is one of horror. And you imagine that you are going to start a new life, without me? Why, I'd sooner kill you, my beauty!"

He had unclenched his fists; and his open hands were clutching on either side of Coralie, close to her head, as though around a prey which they seemed on the point of throttling. A nervous shiver made his jaws clash together. Beads of perspiration gleamed on his bald head.

In front of him, Coralie stood impassive, looking very small and frail. Patrice Belval, in an agony of suspense and ready at any moment to act, could read nothing on her calm features but aversion and contempt.

Mastering himself at last, Essarès said:

"You shall join me, Coralie. Whether you like it or not, I am your husband. You felt it just now, when the lust to murder me made you take up a weapon and left you without the courage to carry out your intention. It will always be like that. Your independent fit will pass away and you will join the man who is your master."

"I shall remain behind to fight against you," she replied, "here, in this house. The work of treason which you have accomplished I shall destroy. I shall do it without hatred, for I am no longer capable of hatred, but I shall do it without intermission, to repair the evil which you have wrought."

He answered, in a low voice:

"I *am* capable of hatred. Beware, Coralie. The very moment when you believe that you have nothing more to fear will perhaps be the moment when I shall call you to account. Take care."

He pushed an electric bell. Old Siméon appeared.

"So the two men-servants have decamped?" asked Essarès. And, without waiting for the answer, he went on, "A good riddance. The housemaid and the cook can do all I want. They heard nothing, did they? No, their bedroom is too far away. No matter, Siméon: you must keep a watch on them after I am gone."

He looked at his wife, surprised to see her still there, and said to his secretary:

"I must be up at six to get everything ready; and I am dead tired. Take me to my room. You can come back and put out the lights afterwards."

He went out, supported by Siméon. Patrice Belval at once perceived that Coralie had done her best to show no weakness in her husband's presence, but that she had come to the end of her strength and was unable to walk. Seized with faintness, she fell on her knees, making the sign of the cross.

When she was able to rise, a few minutes later, she saw on the carpet, between her and the door, a sheet of note-paper with her name on it. She picked it up and read:

"Little Mother Coralie, the struggle is too much for you. Why not appeal to me, your friend? Give a signal and I am with you."

She staggered, dazed by the discovery of the letter and dismayed by Belval's daring. But, making a last effort to summon up her power of will, she left the room, without giving the signal for which Patrice was longing.

6

NINETEEN MINUTES PAST SEVEN

Patrice, in his bedroom at the home, was unable to sleep that night. He had a continual waking sensation of being oppressed and hunted down, as though he were suffering the terrors of some monstrous nightmare. He had an impression that the frantic series of events in which he was playing the combined parts of a bewildered spectator and a helpless actor would never cease so long as he tried to rest; that, on the contrary, they would rage with greater violence and intensity. The leave-taking of the husband and wife did not put an end, even momentarily, to the dangers incurred by Coralie. Fresh perils arose on every side; and Patrice Belval confessed himself incapable of foreseeing and still more of allaying them.

After lying awake for two hours, he switched on his electric light and began hurriedly to write down the story of the past twelve hours. He hoped in this way to some small extent to unravel the tangled knot.

At six o'clock he went and roused Ya-Bon and brought him back with him. Then, standing in front of the astonished negro, he crossed his arms and exclaimed:

"So you consider that your job is over! While I lie tossing about in the dark, my lord sleeps and all's well! My dear man, you have a jolly elastic conscience."

The word elastic amused the Senegalese mightily. His mouth opened wider than ever; and he gave a grunt of enjoyment.

"That'll do, that'll do," said the captain. "There's no getting a word in, once you start talking. Here, take a chair, read this report and give me your reasoned opinion. What? You don't know how to read? Well, upon my word! What was the good, then, of wearing out the seat of your trousers on the benches of the Senegal schools and colleges? A queer education, I must say!"

He heaved a sigh, and, snatching the manuscript, said:

"Listen, reflect, argue, deduct and conclude. This is how the matter briefly stands. First, we have one Essarès Bey, a banker, rich as Croesus, and the lowest of rapscallions, who betrays at one and the same time France, Egypt, England, Turkey, Bulgaria and Greece... as is proved by the fact that his accomplices roast his feet for him. Thereupon he kills one of them and gets rid of four with the aid of as many millions, which millions he orders another accomplice to get back for him before five minutes are passed. And all these bright spirits will duck underground at eleven o'clock this morning, for at twelve o'clock the police propose to enter on the scene. Good."

Patrice Belval paused to take breath and continued:

"Secondly, Little Mother Coralie—upon my word, I can't say why—is married to Rapscallion Bey. She hates him and wants to kill him. He loves her and wants to kill her. There is also a colonel who loves her and for that reason loses his life and a certain Mustapha, who tries to kidnap her on the colonel's account and also loses his life for that reason, strangled by a Senegalese. Lastly, there is a French captain, a dot-and-carry-one, who likewise loves her, but whom she avoids because she is married to a man whom she abhors. And with this captain, in a previous incarnation, she has halved an amethyst bead. Add to all this, by way of accessories, a rusty key, a red silk bowstring, a dog choked to death and a grate filled with red coals. And, if you dare to understand a single word of my explanation, I'll catch you a whack with my wooden leg, for I don't understand it a little bit and I'm your captain."

Ya-Bon laughed all over his mouth and all over the gaping scar that cut one of his cheeks in two. As ordered by his captain, he understood nothing of the business and very little of what Patrice had said; but he always quivered with delight when Patrice addressed him in that gruff tone.

"That's enough," said the captain. "It's my turn now to argue, deduct and conclude."

He leant against the mantelpiece, with his two elbows on the marble shelf and his head tight-pressed between his hands. His merriment, which sprang from temperamental lightness of heart, was this time only a surface merriment. Deep down within himself he did nothing but think of Coralie with sorrowful apprehension. What could he do to protect her? A number of plans occurred to him: which was he to choose? Should he hunt through the numbers in the telephone-book till he hit upon the whereabouts of that Gregoire, with whom Bournef and his companions had taken refuge? Should he inform the police? Should he return to the Rue Raynouard? He did not know. Yes, he was capable of acting, if the act to be performed consisted in flinging himself into the conflict with furious ardour. But to prepare the action, to divine the obstacles, to rend the darkness, and, as he said, to see the invisible and grasp the intangible, that was beyond his powers.

He turned suddenly to Ya-Bon, who was standing depressed by his silence:

"What's the matter with you, putting on that lugubrious air? Of course it's you that throw a gloom over me! You always look at the black side of things... like a nigger!... Be off."

Ya-Bon was going away discomfited, when someone tapped at the door and a voice said:

"Captain Belval, you're wanted on the telephone."

Patrice hurried out. Who on earth could be telephoning to him so early in the morning?

"Who is it?" he asked the nurse.

"I don't know, captain... It's a man's voice; he seemed to want you urgently. The bell had been ringing some time. I was downstairs, in the kitchen..."

Before Patrice's eyes there rose a vision of the telephone in the Rue Raynouard, in the big room at the Essarès' house. He could not help wondering if there was anything to connect the two incidents.

He went down one flight of stairs and along a passage. The telephone was through a small waiting-room, in a room that had been turned into a linen-closet. He closed the door behind him.

"Hullo! Captain Belval speaking. What is it?"

A voice, a man's voice which he did not know, replied in breathless, panting tones:

"Ah!... Captain Belval!... It's you!... Look here... but I'm almost afraid that it's too late... I don't know if I shall have time to finish... Did you get the key and the letter?..."

"Who are you?" asked Patrice.

"Did you get the key and the letter?" the voice insisted.

"The key, yes," Patrice replied, "but not the letter."

"Not the letter? But this is terrible! Then you don't know..."

A hoarse cry struck Patrice's ear and the next thing he caught was incoherent sounds at the other end of the wire, the noise of an altercation. Then the voice seemed to glue itself to the instrument and he distinctly heard it gasping:

"Too late!... Patrice... is that you?... Listen, the amethyst pendant... yes, I have it on me... The pendant... Ah, it's too late!... I should so much have liked to... Patrice... Coralie..."

Then again a loud cry, a heart-rending cry, and confused sounds growing more distant, in which he seemed to distinguish:

"Help!... Help!..."

These grew fainter and fainter. Silence followed. And suddenly there was a little click. The murderer had hung up the receiver.

All this had not taken twenty seconds. But, when Patrice wanted to replace the telephone, his fingers were gripping it so hard that it needed an effort to relax them.

He stood utterly dumfounded. His eyes had fastened on a large clock which he saw, through the window, on one of the buildings in the yard, marking nineteen minutes past seven; and he mechanically repeated these figures, attributing a documentary value to them. Then he asked himself—so unreal did the scene appear to him—if all this was true and if the crime had not been penetrated within himself, in the depths of his aching heart. But the shouting still echoed in his ears; and suddenly he took up the receiver again, like one clinging desperately to some undefined hope:

"Hullo!" he cried. "Exchange!... Who was it rang me up just now?... Are you there? Did you hear the cries?... Are you there?... Are you there?..."

There was no reply. He lost his temper, insulted the exchange, left the linen-closet, met Ya-Bon and pushed him about:

"Get out of this! It's your fault. Of course you ought to have stayed and looked after Coralie. Be off there now and hold yourself at my disposal. I'm going to inform the police. If you hadn't prevented me, it would have been done long ago and we shouldn't be in this predicament. Off you go!"

He held him back:

"No, don't stir. Your plan's ridiculous. Stay here. Oh, not here in my pocket! You're too impetuous for me, my lad!"

He drove him out and returned to the linen-closet, striding up and down and betraying his excitement in irritable gestures and angry words. Nevertheless, in the midst of his confusion, one idea gradually came to light, which was that, after all, he had no proof that the crime which he suspected had happened at the house in the Rue Raynouard. He must not allow himself to be obsessed by the facts that lingered in his memory to the point of always seeing the same vision in the same tragic setting. No doubt the drama was being continued, as he had felt that it would be, but perhaps elsewhere and far away from Coralie.

And this first thought led to another: why not investigate matters at once?

"Yes, why not?" he asked himself. "Before bothering the police, discovering the number of the person who rang me up and thus working back to the start, a process which it will be time enough to employ later, why shouldn't I telephone to the Rue Raynouard at once, on any pretext and in anybody's name? I shall then have a chance of knowing what to think..."

Patrice felt that this measure did not amount to much. Suppose that no one answered, would that prove that the murder had been committed in the house, or merely that no one was yet about? Nevertheless, the need to do something decided him. He looked up Essarès Bey's number in the telephone-directory and resolutely rang up the exchange.

The strain of waiting was almost more than he could bear. And then he was conscious of a thrill which vibrated through him from head to foot. He was connected; and someone at the other end was answering the call.

"Hullo!" he said.

"Hullo!" said a voice. "Who are you?"

It was the voice of Essarès Bey.

Although this was only natural, since at that moment Essarès must be getting his papers ready and preparing his flight, Patrice was so much taken aback that he did not know what to say and spoke the first words that came into his head:

"Is that Essarès Bey?"

"Yes. Who are you?"

"I'm one of the wounded at the hospital, now under treatment at the home..."

"Captain Belval, perhaps?"

Patrice was absolutely amazed. So Coralie's husband knew him by name? He stammered:

"Yes... Captain Belval."

"What a lucky thing!" cried Essarès Bey, in a tone of delight. "I rang you up a moment ago, at the home, Captain Belval, to ask..."

"Oh, it was you!" interrupted Patrice, whose astonishment knew no bounds.

"Yes, I wanted to know at what time I could speak to Captain Belval in order to thank him."

"It was *you*!... It was *you*!..." Patrice repeated, more and more thunderstruck.

Essarès' intonation denoted a certain surprise.

"Yes, wasn't it a curious coincidence?" he said. "Unfortunately, I was cut off, or rather my call was interrupted by somebody else."

"Then you heard?"

"What, Captain Belval?"

"Cries."

"Cries?"

"At least, so it seemed to me; but the connection was very indistinct."

"All that I heard was somebody asking for you, somebody who was in a great hurry; and, as I was not, I hung up the telephone and postponed the pleasure of thanking you."

"Of thanking me?"

"Yes, I have heard how my wife was assaulted last night and how you came to her rescue. And I am anxious to see you and express my gratitude. Shall we make an appointment? Could we meet at the hospital, for instance, at three o'clock this afternoon?"

Patrice made no reply. The audacity of this man, threatened with arrest and preparing for flight, baffled him. At the same time, he was wondering what Essarès' real object had been in telephoning to him without being in any way obliged to. But Belval's silence in no way troubled the banker, who continued his civilities and ended the inscrutable conversation with a monologue in which he replied with the greatest ease to questions which he kept putting to himself.

In spite of everything, Patrice felt more comfortable. He went back to his room, lay down on his bed and slept for two hours. Then he sent for Ya-Bon.

"This time," he said, "try to control your nerves and not to lose your head as you did just now. You were absurd. But don't let's talk about it. Have you had your breakfast? No? No more have I. Have you seen the doctor? No? No more have I. And the surgeon has just promised to take off this beastly bandage. You can imagine how pleased I am. A wooden leg is all very well; but a head wrapped up in lint, for a lover, never! Get on, look sharp. When we're ready, we'll start for the hospital. Little Mother Coralie can't forbid me to see her there!"

Patrice was as happy as a schoolboy. As he said to Ya-Bon an hour later, on their way to the Porte-Maillot, the clouds were beginning to roll by:

"Yes, Ya-Bon, yes, they are. And this is where we stand. To begin with, Coralie is not in danger. As I hoped, the battle is being fought far away from her, among the accomplices no doubt, over their millions. As for the unfortunate man who rang me up and whose dying cries I overheard, he was obviously some unknown friend, for he addressed me familiarly and called me by my Christian name. It was certainly he who sent me the key of the garden. Unfortunately, the letter that came with the key went astray. In the end, he felt constrained to tell me everything. Just at that moment he was attacked. By whom, you ask. Probably by one of the accomplices, who was frightened of his revelations. There you are, Ya-Bon. It's all as clear as noonday. For that matter, the truth may just as easily be the exact opposite of what I suggest. But I don't care. The great thing is to take one's stand upon a theory, true or false. Besides, if mine is false, I reserve the right to shift the responsibility on you. So you know what you're in for..."

At the Porte-Maillot they took a cab and it occurred to Patrice to drive round by the Rue Raynouard. At the junction of this street with the Rue de Passy, they saw Coralie leaving the Rue Raynouard, accompanied by old Siméon.

She had hailed a taxi and stepped inside. Siméon sat down by the driver. They went to the hospital in the Champs-Elysees, with Patrice following. It was eleven o'clock when they arrived.

"All's well," said Patrice. "While her husband is running away, she refuses to make any change in her daily life."

He and Ya-Bon lunched in the neighbourhood, strolled along the avenue, without losing sight of the hospital, and called there at half-past one.

Patrice at once saw old Siméon, sitting at the end of a covered yard where the soldiers used to meet. His head was half wrapped up in the usual comforter; and, with his big yellow spectacles on his nose, he sat smoking his pipe on the chair which he always occupied.

As for Coralie, she was in one of the rooms allotted to her on the first floor, seated by the bedside of a patient whose hand she held between her own. The man was asleep.

Coralie appeared to Patrice to be very tired. The dark rings round her eyes and the unusual pallor of her cheeks bore witness to her fatigue.

"Poor child!" he thought. "All those blackguards will be the death of you."

He now understood, when he remembered the scenes of the night before, why Coralie kept her private life secret and endeavoured, at least to the little world of the hospital, to be merely the kind sister whom people call by her Christian name. Suspecting the web of crime with which she was surrounded, she dropped her husband's name and told nobody where she lived. And so well was she protected by the defences set up by her modesty and determination that Patrice dared not go to her and stood rooted to the threshold.

"Yet surely," he said to himself, as he looked at Coralie without being seen by her, "I'm not going to send her in my card!"

He was making up his mind to enter, when a woman who had come up the stairs, talking loudly as she went, called out:

"Where is madame?... M. Siméon, she must come at once!"

Old Siméon, who had climbed the stairs with her, pointed to where Coralie sat at the far end of the room; and the woman rushed in. She said a few words to Coralie, who seemed upset and at once, ran to the door, passing in front of Patrice, and down the stairs, followed by Siméon and the woman.

"I've got a taxi, ma'am," stammered the woman, all out of breath. "I had the luck to find one when I left the house and I kept it. We must be quick, ma'am... The commissary of police told me to..."

Patrice, who was downstairs by this time, heard nothing more; but the last words decided him. He seized hold of Ya-Bon as he passed; and the two of them leapt into a cab, telling the driver to follow Coralie's taxi.

"There's news, Ya-Bon, there's news!" said Patrice. "The plot is thickening. The woman is obviously one of the Essarès' servants and she has come for her mistress by the commissary's orders. Therefore the colonel's disclosures are having their effect. House searched; magistrate's inquest; every sort of worry for Little Mother Coralie; and you have the cheek to advise me to be careful! You imagine that I would leave her to her own devices at such a moment! What a mean nature you must have, my poor Ya-Bon!"

An idea occurred to him; and he exclaimed:

"Heavens! I hope that ruffian of an Essarès hasn't allowed himself to be caught! That would be a disaster! But he was far too sure of himself. I expect he's been trifling away his time..."

All through the drive this fear excited Captain Belval and removed his last scruples. In the end his certainty was absolute. Nothing short of Essarès' arrest could have produced the servant's attitude of panic or Coralie's precipitate departure. Under these conditions, how could he hesitate to interfere in a matter in which his revelations would enlighten the police? All the more so as, by revealing less or more, according to circumstances, he could make his evidence subservient to Coralie's interests.

The two cabs pulled up almost simultaneously outside the Essarès' house, where a car was already standing. Coralie alighted and disappeared through the carriage-gate. The maid and Siméon also crossed the pavement.

"Come along," said Patrice to the Senegalese.

The front-door was ajar and Patrice entered. In the big hall were two policemen on duty. Patrice acknowledged their presence with a hurried movement of his hand and passed them with the air of a man who belonged to the house and whose importance was so great that nothing done without him could be of any use.

The sound of his footsteps echoing on the flags reminded him of the flight of Bournef and his accomplices. He was on the right road. Moreover, there was a drawing-room on the left, the room, communicating with the library, to which the accomplices had carried the colonel's body. Voices came from the library. He walked across the drawing-room.

At that moment he heard Coralie exclaim in accents of terror:

"Oh, my God, it can't be!..."

Two other policemen barred the doorway.

"I am a relation of Mme. Essarès'," he said, "her only relation..."

"We have our orders, captain..."

"I know, of course. Be sure and let no one in! Ya-Bon, stay here."

And he went in.

But, in the immense room, a group of six or seven gentlemen, no doubt commissaries of police and magistrates, stood in his way, bending over something which he was unable to distinguish. From amidst this group Coralie suddenly appeared and came towards him, tottering and wringing her hands. The housemaid took her round the waist and pressed her into a chair.

"What's the matter?" asked Patrice.

"Madame is feeling faint," replied the woman, still quite distraught. "Oh, I'm nearly off my head!"

"But why? What's the reason?"

"It's the master... just think!... Such a sight!... It gave me a turn, too..."

"What sight?"

One of the gentlemen left the group and approached:

"Is Mme. Essarès ill?"

"It's nothing," said the maid. "A fainting-fit... She is liable to these attacks."

"Take her away as soon as she can walk. We shall not need her any longer."

And, addressing Patrice Belval with a questioning air:

"Captain?..."

Patrice pretended not to understand:

"Yes, sir," he said, "we will take Mme. Essarès away. Her presence, as you say, is unnecessary. Only I must first..."

He moved aside to avoid his interlocutor, and, perceiving that the group of magistrates had opened out a little, stepped forward. What he now saw explained Coralie's fainting-fit and the servant's agitation. He himself felt his flesh creep at a spectacle which was infinitely more horrible than that of the evening before.

On the floor, near the fireplace, almost at the place where he had undergone his torture, Essarès Bey lay upon his back. He was wearing the same clothes as on the previous day: a brown-velvet smoking-suit with a braided jacket. His head and shoulders had been covered with a napkin. But one of the men standing around, a divisional surgeon no doubt, was holding up the napkin with one hand and pointing to the dead man's face with the other, while he offered an explanation in a low voice.

And that face... but it was hardly the word for the unspeakable mass of flesh, part of which seemed to be charred while the other part formed no more than a bloodstained pulp, mixed with bits of bone and skin, hairs and a broken eye-ball.

"Oh," Patrice blurted out, "how horrible! He was killed and fell with his head right in the fire. That's how they found him, I suppose?"

The man who had already spoken to him and who appeared to be the most important figure present came up to him once more:

"May I ask who you are?" he demanded.

"Captain Belval, sir, a friend of Mme. Essarès, one of the wounded officers whose lives she has helped to save..."

"That may be, sir," replied the important figure, "but you can't stay here. Nobody must stay here, for that matter. Monsieur le commissaire, please order everyone to leave the room, except the doctor, and have the door guarded. Let no one enter on any pretext whatever..."

"Sir," Patrice insisted, "I have some very serious information to communicate."

"I shall be pleased to receive it, captain, but later on. You must excuse me now."

7

TWENTY-THREE MINUTES PAST TWELVE

The great hall that ran from Rue Raynouard to the upper terrace of the garden was filled to half its extent by a wide staircase and divided the Essarès house into two parts communicating only by way of the hall.

On the left were the drawing-room and the library, which was followed by an independent block containing a private staircase. On the right were a billiard-room and the dining-room, both with lower ceilings. Above these were Essarès Bey's bedroom, on the street side, and Coralie's, overlooking the garden. Beyond was the servants' wing, where old Siméon also used to sleep.

Patrice was asked to wait in the billiard-room, with the Senegalese. He had been there about a quarter of an hour when Siméon and the maid were shown in.

The old secretary seemed quite paralyzed by the death of his employer and was holding forth under his breath, making queer gestures as he spoke. Patrice asked him how things were going; and the old fellow whispered in his ear:

"It's not over yet... There's something to fear... to fear!... Today... presently."

"Presently?" asked Patrice.

"Yes... yes," said the old man, trembling.

He said nothing more. As for the housemaid, she readily told her story in reply to Patrice' questions:

"The first surprise, sir, this morning was that there was no butler, no footman, no porter. All the three were gone. Then, at half-past six, M. Siméon came and told us from the master that the master had locked himself in his library and that he wasn't to be disturbed even for breakfast. The mistress was not very well. She had her chocolate at nine o'clock... At ten o'clock she went out with M. Siméon. Then, after we had done the bedrooms, we never left the kitchen. Eleven o'clock came, twelve... and, just as the hour was striking, we heard a loud ring at the front-door. I looked out of the window. There was a motor, with four gentlemen inside. I went to the door. The commissary of police explained who he was and wanted to see the master. I showed them the way. The library-door was locked. We knocked: no answer. We shook it: no answer. In the end, one of the gentlemen, who knew how, picked the lock... Then... then... you can imagine what we saw... But you can't, it was much worse, because the poor master at that moment had his head almost under the grate... Oh, what scoundrels they must have been!... For they did kill him, didn't they? I know one of the gentlemen said at once that the master had died of a stroke and fallen into the fire. Only my firm belief is..."

Old Siméon had listened without speaking, with his head still half wrapped up, showing only his bristly grey beard and his eyes hidden behind their yellow spectacles. But at this point of the story he gave a little chuckle, came up to Patrice and said in his ear:

"There's something to fear... to fear!... Mme. Coralie... Make her go away at once... make her go away... If not, it'll be the worse for her..."

Patrice shuddered and tried to question him, but could learn nothing more. Besides, the old man did not remain. A policeman came to fetch him and took him to the library.

His evidence lasted a long time. It was followed by the depositions of the cook and the housemaid. Next, Coralie's evidence was taken, in her own room. At four o'clock another car arrived. Patrice saw two gentlemen pass into the hall, with everybody bowing very low before them. He recognized the minister of justice and the minister of the interior. They conferred in the library for half an hour and went away again.

At last, shortly before five o'clock, a policeman came for Patrice and showed him up to the first floor. The man tapped at a door and stood aside. Patrice entered a small boudoir, lit up by a wood fire by which two persons were seated: Coralie, to whom he bowed, and, opposite her, the gentleman who had spoken to him on his arrival and who seemed to be directing the whole enquiry.

He was a man of about fifty, with a thickset body and a heavy face, slow of movement, but with bright, intelligent eyes.

"The examining-magistrate, I presume, sir?" asked Patrice.

"No," he replied, "I am M. Masseron, a retired magistrate, specially appointed to clear up this affair... not to examine it, as you think, for it does not seem to me that there is anything to examine."

"What?" cried Patrice, in great surprise. "Nothing to examine?"

He looked at Coralie, who kept her eyes fixed upon him attentively. Then she turned them on M. Masseron, who resumed:

"I have no doubt, Captain Belval, that, when we have said what we have to say, we shall be agreed at all points... just as madame and I are already agreed."

"I don't doubt it either," said Patrice. "All the same, I am afraid that many of those points remain unexplained."

"Certainly, but we shall find an explanation, we shall find it together. Will you please tell me what you know?"

Patrice waited for a moment and then said:

"I will not disguise my astonishment, sir. The story which I have to tell is of some importance; and yet there is no one here to take it down. Is it not to count as evidence given on oath, as a deposition which I shall have to sign?"

"You yourself, captain, shall determine the value of your words and the innuendo which you wish them to bear. For the moment, we will look on this as a preliminary conversation, as an exchange of views relating to facts... touching which Mme. Essarès has given me, I believe, the same information that you will be able to give me."

Patrice did not reply at once. He had a vague impression that there was a private understanding between Coralie and the magistrate and that, in face of that understanding, he, both by his presence and by his zeal, was playing the part of an intruder whom they would gladly have dismissed. He resolved therefore to maintain an attitude of reserve until the magistrate had shown his hand.

"Of course," he said, "I daresay madame has told you. So you know of the conversation which I overheard yesterday at the restaurant?"

"Yes."

"And the attempt to kidnap Mme. Essarès?"

"Yes."

"And the murder?..."

"Yes."

"Mme. Essarès has described to you the blackmailing scene that took place last night, with M. Essarès for a victim, the details of the torture, the death of the colonel, the handing over of the four millions, the conversation on the telephone between M. Essarès and a certain Gregoire and, lastly, the threats uttered against madame by her husband?"

"Yes, Captain Belval, I know all this, that is to say, all that you know, and I know, in addition, all that I discovered through my own investigations."

"Of course, of course," Patrice repeated. "I see that my story becomes superfluous and that you are in possession of all the necessary factors to enable you to draw your conclusions." And, continuing to put rather than answer questions, he added, "May I ask what inference you have arrived at?"

"To tell you the truth, captain, my inferences are not definite. However, until I receive some proof to the contrary, I propose to remain satisfied with the actual words of a letter which M. Essarès wrote to his wife at about twelve o'clock this morning and which we found lying on his desk, unfinished. Mme. Essarès asked me to read it and, if necessary, to communicate the contents to you. Listen."

M. Masseron proceeded to read the letter aloud:

"Coralie,

"You were wrong yesterday to attribute my departure to reasons which I dared not acknowledge; and perhaps I also was wrong not to defend myself more convincingly against your accusation. The only motive for my departure is the hatred with which I am surrounded. You have seen how fierce it is. In the face of these enemies who are seeking to despoil me by every possible means, my only hope of salvation lies in flight. That is why I am going away.

"But let me remind you, Coralie, of my clearly expressed wish. You are to join me at the first summons. If you do not leave Paris then, nothing shall protect you against my lawful resentment: nothing, not even my death. I have made all my arrangements so that, even in the contingency..."

"The letter ends there," said M. Masseron, handing it back to Coralie, "and we know by an unimpeachable sign that the last lines were written immediately before M. Essarès' death, because, in falling, he upset a little clock which stood on his desk and which marked twenty-three minutes past twelve. I assume that he felt unwell and that, on trying to rise, he was seized with a fit of giddiness and fell to the floor. Unfortunately, the fireplace was near, with a fierce fire blazing in it; his head struck the grate; and the wound that resulted was so deep—the surgeon testified to this—that he fainted. Then the fire close at hand did its work... with the effects which you have seen..."

Patrice had listened in amazement to this unexpected explanation:

"Then in your opinion," he asked, "M. Essarès died of an accident? He was not murdered?"

"Murdered? Certainly not! We have no clue to support any such theory."

"Still..."

"Captain Belval, you are the victim of an association of ideas which, I admit, is perfectly justifiable. Ever since yesterday you have been witnessing a series of tragic incidents; and your imagination naturally leads you to the most tragic solution, that of murder. Only—reflect—why should a murder have been committed? And by whom? By Bournef and his friends? With what object? They were crammed full with bank-notes; and, even admitting that the man called Grégoire recovered those millions from them, they would certainly not have got them back by killing M. Essarès. Then again, how would they have entered the house? And how can they have gone out?... No, captain, you must excuse me, but M. Essarès died an accidental death. The facts are undeniable; and this is the opinion of the divisional surgeon, who will draw up his report in that sense."

Patrice turned to Coralie:

"Is it Mme. Essarès' opinion also?"

She reddened slightly and answered:

"Yes."

"And old Siméon's?"

"Oh," replied the magistrate, "old Siméon is wandering in his mind! To listen to him, you would think that everything was about to happen all over again, that Mme. Essarès is threatened with danger and that she ought to take to flight at once. That is all that I have been able to get out of him. However, he took me to an old disused door that opens out of the garden on a lane running at right angles with the Rue Raynouard; and here he showed me first the watch-dog's dead body and next some footprints between the door and the flight of steps near the library. But you know those footprints, do you not? They belong to you and your Senegalese. As for the death of the watch-dog, I can put that down to your Senegalese, can't I?"

Patrice was beginning to understand. The magistrate's reticence, his explanation, his agreement with Coralie: all this was gradually becoming plain. He put the question frankly:

"So there was no murder?"

"No."

"Then there will be no magistrate's examination?"

"No."

"And no talk about the matter; it will all be kept quiet, in short, and forgotten?"

"Just so."

Captain Belval began to walk up and down, as was his habit. He now remembered Essarès' prophecy:

"I sha'n't be arrested... If I am, I shall be let go... The matter will be hushed up..."

Essarès was right. The hand of justice was arrested; and there was no way for Coralie to escape silent complicity.

Patrice was intensely annoyed by the manner in which the case was being handled. It was certain that a compact had been concluded between Coralie and M. Masseron. He suspected the magistrate of circumventing Coralie and inducing her to sacrifice her own interests to other considerations. To effect this, the first thing was to get rid of him, Patrice.

"Ugh!" said Patrice to himself. "I'm fairly sick of this sportsman, with his cool ironical ways. It looks as if he were doing a considerable piece of thimblerigging at my expense."

He restrained himself, however, and, with a pretence of wanting to keep on good terms with the magistrate, came and sat down beside him:

"You must forgive me, sir," he said, "for insisting in what may appear to you an indiscreet fashion. But my conduct is explained not only by such sympathy or feeling as I entertain for Mme. Essarès at a moment in her life when she is more lonely than ever, a sympathy and feeling which she seems to repulse even more firmly than she did before. It is also explained by certain mysterious links which unite us to each other and which go back to a period too remote for our eyes to focus. Has Mme. Essarès told you those details? In my opinion, they are most important; and I cannot help associating them with the events that interest us."

M. Masseron glanced at Coralie, who nodded. He answered:

"Yes, Mme. Essarès has informed me and even..."

He hesitated once more and again consulted Coralie, who flushed and seemed put out of countenance. M. Masseron, however, waited for a reply which would enable him to proceed. She ended by saying, in a low voice:

"Captain Belval is entitled to know what we have discovered. The truth belongs as much to him as to me; and I have no right to keep it from him. Pray speak, monsieur."

"I doubt if it is even necessary to speak," said the magistrate. "It will be enough, I think, to show the captain this photograph-album which I have found. Here you are, Captain Belval."

And he handed Patrice a very slender album, covered in grey canvas and fastened with an India-rubber band.

Patrice took it with a certain anxiety. But what he saw on opening it was so utterly unexpected that he gave an exclamation:

"It's incredible!"

On the first page, held in place by their four corners, were two photographs: one, on the right, representing a small boy in an Eton jacket; the other, on the left, representing a very little girl. There was an inscription under each. On the right: "Patrice, at ten." On the left: "Coralie, at three."

Moved beyond expression, Patrice turned the leaf. On the second page they appeared again, he at the age of fifteen, she at the age of eight. And he saw himself at nineteen and at twenty-three and at twenty-eight, always accompanied by Coralie, first as a little girl, then as a young girl, next as a woman.

"This is incredible!" he cried. "How is it possible? Here are portraits of myself which I had never seen, amateur photographs obviously, which trace my whole life. Here's one when I was doing my military training... Here I am on horseback... Who can have ordered these photographs? And who can have collected them together with yours, madame?"

He fixed his eyes on Coralie, who evaded their questioning gaze and lowered her head as though the close connection between their two lives, to which those pages bore witness, had shaken her to the very depths of her being.

"Who can have brought them together?" he repeated. "Do you know? And where does the album come from?"

M. Masseron supplied the answer:

"It was the surgeon who found it. M. Essarès wore a vest under his shirt; and the album was in an inner pocket, a pocket sewn inside the vest. The surgeon felt the boards through it when he was undressing M. Essarès' body."

This time, Patrice's and Coralie's eyes met. The thought that M. Essarès had been collecting both their photographs during the past twenty years and that he wore them next to his breast and that he had lived and died with them upon him, this thought amazed them so much that they did not even try to fathom its strange significance.

"Are you sure of what you are saying, sir?" asked Patrice.

"I was there," said M. Masseron. "I was present at the discovery. Besides, I myself made another which confirms this one and completes it in a really surprising fashion. I found a pendant, cut out of a solid block of amethyst and held in a setting of filigree-work."

"What's that?" cried Captain Belval. "What's that? A pendant? An amethyst pendant?"

"Look for yourself, sir," suggested the magistrate, after once more consulting Mme. Essarès with a glance.

And he handed Captain Belval an amethyst pendant, larger than the ball formed by joining the two halves which Coralie and Patrice possessed, she on her rosary and he on his bunch of seals; and this new ball was encircled with a specimen of gold filigreework exactly like that on the rosary and on the seal.

The setting served as a clasp.

"Am I to open it?" he asked.

Coralie nodded. He opened the pendant. The inside was divided by a movable glass disk, which separated two miniature photographs, one of Coralie as a nurse, the other of himself, wounded, in an officer's uniform.

Patrice reflected, with pale cheeks. Presently he asked:

"And where does this pendant come from? Did you find it, sir?"

"Yes, Captain Belval."

"Where?"

The magistrate seemed to hesitate. Coralie's attitude gave Patrice the impression that she was unaware of this detail. M. Masseron at last said:

"I found it in the dead man's hand."

"In the dead man's hand? In M. Essarès' hand?"

Patrice had given a start, as though under an unexpected blow, and was now leaning over the magistrate, greedily awaiting a reply which he wanted to hear for the second time before accepting it as certain.

"Yes, in his hand. I had to force back the clasped fingers in order to release it."

Belval stood up and, striking the table with his fist, exclaimed:

"Well, sir, I will tell you one thing which I was keeping back as a last argument to prove to you that my collaboration is of use; and this thing becomes of great importance after what we have just learnt. Sir, this morning someone asked to speak to me on the telephone; and I had hardly answered the call when this person, who seemed greatly excited, was the victim of a murderous assault, committed in my hearing. And, amid the sound of the scuffle and the cries of agony, I caught the following words, which the unhappy man insisted on trying to get to me as so many last instructions: 'Patrice!... Coralie!... The amethyst pendant... Yes, I have it on me... The pendant... Ah, it's too late!... I should so much have liked... Patrice... Coralie... 'There's what I heard, sir, and here are the two facts which we cannot escape. This morning, at nineteen minutes past seven, a man was murdered having upon him an amethyst pendant. This is the first undeniable fact. A few hours later, at twenty-three minutes past twelve, this same amethyst pendant is discovered clutched in the hand of another man. This is the second undeniable fact. Place these facts side by side and you are bound to come to the conclusion that the first murder, the one of which I caught the distant echo, was committed here, in this house, in the same library which, since yesterday evening, witnessed the end of every scene in the tragedy which we are contemplating."

This revelation, which in reality amounted to a fresh accusation against Essarès, seemed to affect the magistrate profoundly. Patrice had flung himself into the discussion with a passionate vehemence and a logical reasoning which it was impossible to disregard without evident insincerity.

Coralie had turned aside slightly and Patrice could not see her face; but he suspected her dismay in the presence of all this infamy and shame.

M. Masseron raised an objection:

"Two undeniable facts, you say, Captain Belval? As to the first point, let me remark that we have not found the body of the man who is supposed to have been murdered at nineteen minutes past seven this morning."

"It will be found in due course."

"Very well. Second point: as regards the amethyst pendant discovered in Essarès' hand, how can we tell that Essarès Bey found it in the murdered man's hand and not somewhere else? For, after all, we do not know if he was at home at that time and still less if he was in his library."

"But I do know."

"How?"

"I telephoned to him a few minutes later and he answered. More than that, to sweep away any trace of doubt, he told me that he had rung me up but that he had been cut off."

M. Masseron thought for a moment and then said:

"Did he go out this morning?"

"Ask Mme. Essarès."

Without turning round, manifestly wishing to avoid Belval's eyes, Coralie answered:

"I don't think that he went out. The suit he was wearing at the time of his death was an indoor suit."

"Did you see him after last night?"

"He came and knocked at my room three times this morning, between seven and nine o'clock. I did not open the door. At about eleven o'clock I started off alone; I heard him call old

Siméon and tell him to go with me. Siméon caught me up in the street. That is all I know."

A prolonged silence ensued. Each of the three was meditating upon this strange series of adventures. In the end, M. Masseron, who had realized that a man of Captain Belval's stamp was not the sort to be easily thrust aside, spoke in the tone of one who, before coming to terms, wishes to know exactly what his adversary's last word is likely to be:

"Let us come to the point, captain. You are building up a theory which strikes me as very vague. What is it precisely? And what are you proposing to do if I decline to accept it? I have asked you two very plain questions. Do you mind answering them?"

"I will answer them, sir, as plainly as you put them."

He went up to the magistrate and said:

"Here, sir, is the field of battle and of attack—yes, of attack, if need be—which I select. A man who used to know me, who knew Mme. Essarès as a child and who was interested in both of us, a man who used to collect our portraits at different ages, who had reasons for loving us unknown to me, who sent me the key of that garden and who was making arrangements to bring us together for a purpose which he would have told us, this man was murdered at the moment when he was about to execute his plan. Now everything tells me that he was murdered by M. Essarès. I am therefore resolved to lodge an information, whatever the results of my action may be. And believe me, sir, my charge will not be hushed up. There are always means of making one's self heard... even if I am reduced to shouting the truth from the house-tops."

M. Masseron burst out laughing:

"By Jove, captain, but you're letting yourself go!"

"I'm behaving according to my conscience; and Mme. Essarès, I feel sure, will forgive me. She knows that I am acting for her good. She knows that all will be over with her if this case is hushed up and if the authorities do not assist her. She knows that the enemies who threaten her are implacable. They will stop at nothing to attain their object and to do away with her, for she stands in their way. And the terrible thing about it is that the most clear-seeing eyes are unable to make out what that object is. We are playing the most formidable game against these enemies; and we do not even know what the stakes are. Only the police can discover those stakes."

M. Masseron waited for a second or two and then, laying his hand on Patrice's shoulder, said, calmly:

"And, suppose the authorities knew what the stakes were?"

Patrice looked at him in surprise:

"What? Do you mean to say you know?"

"Perhaps."

"And can you tell me?"

"Oh, well, if you force me to!"

"What are they?"

"Not much! A trifle!"

"But what sort of trifle?"

"A thousand million francs."

"A thousand millions?"

"Just that. A thousand millions, of which two-thirds, I regret to say, if not three-quarters, had already left France before the war. But the remaining two hundred and fifty or three hundred millions are worth more than a thousand millions all the same, for a very good reason."

"What reason?"

"They happen to be in gold."

8

ESSARÈS BEY'S WORK

This time Captain Belval seemed to relax to some extent. He vaguely perceived the consideration that compelled the authorities to wage the battle prudently.

"Are you sure?" he asked.

"Yes, I was instructed to investigate this matter two years ago; and my enquiries proved that really remarkable exports of gold were being effected from France. But, I confess, it is only since my conversation with Mme. Essarès that I have seen where the leakage came from and who it was that set on foot, all over France, down to the least important market-towns, the formidable organization through which the indispensable metal was made to leave the country."

"Then Mme. Essarès knew?"

"No, but she suspected a great deal; and last night, before you arrived, she overheard some words spoken between Essarès and his assailants which she repeated to me, thus giving me the key to the riddle. I should have been glad to work out the complete solution without your assistance—for one thing, those were the orders of the minister of the interior; and Mme. Essarès displayed the same wish—but your impetuosity overcomes my hesitation; and, since I can't manage to get rid of you, Captain

Belval, I will tell you the whole story frankly... especially as your cooperation is not to be despised."

"I am all ears," said Patrice, who was burning to know more.

"Well, the motive force of the plot was here, in this house. Essarès Bey, president of the Franco-Oriental Bank, 6, Rue Lafayette, apparently an Egyptian, in reality a Turk, enjoyed the greatest influence in the Paris financial world. He had been naturalized an Englishman, but had kept up secret relations with the former possessors of Egypt; and he had received instructions from a foreign power, which I am not yet able to name with certainty, to bleed—there is no other word for it—to bleed France of all the gold that he could cause to flow into his coffers. According to documents which I have seen, he succeeded in exporting in this way some seven hundred million francs in two years. A last consignment was preparing when war was declared. You can understand that thenceforth such important sums could not be smuggled out of the country so easily as in times of peace. The railway-wagons are inspected on the frontiers; the outgoing vessels are searched in the harbours. In short, the gold was not sent away. Those two hundred and fifty or three hundred millions remained in France. Ten months passed; and the inevitable happened, which was that Essarès Bey, having this fabulous treasure at his disposal, clung to it, came gradually to look upon it as his own and, in the end, resolved to appropriate it. Only there were accomplices..."

"The men I saw last night?"

"Yes, half-a-dozen shady Levantines, sham naturalized French citizens, more or less well-disguised Bulgarians, secret agents of the little German courts in the Balkans. This gang ran provincial branches of Essarès' bank. It had in its pay, on Essarès' account, hundreds of minor agents, who scoured the villages, visited the fairs, were hail-fellow-well-met with the peasants, offered them bank-notes and government securities in exchange for French gold and trousered all their savings. When war broke out the gang shut up shop and gathered round Essarès Bey, who also had closed his offices in the Rue Lafayette."

"What happened then?"

"Things that we don't know. No doubt the accomplices learnt from their governments that the last despatch of gold had never taken place; and no doubt they also guessed that Essarès Bey was trying to keep for himself the three hundred millions collected by the gang. One thing is certain, that a struggle began between the former partners, a fierce, implacable struggle, the accomplices wanting their share of the plunder, while Essarès Bey was resolved to part with none of it and pretended that the millions had left the country. Yesterday the struggle attained its culminating-point. In the afternoon the accomplices tried to get hold of Mme. Essarès so that they might have a hostage to use against her husband. In the evening... in the evening you yourself witnessed the final episode."

"But why yesterday evening rather than another?"

"Because the accomplices had every reason to think that the millions were intended to disappear yesterday evening. Though they did not know the methods employed by Essarès Bey when he made his last remittances, they believed that each of the remittances, or rather each removal of the sacks, was preceded by a signal."

"Yes, a shower of sparks, was it not?"

"Exactly. In a corner of the garden are some old conservatories, above which stands the furnace that used to heat them. This grimy furnace, full of soot and rubbish, sends forth, when you light it, flakes of fire and sparks which are seen at a distance and serve as an intimation. Essarès Bey lit it last night himself. The accomplices at once took alarm and came prepared to go any lengths."

"And Essarès' plan failed."

"Yes. But so did theirs. The colonel is dead. The others were only able to get hold of a few bundles of notes which have probably been taken from them by this time. But the struggle was not finished; and its dying agony has been a most shocking tragedy. According to your statement, a man who knew you and who was seeking to get into touch with you, was killed at nineteen minutes past seven, most likely by Essarès Bey, who dreaded his intervention. And, five hours later, at twenty-three past twelve, Essarès Bey himself was murdered, presumably by one of his accomplices. There is the whole story, Captain Belval. And, now that you know as much of it as I do, don't you think that the investigation of this case should remain secret and be pursued not quite in accordance with the ordinary rules?"

After a moment's reflection Patrice said:

"Yes, I agree."

"There can be no doubt about it!" cried M. Masseron. "Not only will it serve no purpose to publish this story of gold which has disappeared and which can't be found, which would startle the public and excite their imaginations, but you will readily imagine that an operation which consisted in draining off such a quantity of gold in two years cannot have been effected without compromising a regrettable number of people. I feel certain that my own enquiries will reveal a series of weak concessions and unworthy bargains on the part of certain more or less important banks and credit-houses, transactions on which I do not wish to insist, but which it would be the gravest of blunders to publish. Therefore, silence."

"But is silence possible?"

"Why not?"

"Bless my soul, there are a good few corpses to be explained away! Colonel Fakhi's, for instance?"

"Suicide."

"Mustapha's, which you will discover or which you have already discovered in the Galliéra garden?"

"Found dead."

"Essarès Bey's?"

"An accident."

"So that all these manifestations of the same power will remain separated?"

"There is nothing to show the link that connects them."

"Perhaps the public will think otherwise."

"The public will think what we wish it to think. This is war-time."

"The press will speak."

"The press will do nothing of the kind. We have the censorship."

"But, if some fact or, rather, a fresh crime...?"

"Why should there be a fresh crime? The matter is finished, at least on its active and dramatic side. The chief actors are dead. The curtain falls on the murder of Essarès Bey. As for the supernumeraries, Bournef and the others, we shall have them stowed away in an internment-camp before a week is past. We therefore find ourselves in the presence of a certain number of millions, with no owner, with no one who dares to claim them, on which France is entitled to lay hands. I shall devote my activity to securing the money for the republic."

Patrice Belval shook his head:

"Mme. Essarès remains, sir. We must not forget her husband's threats."

"He is dead."

"No matter, the threats are there. Old Siméon tells you so in a striking fashion."

"He's half mad."

"Exactly, his brain retains the impression of great and imminent danger. No, the struggle is not ended. Perhaps indeed it is only beginning."

"Well, captain, are we not here? Make it your business to protect and defend Mme. Essarès by all the means in your power and by all those which I place at your disposal. Our collaboration will be uninterrupted, because my task lies here and because, if the battle—which you expect and I do not—takes place, it will be within the walls of this house and garden."

"What makes you think that?"

"Some words which Mme. Essarès overheard last night. The colonel repeated several times, 'The gold is here, Essarès.' He added, 'For years past, your car brought to this house all that there was at your bank in the Rue Lafayette. Siméon, you and the chauffeur used to let the sacks down the last grating on the left. How you used to send it away I do not know. But of what was here on the day when the war broke out, of the seventeen or eighteen hundred bags which they were expecting out yonder, none has left your place. I suspected the trick; and we kept watch night and day. The gold is here.'"

"And have you no clue?"

"Not one. Or this at most; but I attach comparatively little value to it."

He took a crumpled paper from his pocket, unfolded it and continued:

"Besides the pendant, Essarès Bey held in his hand this bit of blotted paper, on which you can see a few straggling, hurriedly-written words. The only ones that are more or less legible are these: 'golden triangle.' What this golden triangle means, what it has to do with the case in hand, I can't for the present tell. The most that I am able to presume is that, like the pendant, the scrap of paper was snatched by Essarès Bey from the man who died at nineteen minutes past seven this morning and that, when he himself was killed at twenty-three minutes past twelve, he was occupied in examining it."

"And then there is the album," said Patrice, making his last point. "You see how all the details are linked together. You may safely believe that it is all one case."

"Very well," said M. Masseron. "One case in two parts. You, captain, had better follow up the second. I grant you that nothing could be stranger than this discovery of photographs of Mme. Essarès and yourself in the same album and in the same pendant. It sets a problem the solution of which will no doubt bring us very near to the truth. We shall meet again soon, Captain Belval, I hope. And, once more, make use of me and of my men."

He shook Patrice by the hand. Patrice held him back:

"I shall make use of you, sir, as you suggest. But is this not the time to take the necessary precautions?"

"They are taken, captain. We are in occupation of the house."

"Yes... yes... I know; but, all the same... I have a sort of presentiment that the day will not end without... Remember old Siméon's strange words..."

M. Masseron began to laugh:

"Come, Captain Belval, we mustn't exaggerate things. If any enemies remain for us to fight, they must stand in great need, for the moment, of taking council with themselves. We'll talk about this tomorrow, shall we, captain?"

He shook hands with Patrice again, bowed to Mme. Essarès and left the room.

Belval had at first made a discreet movement to go out with him. He stopped at the door and walked back again. Mme. Essarès, who seemed not to hear him, sat motionless, bent in two, with her head turned away from him.

"Coralie," he said.

She did not reply; and he uttered her name a second time, hoping that again she might not answer, for her silence suddenly appeared to him to be the one thing in the world for him to desire. That silence no longer implied either constraint or rebellion. Coralie accepted the fact that he was there, by her side, as a helpful friend. And Patrice no longer thought of all the problems that harassed him, nor of the murders that had mounted up, one after another, around them, nor of the dangers that might still encompass them. He thought only of Coralie's yielding gentleness.

"Don't answer, Coralie, don't say a word. It is for me to speak. I must tell you what you do not know, the reasons that made you wish to keep me out of this house... out of this house and out of your very life."

He put his hand on the back of the chair in which she was sitting; and his hand just touched Coralie's hair.

"Coralie, you imagine that it is the shame of your life here that keeps you away from me. You blush at having been that man's wife; and this makes you feel troubled and anxious, as though you yourself had been guilty. But why should you? It was not your fault. Surely you know that I can guess the misery and hatred that must have passed between you and him and the constraint that was brought to bear upon you, by some machination, in order to force your consent to the marriage! No, Coralie, there is something else; and I will tell you what it is. There is something else..."

He was bending over her still more. He saw her beautiful profile lit up by the blazing logs and, speaking with increasing fervour and adopting the familiar *tu* and *toi* which, in his mouth, retained a note of affectionate respect, he cried:

"Am I to speak, Little Mother Coralie? I needn't, need I? You have understood; and you read yourself clearly. Ah, I feel you trembling from head to foot! Yes, yes, I tell you, I knew your secret from the very first day. From the very first day you loved your great beggar of a wounded man, all scarred and maimed though he was. Hush! Don't deny it!... Yes, I understand: you are rather shocked to hear such words as these spoken today. I ought perhaps to have waited. And yet why should I? I am asking you nothing. I know; and that is enough for me. I sha'n't speak of it again for a long time to come, until the inevitable hour arrives when you are forced to tell it to me yourself. Till then I shall keep silence. But our love will always be between us; and it will be exquisite, Little Mother Coralie, it will be exquisite for me to know that you love me. Coralie... There, now you're crying! And you would still deny the truth? Why, when you cry—I know you, Little Mother—it means that your dear heart is overflowing with tenderness and love! You are crying? Ah, Little Mother, I never thought you loved me to that extent!"

Patrice also had tears in his eyes. Coralie's were coursing down her pale cheeks; and he would have given much to kiss that wet face. But the least outward sign of affection appeared to him an offense at such a moment. He was content to gaze at her passionately.

And, as he did so, he received an impression that her thoughts were becoming detached from his own, that her eyes were being attracted by an unexpected sight and that, amid the great silence of their love, she was listening to something that he himself had not heard.

And suddenly he too heard that thing, though it was almost imperceptible. It was not so much a sound as the sensation of a presence mingling with the distant rumble of the town. What could be happening?

The light had begun to fade, without his noticing it. Also unperceived by Patrice, Mme. Essarès had opened the window a little way, for the boudoir was small and the heat of the fire was becoming oppressive. Nevertheless, the two casements were almost touching. It was at this that she was staring; and it was from there that the danger threatened.

Patrice's first impulse was to run to the window, but he restrained himself. The danger was becoming defined. Outside, in the twilight, he distinguished through the slanting panes a human form. Next, he saw between the two casements something which gleamed in the light of the fire and which looked like the barrel of a revolver.

"Coralie is done for," he thought, "if I allow it to be suspected for an instant that I am on my guard."

She was in fact opposite the window, with no obstacle intervening. He therefore said aloud, in a careless tone:

"Coralie, you must be a little tired. We will say goodbye."

At the same time, he went round her chair to protect her.

But he had not the time to complete his movement. She also no doubt had seen the glint of the revolver, for she drew back abruptly, stammering:

"Oh, Patrice!... Patrice!..."

Two shots rang out, followed by a moan.

"You're wounded!" cried Patrice, springing to her side.

"No, no," she said, "but the fright..."

"Oh, if he's touched you, the scoundrel!"

"No, he hasn't."

"Are you quite sure?"

He lost thirty or forty seconds, switching on the electric light, looking at Coralie for signs of a wound and waiting in an agony of suspense for her to regain full consciousness. Only then did he rush to the window, open it wide and climb over the balcony. The room was on the first floor. There was plenty of lattice-work on the wall. But, because of his leg, Patrice had some difficulty in making his way down.

Below, on the terrace, he caught his foot in the rungs of an overturned ladder. Next, he knocked against some policemen who were coming from the ground-floor. One of them shouted:

"I saw the figure of a man making off that way."

"Which way?" asked Patrice.

The man was running in the direction of the lane. Patrice followed him. But, at that moment, from close beside the little door, there came shrill cries and the whimper of a choking voice:

"Help!... Help!..."

When Patrice came up, the policeman was already flashing his electric lantern over the ground; and they both saw a human form writhing in the shrubbery.

"The door's open!" shouted Patrice. "The assassin has escaped! Go after him!"

The policeman vanished down the lane; and, Ya-Bon appearing on the scene, Patrice gave him his orders:

"Quick as you can, Ya-Bon!... If the policeman is going up the lane, you go down. Run! I'll look after the victim."

All this time, Patrice was stooping low, flinging the light of the policeman's lantern on the man who lay struggling on the ground. He recognized old Siméon, nearly strangled, with a red-silk cord round his neck.

"How do you feel?" he asked. "Can you understand what I'm saying?"

He unfastened the cord and repeated his question. Siméon stuttered out a series of incoherent syllables and then suddenly began to sing and laugh, a very low, jerky laugh, alternating with hiccoughs. He had gone mad.

When M. Masseron arrived, Patrice told him what had happened:

"Do you really believe it's all over?" he asked.

"No. You were right and I was wrong," said M. Masseron. "We must take every precaution to ensure Mme. Essarès' safety. The house shall be guarded all night."

A few minutes later the policeman and Ya-Bon returned, after a vain search. The key that had served to open the door was found in the lane. It was exactly similar to the one in Patrice Belval's possession, equally old and equally rusty. The would-be murderer had thrown it away in the course of his flight.

It was seven o'clock when Patrice, accompanied by Ya-Bon, left the house in the Rue Raynouard and turned towards Neuilly. As usual, Patrice took Ya-Bon's arm and, leaning upon him for support as he walked, he said:

"I can guess what you're thinking, Ya-Bon."

Ya-Bon grunted.

"That's it," said Captain Belval, in a tone of approval. "We are entirely in agreement all along the line. What strikes you first and foremost is the utter incapacity displayed by the police. A pack of addle-pates, you say? When you speak like that, Master Ya-Bon, you are talking impertinent nonsense, which, coming from you, does not astonish me and which might easily make me give you the punishment you deserve. But we will overlook it this time. Whatever you may say, the police do what they can, not to mention that, in war-time, they have other things to do than to occupy themselves with the mysterious relations between Captain Belval and Mme. Essarès. It is I therefore who will have to act; and I have hardly anyone to reckon on but myself. Well, I wonder if I am a match for such adversaries. To think that here's one who has the cheek to come back to the house while it is being watched by the police, to put up a ladder, to listen no doubt to my conversation with M. Masseron and afterwards to what I said to Little Mother Coralie and, lastly, to send a couple of bullets whizzing past our ears! What do you say? Am I the man for the job? And could all the French police, overworked as they are, give me the indispensable assistance? No, the man I need for clearing up a thing like this is an exceptional sort of chap, one who unites every quality in himself, in short the type of man one never sees."

Patrice leant more heavily on his companion's arm:

"You, who know so many good people, haven't you the fellow I want concealed about your person? A genius of sorts? A demigod?"

Ya-Bon grunted again, merrily this time, and withdrew his arm. He always carried a little electric lamp. Switching on the light, he put the handle between his teeth. Then he took a bit of chalk out of his jacket-pocket.

A grimy, weather-beaten plaster wall ran along the street. Ya-Bon took his stand in front of the wall and, turning the light upon it, began to write with an unskilful hand, as though each letter cost him a measureless effort and as though the sum total of those letters were the only one that he had ever succeeded in composing and remembering. In this way he wrote two words which Patrice read out:

Arsène Lupin.

"Arsène Lupin," said Patrice, under his breath. And, looking at Ya-Bon in amazement, "Are you in your right mind? What do you mean by Arsène Lupin? Are you suggesting Arsène Lupin to me?"

Ya-Bon nodded his head.

"Arsène Lupin? Do you know him?"

"Yes," Ya-Bon signified.

Patrice then remembered that the Senegalese used to spend his days at the hospital getting his good-natured comrades to read all the adventures of Arsène Lupin aloud to him; and he grinned:

"Yes, you know him as one knows somebody whose history one has read."

"No," protested Ya-Bon.

"Do you know him personally?"

"Yes."

"Get out, you silly fool! Arsène Lupin is dead. He threw himself into the sea from a rock; and you pretend that you know him?"

"Yes."

"Do you mean to say that you have met him since he died?"

"Yes."

"By Jove! And Master Ya-Bon's influence with Arsène Lupin is enough to make him come to life again and put himself out at a sign from Master Ya-Bon?"

"Yes."

"I say! I had a high opinion of you as it was, but now there is nothing for me but to make you my bow. A friend of the late Arsène Lupin! We're going it!... And how long will it take you to place his ghost at our disposal? Six months? Three months? One month? A fortnight?"

Ya-Bon made a gesture.

"About a fortnight," Captain Belval translated. "Very well, evoke your friend's spirit; I shall be delighted to make his acquaintance. Only, upon my word, you must have a very poor idea of me to imagine that I need a collaborator! What next! Do you take me for a helpless dunderhead?"

9

PATRICE AND CORALIE

Everything happened as M. Masseron had foretold. The press did not speak. The public did not become excited. The various deaths were casually paragraphed. The funeral of Essarès Bey, the wealthy banker, passed unnoticed.

But, on the day following the funeral, after Captain Belval, with the support of the police, had made an application to the military authorities, a new order of things was established in the house in the Rue Raynouard. It was recognized as Home No. 2 attached to the hospital in the Champs-Élysées; Mme. Essarès was appointed matron; and it became the residence of Captain Belval and his seven wounded men exclusively.

Coralie, therefore, was the only woman remaining. The cook and housemaid were sent away. The seven cripples did all the work of the house. One acted as hall-porter, another as cook, a third as butler. Ya-Bon, promoted to parlour-maid, made it his business to wait on Little Mother Coralie. At night he slept in the passage outside her door. By day he mounted guard outside her window.

"Let no one near that door or that window!" Patrice said to him. "Let no one in! You'll catch it if so much as a mosquito succeeds in entering her room."

Nevertheless, Patrice was not easy in his mind. The enemy had given him too many proofs of reckless daring to let him imagine that he could take any steps to ensure her perfect protection. Danger always creeps in where it is least expected; and it was all the more difficult to ward off in that no one knew whence it threatened. Now that Essarès Bey was dead, who was continuing his work? Who had inherited the task of revenge upon Coralie announced in his last letter?

M. Masseron had at once begun his work of investigation, but the dramatic side of the case seemed to leave him indifferent. Since he had not found the body of the man whose dying cries reached Patrice Belval's ears, since he had discovered no clue to the mysterious assailant who had fired at Patrice and Coralie later in the day, since he was not able to trace where the assailant had obtained his ladder, he dropped these questions and confined his efforts entirely to the search of the eighteen hundred bags of gold. These were all that concerned him.

"We have every reason to believe that they are here," he said, "between the four sides of the quadrilateral formed by the garden and the house. Obviously, a bag of gold weighing a hundredweight does not take up as much room, by a long way, as a sack of coal of the same weight. But, for all that, eighteen hundred bags represent a cubic content; and a content like that is not easily concealed."

In two days he had assured himself that the treasure was hidden neither in the house nor under the house. On the evenings when Essarès Bey's car brought the gold out of the coffers of the Franco-Oriental Bank to the Rue Raynouard, Essarès, the chauffeur and the man known as Grégoire used to pass a thick wire through the grating of which the accomplices spoke. This wire was found. Along the wire ran hooks, which were also found; and on these the bags were slung and afterwards stacked in a large cellar situated exactly under the library. It is needless to say that M. Masseron and his detectives devoted all their ingenuity and all the painstaking patience of which they were capable to the task of searching every corner of this cellar. Their efforts only established beyond doubt that it contained no secret, save that of a staircase which ran down from the library and which was closed at the top by a trapdoor concealed by the carpet.

In addition to the grating on the Rue Raynouard, there was another which overlooked the garden, on the level of the first terrace. These two openings were barricaded on the inside by very heavy shutters, so that it was an easy matter to stack thousands and thousands of rouleaus of gold in the cellar before sending them away.

"But how were they sent away?" M. Masseron wondered. "That's the mystery. And why this intermediate stage in the basement, in the Rue Raynouard? Another mystery. And now we have Fakhi, Bournef and Co. declaring that, this time, it was not sent away, that the gold is here and that it can be found for the searching. We have searched the house. There is still the garden. Let us look there."

It was a beautiful old garden and had once formed part of the wide-stretching estate where people were in the habit, at the end of the eighteenth century, of going to drink the Passy waters. With a two-hundred-yard frontage, it ran from the Rue Raynouard to the quay of the river-side and led, by four successive terraces, to an expanse of lawn as old as the rest of the garden, fringed with thickets of evergreens and shaded by groups of tall trees.

But the beauty of the garden lay chiefly in its four terraces and in the view which they afforded of the river, the low ground on the left bank and the distant hills. They were united by twenty sets of steps; and twenty paths climbed from the one to the other, paths cut between the buttressing walls and sometimes hidden in the floods of ivy that dashed from top to bottom.

Here and there a statue stood out, a broken column, or the fragments of a capital. The stone balcony that edged the upper terrace was still adorned with all its old terracotta vases. On this terrace also were the ruins of two little round temples where, in the old days, the springs bubbled to the surface. In front of the library windows was a circular basin, with in the centre the figure of a child shooting a slender thread of water through the funnel of a shell. It was the overflow from this basin, forming a little stream, that trickled over the rocks against which Patrice had stumbled on the first evening.

"Ten acres to explore before we've done," said M. Masseron to himself.

He employed upon this work, in addition to Belval's cripples, a dozen of his own detectives. It was not a difficult business and was bound to lead to some definite result. As M. Masseron never ceased saying, eighteen hundred bags cannot remain invisible. An excavation leaves traces. You want a hole to go in and out by. But neither the grass of the lawns nor the sand of the paths showed any signs of earth recently disturbed. The ivy? The buttressing-walls? The terraces? Everything was inspected, but in vain. Here and there, in cutting up the ground, old conduit pipes were found, running towards the Seine, and remains of aqueducts that had once served to carry off the Passy waters. But there was no such thing as a cave, an underground chamber, a brick arch or anything that looked like a hiding-place.

Patrice and Coralie watched the progress of the search. And yet, though they fully realized its importance and though, on the other hand, they were still feeling the strain of the recent dramatic hours, in reality they were engrossed only in the inexplicable problem of their fate; and their conversation nearly always turned upon the mystery of the past.

Coralie's mother was the daughter of a French consul at Salonica, where she married a very rich man of a certain age, called Count Odolavitch, the head of an ancient Servian family. He died a year after Coralie was born. The widow and child were at that time in France, at this same house in the Rue Raynouard, which Count Odolavitch had purchased through a young Egyptian called Essarès, his secretary and factotum.

Coralie here spent three years of her childhood. Then she suddenly lost her mother and was left alone in the world. Essarès took her to Salonica, to a surviving sister of her grandfather the consul, a woman many years younger than her brother. This lady took charge of Coralie. Unfortunately, she fell under Essarès' influence, signed papers and made her little grand-niece sign papers, until the child's whole fortune, administered by the Egyptian, gradually disappeared.

At last, when she was about seventeen, Coralie became the victim of an adventure which left the most hideous memory in her mind and which had a fatal effect on her life. She was kidnapped one morning by a band of Turks on the plains of Salonica and spent a fortnight in the palace of the governor of the province, exposed to his desires. Essarès released her. But the release was brought about in so fantastic a fashion that Coralie must have often wondered afterwards whether the Turk and the Egyptian were not in collusion.

At any rate, sick in body and depressed in spirits, fearing a fresh assault upon her liberty and yielding to her aunt's wishes, a month later she married this Essarès, who had already been paying her his addresses and who now definitely assumed in her eyes the figure of a deliverer. It was a hopeless union, the horror of which became manifest to her on the very day on which it was cemented. Coralie was the wife of a man whom she hated and whose love only grew with the hatred and contempt which she showed for it.

Before the end of the year they came and took up their residence at the house in the Rue Raynouard. Essarès, who had long ago established and was at that time managing the

Salonica branch of the Franco-Oriental Bank, bought up almost all the shares of the bank itself, acquired the building in the Rue Lafayette for the head office, became one of the financial magnates of Paris and received the title of Bey in Egypt.

This was the story which Coralie told Patrice one day in the beautiful garden at Passy; and, in this unhappy past which they explored together and compared with Patrice Belval's own, neither he nor Coralie was able to discover a single point that was common to both. The two of them had lived in different parts of the world. Not one name evoked the same recollection in their minds. There was not a detail that enabled them to understand why each should possess a piece of the same amethyst bead nor why their joint images should be contained in the same medallion-pendant or stuck in the pages of the same album.

"Failing everything else," said Patrice, "we can explain that the pendant found in the hand of Essarès Bey was snatched by him from the unknown friend who was watching over us and whom he murdered. But what about the album, which he wore in a pocket sewn inside his vest?"

Neither attempted to answer the question. Then Patrice asked:

"Tell me about Siméon."

"Siméon has always lived here."

"Even in your mother's time?"

"No, it was one or two years after my mother's death and after I went to Salonica that Essarès put him to look after this property and keep it in good condition."

"Was he Essarès' secretary?"

"I never knew what his exact functions were. But he was not Essarès' secretary, nor his confidant either. They never talked together intimately. He came to see us two or three times at Salonica. I remember one of his visits. I was quite a child and

I heard him speaking to Essarès in a very angry tone, apparently threatening him."

"With what?"

"I don't know. I know nothing at all about Siméon. He kept himself very much to himself and was nearly always in the garden, smoking his pipe, dreaming, tending the trees and flowers, sometimes with the assistance of two or three gardeners whom he would send for."

"How did he behave to you?"

"Here again I can't give any definite impression. We never talked; and his occupations very seldom brought him into contact with me. Nevertheless I sometimes thought that his eyes used to seek me, through their yellow spectacles, with a certain persistency and perhaps even a certain interest. Moreover, lately, he liked going with me to the hospital; and he would then, either there or on the way, show himself more attentive, more eager to please... so much so that I have been wondering this last day or two..."

She hesitated for a moment, undecided whether to speak, and then continued:

"Yes, it's a very vague notion... but, all the same... Look here, there's one thing I forgot to tell you. Do you know why I joined the hospital in the Champs-Élysées, the hospital where you were lying wounded and ill? It was because Siméon took me there. He knew that I wanted to become a nurse and he suggested this hospital... And then, if you think, later on, the photograph in the pendant, the one showing you in uniform and me as a nurse, can only have been taken at the hospital. Well, of the people here, in this house, no one except Siméon ever went there... You will also remember that he used to come to Salonica, where he saw me as a child and afterwards as a girl, and that there also he may have taken the snapshots in the album. So that, if we allow that he had some correspondent who on his side followed your footsteps in life, it would not be impossible to believe that the unknown friend whom you assume to have intervened between us, the one who sent you the key of the garden..."

"Was old Siméon?" Patrice interrupted. "The theory won't hold water."

"Why not?"

"Because this friend is dead. The man who, as you say, sought to intervene between us, who sent me the key of the garden, who called me to the telephone to tell me the truth, that man was murdered. There is not the least doubt about it. I heard the cries of a man who is being killed, dying cries, the cries which a man utters when at the moment of death."

"You can never be sure."

"I am, absolutely. There is no shadow of doubt in my mind. The man whom I call our unknown friend died before finishing his work; he died murdered, whereas Siméon is alive. Besides," continued Patrice, "this man had a different voice from Siméon, a voice which I had never heard before and which I shall never hear again."

Coralie was convinced and did not insist.

They were seated on one of the benches in the garden, enjoying the bright April sunshine. The buds of the chestnut-trees shone at the tips of the branches. The heavy scent of the wall-flowers rose from the borders; and their brown and yellow blossoms, like a cluster of bees and wasps pressed close together, swayed to the light breeze.

Suddenly Patrice felt a thrill. Coralie had placed her hand on his, with engaging friendliness; and, when he turned to look at her, he saw that she was in tears.

"What's the matter, Little Mother Coralie?"

Coralie's head bent down and her cheek touched the officer's shoulder. He dared not move. She was treating him as a protecting elder brother; and he shrank from showing any warmth of affection that might annoy her.

"What is it, dear?" he repeated. "What's the matter?"

"Oh, it is so strange!" she murmured. "Look, Patrice, look at those flowers."

They were on the third terrace, commanding a view of the fourth; and this, the lowest of the terraces, was adorned not with borders of wallflowers but with beds in which were mingled all manner of spring flowers; tulips, silvery alyssums, hyacinths, with a great round plot of pansies in the middle.

"Look over there," she said, pointing to this plot with her outstretched arm. "Do you see?... Letters..."

Patrice looked and gradually perceived that the clumps of pansies were so arranged as to form on the ground some letters that stood out among the other flowers. It did not appear at the first glance. It took a certain time to see; but, once seen, the letters grouped themselves of their own accord, forming three words set down in a single line:

Patrice and Coralie

"Ah," he said, in a low voice, "I understand what you mean!"

It gave them a thrill of inexpressible excitement to read their two names, which a friendly hand had, so to speak, sown; their two names united in pansy-flowers. It was inexpressibly exciting too that he and she should always find themselves thus linked together, linked together by events, linked together by their portraits, linked together by an unseen force of will, linked together now by the struggling effort of little flowers that spring up, waken into life and blossom in predetermined order.

Coralie, sitting up, said:

"It's Siméon who attends to the garden."

"Yes," he said, wavering slightly. "But surely that does not affect my opinion. Our unknown friend is dead, but Siméon may have known him. Siméon perhaps was acting with him in certain matters and must know a good deal. Oh, if he could only put us on the right road!"

An hour later, as the sun was sinking on the horizon, they climbed the terraces. On reaching the top they saw M. Masseron beckoning to them.

"I have something curious to show you," he said, "something I have found which will interest both you, madame, and you, captain, particularly."

He led them to the very end of the terrace, outside the occupied part of the house next to the library. Two detectives were standing mattock in hand. In the course of their searching, M. Masseron explained, they had begun by removing the ivy from the low wall adorned with terracotta vases. Thereupon M. Masseron's attention was attracted by the fact that this wall was covered, for a length of some yards, by a layer of plaster which appeared to be more recent in date than the stone.

"What did it mean?" said M. Masseron. "I had to presuppose some motive. I therefore had this layer of plaster demolished; and underneath it I found a second layer, not so thick as the first and mingled with the rough stone. Come closer... or, rather, no, stand back a little way: you can see better like that."

The second layer really served only to keep in place some small white pebbles, which constituted a sort of mosaic set in black pebbles and formed a series of large, written letters, spelling three words. And these three words once again were:

Patrice and Coralie

"What do you say to that?" asked M. Masseron. "Observe that the inscription goes several years back, at least ten years, when we consider the condition of the ivy clinging to this part of the wall."

"At least ten years," Patrice repeated, when he was once more alone with Coralie. "Ten years ago was when you were not married, when you were still at Salonica and when nobody used to come to this garden... nobody except Siméon and such people as he chose to admit. And among these," he concluded, "was our unknown friend who is now dead. And Siméon knows the truth, Coralie."

They saw old Siméon, late that afternoon, as they had seen him constantly since the tragedy, wandering in the garden or along the passages of the house, restless and distraught, with his comforter always wound round his head and his spectacles on his nose, stammering words which no one could understand. At night, his neighbour, one of the maimed soldiers, would often hear him humming to himself.

Patrice twice tried to make him speak. He shook his head and did not answer, or else laughed like an idiot.

The problem was becoming complicated; and nothing pointed to a possible solution. Who was it that, since their childhood, had promised them to each other as a pair betrothed long beforehand by an inflexible ordinance? Who was it that arranged the pansybed last autumn, when they did not know each other? And who was it that had written their two names, ten years ago, in white pebbles, within the thickness of a wall?

These were haunting questions for two young people in whom love had awakened quite spontaneously and who suddenly saw stretching behind them a long past common to them both. Each step that they took in the garden seemed to them a pilgrimage amid forgotten memories; and, at every turn in a path, they were prepared to discover some new proof of the bond that linked them together unknown to themselves.

As a matter of fact, during those few days, they saw their initials interlaced twice on the trunk of a tree, once on the back of a bench. And twice again their names appeared inscribed on old walls and concealed behind a layer of plaster overhung with ivy.

On these two occasions their names were accompanied by two separate dates:

Patrice and Coralie, 1904
Patrice and Coralie, 1907

"Eleven years ago and eight years ago," said the officer. "And always our two names: Patrice and Coralie."

Their hands met and clasped each other. The great mystery of their past brought them as closely together as did the great love which filled them and of which they refrained from speaking.

In spite of themselves, however, they sought out solitude; and it was in this way that, a fortnight after the murder of Essarès Bey, as they passed the little door opening on the lane, they decided to go out by it and to stroll down to the river bank. No one saw them, for both the approach to the door and the path leading to it were hidden by a screen of tall bushes; and M. Masseron and his men were exploring the old green-houses, which stood at the other side of the garden, and the old furnace and chimney which had been used for signalling.

But, when he was outside, Patrice stopped. Almost in front of him, in the opposite wall, was an exactly similar door. He called Coralie's attention to it, but she said:

"There is nothing astonishing about that. This wall is the boundary of another garden which at one time belonged to the one we have just left."

"But who lives there?"

"Nobody. The little house which overlooks it and which comes before mine, in the Rue Raynouard, is always shut up."

"Same door, same key, perhaps," Patrice murmured, half to himself.

He inserted in the lock the rusty key, which had reached him by messenger. The lock responded.

"Well," he said, "the series of miracles is continuing. Will this one be in our favour?"

The vegetation had been allowed to run riot in the narrow strip of ground that faced them. However, in the middle of the exuberant grass, a well-trodden path, which looked as if it were often used, started from the door in the wall and rose obliquely to the single terrace, on which stood a dilapidated lodge with closed shutters. It was built on one floor, but was surmounted by a small lantern-shaped belvedere. It had its own entrance in the Rue Raynouard, from which it was separated by a yard and a very high wall. This entrance seemed to be barricaded with boards and posts nailed together.

They walked round the house and were surprised by the sight that awaited them on the right-hand side. The foliage had been trained into rectangular cloisters, carefully kept, with regular arcades cut in yew-and box-hedges. A miniature garden was laid out in this space, the very home of silence and tranquillity. Here also were wall-flowers and pansies and hyacinths. And four paths, coming from four corners of the cloisters, met round a central space, where stood the five columns of a small, open temple, rudely constructed of pebbles and unmortared building-stones.

Under the dome of this little temple was a tombstone and, in front of it, an old wooden praying-chair, from the bars of which hung, on the left, an ivory crucifix and, on the right, a rosary composed of amethyst beads in a gold filigree setting.

"Coralie, Coralie," whispered Patrice, in a voice trembling with emotion, "who can be buried here?"

They went nearer. There were bead wreaths laid in rows on the tombstone. They counted nineteen, each bearing the date of one of the last nineteen years. Pushing them aside, they read the following inscription in gilt letters worn and soiled by the rain:

HERE LIE
PATRICE AND CORALIE,
BOTH OF WHOM WERE MURDERED
ON THE 14th OF APRIL, 1895.
REVENGE TO ME: I WILL REPAY.

10

THE RED CORD

Coralie, feeling her legs give way beneath her, had flung herself on the prie-dieu and there knelt praying fervently and wildly. She could not tell on whose behalf, for the repose of what unknown soul her prayers were offered; but her whole being was afire with fever and exaltation and the very action of praying seemed able to assuage her.

"What was your mother's name, Coralie?" Patrice whispered.

"Louise," she replied.

"And my father's name was Armand. It cannot be either of them, therefore; and yet..."

Patrice also was displaying the greatest agitation. Stooping down, he examined the nineteen wreaths, renewed his inspection of the tombstone and said:

"All the same, Coralie, the coincidence is really too extraordinary. My father died in 1895."

"And my mother died in that year too," she said, "though I do not know the exact date."

"We shall find out, Coralie," he declared. "These things can all be verified. But meanwhile one truth becomes clear. The man who used to interlace the names of Patrice and Coralie was not thinking only of us and was not considering only the future. Perhaps he thought even more of the past, of that

Coralie and Patrice whom he knew to have suffered a violent death and whom he had undertaken to avenge. Come away, Coralie. No one must suspect that we have been here."

They went down the path and through the two doors on the lane. They were not seen coming in. Patrice at once brought Coralie indoors, urged Ya-Bon and his comrades to increase their vigilance and left the house.

He came back in the evening only to go out again early the next day; and it was not until the day after, at three o'clock in the afternoon, that he asked to be shown up to Coralie.

"Have you found out?" she asked him at once.

"I have found out a great many things which do not dispel the darkness of the present. I am almost tempted to say that they increase it. They do, however, throw a very vivid light on the past."

"Do they explain what we saw two days ago?" she asked, anxiously.

"Listen to me, Coralie."

He sat down opposite her and said:

"I shall not tell you all the steps that I have taken. I will merely sum up the result of those which led to some result. I went, first of all, to the Mayor of Passy's office and from there to the Servian Legation."

"Then you persist in assuming that it was my mother?"

"Yes. I took a copy of her death-certificate, Coralie. Your mother died on the fourteenth of April, 1895."

"Oh!" she said. "That is the date on the tomb!"

"The very date."

"But the name? Coralie? My father used to call her Louise."

"Your mother's name was Louise Coralie Countess Odolavitch."

"Oh, my mother!" she murmured. "My poor darling mother! Then it was she who was murdered. It was for her that I was praying over the way?"

"For her, Coralie, and for my father. I discovered his full name at the mayor's office in the Rue Drouot. My father was Armand Patrice Belval. He died on the fourteenth of April, 1895."

Patrice was right in saying that a singular light had been thrown upon the past. He had now positively established that the inscription on the tombstone related to his father and Coralie's mother, both of whom were murdered on the same day. But by whom and for what reason, in consequence of what tragedies? This was what Coralie asked him to tell her.

"I cannot answer your questions yet," he replied. "But I addressed another to myself, one more easily solved; and that I did solve. This also makes us certain of an essential point. I wanted to know to whom the lodge belonged. The outside, in the Rue Raynouard, affords no clue. You have seen the wall and the door of the yard: they show nothing in particular. But the number of the property was sufficient for my purpose. I went to the local receiver and learnt that the taxes were paid by a notary in the Avenue de l'Opéra. I called on this notary, who told me..."

He stopped for a moment and then said:

"The lodge was bought twenty-one years ago by my father. Two years later my father died; and the lodge, which of course formed part of his estate, was put up for sale by the present notary's predecessor and bought by one Siméon Diodokis, a Greek subject."

"It's he!" cried Coralie. "Siméon's name is Diodokis."

"Well, Siméon Diodokis," Patrice continued, "was a friend of my father's, because my father appointed him the sole executor of his will and because it was Siméon Diodokis who, through the notary in question and a London solicitor, paid my school-fees and, when I attained my majority, made over to me the sum of two hundred thousand francs, the balance of my inheritance."

They maintained a long silence. Many things were becoming manifest, but indistinctly, as yet, and shaded, like things seen in the evening mist. And one thing stood in sharper outline than the rest, for Patrice murmured:

"Your mother and my father loved each other, Coralie."

The thought united them more closely and affected them profoundly. Their love was the counterpart of another love, bruised by trials, like theirs, but still more tragic and ending in bloodshed and death.

"Your mother and my father loved each other," he repeated. "I should say they must have belonged to that class of rather enthusiastic lovers whose passion indulges in charming little childish ways, for they had a trick of calling each other, when alone, by names which nobody else used to them; and they selected their second Christian names, which were also yours and mine. One day your mother dropped her amethyst rosary. The largest of the beads broke in two pieces. My father had one of the pieces mounted as a trinket which he hung on his watch-chain. Both were widowed. You were two years old and I was eight. In order to devote himself altogether to the woman he loved, my father sent me to England and bought the lodge in which your mother, who lived in the big house next door, used to go and see him, crossing the lane and using the same key for both doors. It was no doubt in this lodge, or in the garden round it, that they were murdered. We shall find that out, because there must be visible proofs of the murder, proofs which Siméon Diodokis discovered, since he was not afraid to say so in the inscription on the tombstone."

"And who was the murderer?" Coralie asked, under her breath.

"You suspect it, Coralie, as I do. The hated name comes to your mind, even though we have no grounds for speaking with certainty."

"Essarès!" she cried, in anguish.

"Most probably."

She hid her face in her hands:

"No, no, it is impossible. It is impossible that I should have been the wife of the man who killed my mother."

"You bore his name, but you were never his wife. You told him so the evening before his death, in my presence. Let us say nothing that we are unable to say positively; but all the same let us remember that he was your evil genius. Remember also that Siméon, my father's friend and executor, the man who bought the lovers' lodge, the man who swore upon their tomb to avenge them: remember that Siméon, a few months after your mother's death, persuaded Essarès to engage him as caretaker of the estate, became his secretary and gradually made his way into Essarès' life. His only object must have been to carry out a plan of revenge."

"There has been no revenge."

"What do we know about it? Do we know how Essarès met his death? Certainly it was not Siméon who killed him, as Siméon was at the hospital. But he may have caused him to be killed. And revenge has a thousand ways of manifesting itself. Lastly, Siméon was most likely obeying instructions that came from my father. There is little doubt that he wanted first to achieve an aim which my father and your mother had at heart: the union of our destinies, Coralie. And it was this aim that ruled his life. It was he evidently who placed among the knick-knacks which I collected as a child this amethyst of which the other half formed a bead in your rosary. It was he who collected our photographs. He lastly was our unknown friend and protector, the one who sent me the key, accompanied by a letter which I never received, unfortunately."

"Then, Patrice, you no longer believe that he is dead, this unknown friend, or that you heard his dying cries?"

"I cannot say. Siméon was not necessarily acting alone. He may have had a confidant, an assistant in the work which he undertook. Perhaps it was this other man who died at nineteen minutes past seven. I cannot say. Everything that happened on that ill-fated morning remains involved in the deepest mystery. The only conviction that we are able to hold is that for twenty years Siméon Diodokis has worked unobtrusively and patiently on our behalf, doing his utmost to defeat the murderer, and that Siméon Diodokis is alive. Alive, but mad!" Patrice added. "So that we can neither thank him nor question him about the grim story which he knows or about the dangers that threaten you."

Patrice resolved once more to make the attempt, though he felt sure of a fresh disappointment. Siméon had a bedroom, next to that occupied by two of the wounded soldiers, in the wing which formerly contained the servants' quarters. Here Patrice found him.

He was sitting half-asleep in a chair turned towards the garden. His pipe was in his mouth; he had allowed it to go out. The room was small, sparsely furnished, but clean and light. Hidden from view, the best part of the old man's life was spent here. M. Masseron had often visited the room, in Siméon's absence, and so had Patrice, each from his own point of view.

The only discovery worthy of note consisted of a crude diagram in pencil, on the white wall-paper behind a chest of drawers: three lines intersecting to form a large equilateral triangle. In the middle of this geometrical figure were three words clumsily inscribed in adhesive gold-leaf:

The Golden Triangle

There was nothing more, not another clue of any kind, to further M. Masseron's search.

Patrice walked straight up to the old man and tapped him on the shoulder:

"Siméon!" he said.

The other lifted his yellow spectacles to him, and Patrice felt a sudden wish to snatch away this glass obstacle which concealed the old fellow's eyes and prevented him from looking into his soul and his distant memories. Siméon began to laugh foolishly.

"So this," thought Patrice, "is my friend and my father's friend. He loved my father, respected his wishes, was faithful to his memory, raised a tomb to him, prayed on it and swore to avenge him. And now his mind has gone."

Patrice felt that speech was useless. But, though the sound of his voice roused no echo in that wandering brain, it was possible that the eyes were susceptible to a reminder. He wrote on a clean sheet of paper the words that Siméon had gazed upon so often:

Patrice and Coralie
14 April, 1895

The old man looked, shook his head and repeated his melancholy, foolish chuckle.

The officer added a new line:
Armand Belval

The old man displayed the same torpor. Patrice continued the test. He wrote down the names of Essarès Bey and Colonel Fakhi. He drew a triangle. The old man failed to understand and went on chuckling.

But suddenly his laughter lost some of its childishness. Patrice had written the name of Bournef, the accomplice, and this time the old secretary appeared to be stirred by a recollection. He tried to get up, fell back in his chair, then rose to his feet again and took his hat from a peg on the wall.

He left his room and, followed by Patrice, marched out of the house and turned to the left, in the direction of Auteuil. He moved like a man in a trance who is hypnotized into walking without knowing where he is going. He led the way along the Rue de Boulainvilliers, crossed the Seine and turned down the Quai de Grenelle with an unhesitating step. Then, when he reached the boulevard, he stopped, putting out his arm, made a sign to Patrice to do likewise. A kiosk hid them from view. He put his head round it. Patrice followed his example.

Opposite, at the corner of the boulevard and a side-street, was a cafe, with a portion of the pavement in front of it marked out by dwarf shrubs in tubs. Behind these tubs four men sat drinking. Three of them had their backs turned to Patrice. He saw the only one that faced him, and he at once recognized Bournef.

By this time Siméon was some distance away, like a man whose part is played and who leaves it to others to complete the work. Patrice looked round, caught sight of a post-office and went in briskly. He knew that M. Masseron was at the Rue Raynouard. He telephoned and told him where Bournef was. M. Masseron replied that he would come at once.

Since the murder of Essarès Bey, M. Masseron's enquiry had made no progress in so far as Colonel Fakhi's four accomplices were concerned. True, they discovered the man Grégoire's sanctuary and the bedrooms with the wall-cupboards; but the whole place was empty. The accomplices had disappeared.

"Old Siméon," said Patrice to himself, "was acquainted with their habits. He must have known that they were accustomed to meet at this café on a certain day of the week, at a fixed hour, and he suddenly remembered it all at the sight of Bournef's name."

A few minutes later M. Masseron alighted from his car with his men. The business did not take long. The open front of the cafe was surrounded. The accomplices offered no resistance.

M. Masseron sent three of them under a strong guard to the Depot and hustled Bournef into a private room.

"Come along," he said to Patrice. "We'll question him."

"Mme. Essarès is alone at the house," Patrice objected.

"Alone? No. There are all your soldier-men."

"Yes, but I would rather go back, if you don't mind. It's the first time that I've left her and I'm justified in feeling anxious."

"It's only a matter of a few minutes," M. Masseron insisted. "One should always take advantage of the fluster caused by the arrest."

Patrice followed him, but they soon saw that Bournef was not one of those men who are easily put out. He simply shrugged his shoulders at their threats:

"It is no use, sir," he said, "to try and frighten me. I risk nothing. Shot, do you say? Nonsense! You don't shoot people in France for the least thing; and we are all four subjects of a neutral country. Tried? Sentenced? Imprisoned? Never! You forget that you have kept everything dark so far; and, when you hushed up the murder of Mustapha, of Fakhi and of Essarès, it was not done with the object of reviving the case for no valid reason. No, sir, I am quite easy. The internment-camp is the worst that can await me."

"Then you refuse to answer?" said M. Masseron.

"Not a bit of it! I accept internment. But there are twenty different ways of treating a man in these camps, and I should like to earn your favour and, in so doing, make sure of reasonable comfort till the end of the war. But first of all, what do you know?"

"Pretty well everything."

"That's a pity: it decreases my value. Do you know about Essarès' last night?"

"Yes, with the bargain of the four millions. What's become of the money?"

Bournef made a furious gesture:

"Taken from us! Stolen! It was a trap!"

"Who took it?"

"One Grégoire."

"Who was he?"

"His familiar, as we have since learnt. We discovered that this Grégoire was no other than a fellow who used to serve as his chauffeur on occasion."

"And who therefore helped him to convey the bags of gold from the bank to his house."

"Yes. And we also think, we know... Look here, you may as well call it a certainty. Grégoire... is a woman."

"A woman!"

"Exactly. His mistress. We have several proofs of it. But she's a trustworthy, capable woman, strong as a man and afraid of nothing."

"Do you know her address?"

"No."

"As to the gold: have you no clue to its whereabouts, no suspicion?"

"No. The gold is in the garden or in the house in the Rue Raynouard. We saw it being taken in every day for a week. It has not been taken out since. We kept watch every night. The bags are there."

"No clue either to Essarès' murderer?"

"No, none."

"Are you quite sure?"

"Why should I tell a lie?"

"Suppose it was yourself? Or one of your friends?"

"We thought that you would suspect us. Fortunately, we happen to have an alibi."

"Easy to prove?"

"Impossible to upset."

"We'll look into it. So you have nothing more to reveal?"

"No. But I have an idea... or rather a question which you will answer or not, as you please. Who betrayed us? Your reply may throw some useful light, for one person only knew of our weekly meetings here from four to five o'clock, one person only, Essarès Bey; and he himself often came here to confer with us. Essarès is dead. Then who gave us away?"

"Old Siméon."

Bournef started with astonishment:

"What! Siméon? Siméon Diodokis?"

"Yes. Siméon Diodokis, Essarès Bey's secretary."

"He? Oh, I'll make him pay for this, the blackguard! But no, it's impossible."

"What makes you say that it's impossible?'"

"Why, because..."

He stopped and thought for some time, no doubt to convince himself that there was no harm in speaking. Then he finished his sentence:

"Because old Siméon was on our side."

"What's that you say?" exclaimed Patrice, whose turn it was to be surprised.

"I say and I swear that Siméon Diodokis was on our side. He was our man. It was he who kept us informed of Essarès Bey's shady tricks. It was he who rang us up at nine o'clock in the evening to tell us that Essarès had lit the furnace of the old hothouses and that the signal of the sparks was going to work. It was he who opened the door to us, pretending to resist, of course, and allowed us to tie him up in the porter's lodge. It was he, lastly, who paid and dismissed the men-servants."

"But why? Why this treachery? For the sake of money?"

"No, from hatred. He bore Essarès Bey a hatred that often gave us the shudders."

"What prompted it?"

"I don't know. Siméon keeps his own counsel. But it dated a long way back."

"Did he know where the gold was hidden?" asked M. Masseron.

"No. And it was not for want of hunting to find out. He never knew how the bags got out the cellar, which was only a temporary hiding-place."

"And yet they used to leave the grounds. If so, how are we to know that the same thing didn't happen this time?"

"This time we were keeping watch the whole way round outside, a thing which Siméon could not do by himself."

Patrice now put the question:

"Can you tell us nothing more about him?"

"No, I can't. Wait, though; there was one rather curious thing. On the afternoon of the great day, I received a letter in which Siméon gave me certain particulars. In the same envelope was another letter, which had evidently got there by some incredible mistake, for it appeared to be highly important."

"What did it say?" asked Patrice, anxiously.

"It was all about a key."

"Don't you remember the details?"

"Here is the letter. I kept it in order to give it back to him and warn him what he had done. Here, it's certainly his writing..."

Patrice took the sheet of notepaper; and the first thing that he saw was his own name. The letter was addressed to him, as he anticipated:

"*Patrice,*

"You will this evening receive a key. The key opens two doors midway down a lane leading to the river: one, on the right, is that of the garden of the woman you love; the other, on the left, that of a garden where I want you to meet me at nine o'clock in the morning on the 14th of April. She will be there also. You shall learn who I am and the object which I intend to attain.

You shall both hear things about the past that will bring you still closer together.

"From now until the 14th the struggle which begins tonight will be a terrible one. If anything happens to me, it is certain that the woman you love will run the greatest dangers. Watch over her, Patrice; do not leave her for an instant unprotected. But I do not intend to let anything happen to me; and you shall both know the happiness which I have been preparing for you so long.

"My best love to you."

"It's not signed," said Bournef, "but, I repeat, it's in Siméon's handwriting. As for the lady, she is obviously Mme. Essarès."

"But what danger can she be running?" exclaimed Patrice, uneasily. "Essarès is dead, so there is nothing to fear."

"I wouldn't say that. He would take some killing."

"Whom can he have instructed to avenge him? Who would continue his work?"

"I can't say, but I should take no risks."

Patrice waited to hear no more. He thrust the letter into M. Masseron's hand and made his escape.

"Rue Raynouard, fast as you can," he said, springing into a taxi.

He was eager to reach his destination. The dangers of which old Siméon spoke seemed suddenly to hang over Coralie's head.

Already the enemy, taking advantage of Patrice's absence, might be attacking his beloved. And who could defend her?

"If anything happens to me," Siméon had said.

And the supposition was partly realized, since he had lost his wits.

"Come, come," muttered Patrice, "this is sheer idiocy... I am fancying things... There is no reason..."

But his mental anguish increased every minute. He reminded himself that old Siméon was still in full possession of his faculties at the time when he wrote that letter and gave the advice which it contained. He reminded himself that old Siméon had purposely informed him that the key opened the door of Coralie's garden, so that he, Patrice, might keep an effective watch by coming to her in case of need.

He saw Siméon some way ahead of him. It was growing late, and the old fellow was going home. Patrice passed him just outside the porter's lodge and heard him humming to himself.

"Any news?" Patrice asked the soldier on duty.

"No, sir."

"Where's Little Mother Coralie?"

"She had a walk in the garden and went upstairs half an hour ago."

"Ya-Bon?"

"Ya-Bon went up with Little Mother Coralie. He should be at her door."

Patrice climbed the stairs, feeling a good deal calmer. But, when he came to the first floor, he was astonished to find that the electric light was not on. He turned on the switch. Then he saw, at the end of the passage, Ya-Bon on his knees outside Coralie's room, with his head leaning against the wall. The door was open.

"What are you doing there?" he shouted, running up.

Ya-Bon made no reply. Patrice saw that there was blood on the shoulder of his jacket. At that moment the Senegalese sank to the floor.

"Damn it! He's wounded! Dead perhaps."

He leapt over the body and rushed into the room, switching on the light at once.

Coralie was lying at full length on a sofa. Round her neck was the terrible little red-silk cord. And yet Patrice did not experience that awful, numbing despair which we feel in the presence of irretrievable misfortunes. It seemed to him that Coralie's face had not the pallor of death.

He found that she was in fact breathing:

"She's not dead. She's not dead," said Patrice to himself. "And she's not going to die, I'm sure of it... nor Ya-Bon either... They've failed this time."

He loosened the cords. In a few seconds Coralie heaved a deep breath and recovered consciousness. A smile lit up her eyes at the sight of him. But, suddenly remembering, she threw her arms, still so weak, around him:

"Oh, Patrice," she said, in a trembling voice, "I'm frightened... frightened for you!"

"What are you frightened of, Coralie? Who is the scoundrel?"

"I didn't see him... He put out the light, caught me by the throat and whispered, 'You first... Tonight it will be your lover's turn!'... Oh, Patrice, I'm frightened for you!..."

11

ON THE BRINK

Patrice at once made up his mind what to do. He lifted Coralie to her bed and asked her not to move or call out. Then he made sure that Ya-Bon was not seriously wounded. Lastly, he rang violently, sounding all the bells that communicated with the posts which he had placed in different parts of the house.

The men came hurrying up.

"You're a pack of nincompoops," he said. "Someone's been here. Little Mother Coralie and Ya-Bon have had a narrow escape from being killed."

They began to protest loudly.

"Silence!" he commanded. "You deserve a good hiding, every one of you. I'll forgive you on one condition, which is that, all this evening and all tonight, you speak of Little Mother Coralie as though she were dead."

"But whom are we to speak to, sir?" one of them objected. "There's nobody here."

"Yes, there is, you silly fool, since Little Mother Coralie and Ya-Bon have been attacked. Unless it was yourselves who did it!... It wasn't? Very well then... And let me have no more nonsense. It's not a question of speaking to others, but of talking among yourselves... and of thinking, even, without speaking. There are people listening to you, spying on you, people who hear what you say and who guess what you don't say. So, until tomorrow, Little Mother Coralie will not leave her room. You shall keep watch over her by turns. Those who are not watching will go to bed immediately after dinner. No moving about the house, do you understand? Absolute silence and quiet."

"And old Siméon, sir?"

"Lock him up in his room. He's dangerous because he's mad. They may have taken advantage of his madness to make him open the door to them. Lock him up!"

Patrice's plan was a simple one. As the enemy, believing Coralie to be on the point of death, had revealed to her his intention, which was to kill Patrice as well, it was necessary that he should think himself free to act, with nobody to suspect his schemes or to be on his guard against him. He would enter upon the struggle and would then be caught in a trap.

Pending this struggle, for which he longed with all his might, Patrice saw to Ya-Bon's wound, which proved to be only slight, and questioned him and Coralie. Their answers tallied at all points. Coralie, feeling a little tired, was lying down reading. Ya-Bon remained in the passage, outside the open door, squatting on the floor, Arab-fashion. Neither of them heard anything suspicious. And suddenly Ya-Bon saw a shadow between himself and the light in the passage. This light, which came from an electric lamp, was put out at just about the same time as the light in the bed-room. Ya-Bon, already half-erect, felt a violent blow in the back of the neck and lost consciousness. Coralie tried to escape by the door of her boudoir, was unable to open it, began to cry out and was at once seized and thrown down. All this had happened within the space of a few seconds.

The only hint that Patrice succeeded in obtaining was that the man came not from the staircase but from the servants' wing. This had a smaller staircase of its own, communicating with the kitchen through a pantry by which the tradesmen entered from the Rue Raynouard. The door leading to the street was locked. But someone might easily possess a key.

After dinner Patrice went in to see Coralie for a moment and then, at nine o'clock, retired to his bedroom, which was situated a little lower down, on the same side. It had been used, in Essarès Bey's lifetime, as a smoking-room.

As the attack from which he expected such good results was not likely to take place before the middle of the night, Patrice sat down at a roll-top desk standing against the wall and took out the diary in which he had begun his detailed record of recent events. He wrote on for half an hour or forty minutes and was about to close the book when he seemed to hear a vague rustle, which he would certainly not have noticed if his nerves had not been stretched to their utmost state of tension. And he remembered the day when he and Coralie had once before been shot at. This time, however, the window was not open nor even ajar.

He therefore went on writing without turning his head or doing anything to suggest that his attention had been aroused; and he set down, almost unconsciously, the actual phases of his anxiety:

"He is here. He is watching me. I wonder what he means to do. I doubt if he will smash a pane of glass and fire a bullet at me. He has tried that method before and found it uncertain and a failure. No, his plan is thought out, I expect, in a different and more intelligent fashion. He is more likely to wait for me to go to bed, when he can watch me sleeping and effect his entrance by some means which I can't guess.

"Meanwhile, it's extraordinarily exhilarating to know that his eyes are upon me. He hates me; and his hatred is coming nearer and nearer to mine, like one sword feeling its way towards another before clashing. He is watching me as a wild animal, lurking in the dark, watches its prey and selects the spot on which to fasten its fangs. But no, I am certain that it's he who is the prey, doomed beforehand to defeat and destruction. He is preparing his knife or his red-silk cord. And it's these two hands of mine that will finish the battle. They are strong and powerful and are already enjoying their victory. They will be victorious."

Patrice shut down the desk, lit a cigarette and smoked it quietly, as his habit was before going to bed. Then he undressed, folded his clothes carefully over the back of a chair, wound up his watch, got into bed and switched off the light.

"At last," he said to himself, "I shall know the truth. I shall know who this man is. Some friend of Essarès', continuing his work? But why this hatred of Coralie? Is he in love with her, as he is trying to finish me off too? I shall know... I shall soon know..."

An hour passed, however, and another hour, during which nothing happened on the side of the window. A single creaking came from somewhere beside the desk. But this no doubt was one of those sounds of creaking furniture which we often hear in the silence of the night.

Patrice began to lose the buoyant hope that had sustained him so far. He perceived that his elaborate sham regarding Coralie's death was a poor thing after all and that a man of his enemy's stamp might well refuse to be taken in by it. Feeling rather put out, he was on the point of going to sleep, when he heard the same creaking sound at the same spot.

The need to do something made him jump out of bed. He turned on the light. Everything seemed to be as he had left it. There was no trace of a strange presence.

"Well," said Patrice, "one thing's certain: I'm no good. The enemy must have smelt a rat and guessed the trap I laid for him. Let's go to sleep. There will be nothing happening tonight."

There was in fact no alarm.

Next morning, on examining the window, he observed that a stone ledge ran above the ground-floor all along the garden front of the house, wide enough for a man to walk upon by holding on to the balconies and rain-pipes. He inspected all the rooms to which the ledge gave access. None of them was old Siméon's room.

"He hasn't stirred out, I suppose?" he asked the two soldiers posted on guard.

"Don't think so, sir. In any case, we haven't unlocked the door."

Patrice went in and, paying no attention to the old fellow, who was still sucking at his cold pipe, he searched the room, having it at the back of his mind that the enemy might take refuge there. He found nobody. But what he did discover, in a press in the wall, was a number of things which he had not seen on the occasion of his investigations in M. Masseron's company. These consisted of a rope-ladder, a coil of lead pipes, apparently gas-pipes, and a small soldering-lamp.

"This all seems devilish odd," he said to himself. "How did the things get in here? Did Siméon collect them without any definite object, mechanically? Or am I to assume that Siméon is merely an instrument of the enemy's? He used to know the enemy before he lost his reason; and he may be under his influence at present."

Siméon was sitting at the window, with his back to the room. Patrice went up to him and gave a start. In his hands the old man held a funeral-wreath made of black and white beads. It bore a date, "14 April, 1915," and made the twentieth, the one which Siméon was preparing to lay on the grave of his dead friends.

"He will lay it there," said Patrice, aloud. "His instinct as an avenging friend, which has guided his steps through life, continues in spite of his insanity. He will lay it on the grave. That's so, Siméon, isn't it: you will take it there tomorrow? For tomorrow is the fourteenth of April, the sacred anniversary..."

He leant over the incomprehensible being who held the key to all the plots and counterplots, to all the treachery and benevolence that constituted the inextricable drama. Siméon thought that Patrice wanted to take the wreath from him and pressed it to his chest with a startled gesture.

"Don't be afraid," said Patrice. "You can keep it. Tomorrow, Siméon, tomorrow, Coralie and I will be faithful to the appointment which you gave us. And tomorrow perhaps the memory of the horrible past will unseal your brain."

The day seemed long to Patrice, who was eager for something that would provide a glimmer in the surrounding darkness. And now this glimmer seemed about to be kindled by the arrival of this twentieth anniversary of the fourteenth of April.

At a late hour in the afternoon M. Masseron called at the Rue Raynouard.

"Look what I've just received," he said to Patrice. "It's rather curious: an anonymous letter in a disguised hand. Listen:

"'*Sir*, be warned. They're going away. Take care. Tomorrow evening the 1800 bags will be on their way out of the country.

A Friend of France.'"

"And tomorrow is the fourteenth of April," said Patrice, at once connecting the two trains of thought in his mind.

"Yes. What makes you say that?"

"Nothing... Something that just occurred to me..."

He was nearly telling M. Masseron all the facts associated with the fourteenth of April and all those concerning the strange personality of old Siméon. If he did not speak, it was for obscure reasons, perhaps because he wished to work out this part of the case alone, perhaps also because of a sort of shyness which prevented him from admitting M. Masseron into all the secrets of the past. He said nothing about it, therefore, and asked:

"What do you think of the letter?"

"Upon my word, I don't know what to think. It may be a warning with something to back it, or it may be a trick to make us adopt one course of conduct rather than another. I'll talk about it to Bournef."

"Nothing fresh on his side?"

"No; and I don't expect anything in particular. The alibi which he has submitted is genuine. His friends and he are so many supers. Their parts are played."

The coincidence of dates was all that stuck in Patrice's mind. The two roads which M. Masseron and he were following suddenly met on this day so long since marked out by fate. The past and the present were about to unite. The catastrophe was at hand. The fourteenth of April was the day on which the gold was to disappear for good and also the day on which an unknown voice had summoned Patrice and Coralie to the same tryst which his father and her mother had kept twenty years ago.

And the next day was the fourteenth of April.

At nine o'clock in the morning Patrice asked after old Siméon.

"Gone out, sir. You had countermanded your orders."

Patrice entered the room and looked for the wreath. It was not there. Moreover, the three things in the cupboard, the rope-ladder, the coil of lead and the glazier's lamp, were not there either.

"Did Siméon take anything with him?"

"Yes, sir, a wreath."

"Nothing else?"

"No, sir."

The window was open. Patrice came to the conclusion that the things had gone by this way, thus confirming his theory that the old fellow was an unconscious confederate.

Shortly before ten o'clock Coralie joined him in the garden. Patrice had told her the latest events. She looked pale and anxious.

They went round the lawns and, without being seen, reached the clumps of dwarf shrubs which hid the door on the lane. Patrice opened the door. As he started to open the other his hand hesitated. He felt sorry that he had not told M. Masseron and that he and Coralie were performing by themselves a pilgrimage which certain signs warned him to be dangerous. He shook off the obsession, however. He had two revolvers with him. What had he to fear?

"You're coming in, aren't you, Coralie?"

"Yes," she said.

"I somehow thought you seemed undecided, anxious..."

"It's quite true," said Coralie. "I feel a sort of hollowness."

"Why? Are you afraid?"

"No. Or rather yes. I'm not afraid for today, but in some way for the past. I think of my poor mother, who went through this door, as I am doing, one April morning. She was perfectly happy, she was going to meet her love... And then I feel as if I wanted to hold her back and cry, 'Don't go on... Death is lying in wait for you... Don't go on...' And it's I who hear those words of terror, they ring in my ears; it's I who hear them and I dare not go on. I'm afraid."

"Let's go back, Coralie."

She only took his arm:

"No," she said, in a firm voice. "We'll walk on. I want to pray. It will do me good."

Boldly she stepped along the little slanting path which her mother had followed and climbed the slope amid the tangled weeds and the straggling branches. They passed the lodge on their left and reached the leafy cloisters where each had a parent lying buried. And at once, at the first glance, they saw that the twentieth wreath was there.

"Siméon has come," said Patrice. "An all-powerful instinct obliged him to come. He must be somewhere near."

While Coralie knelt down beside the tombstone, he hunted around the cloisters and went as far as the middle of the garden. There was nothing left but to go to the lodge, and this was evidently a dread act which they put off performing, if not from fear, at least from the reverent awe which checks a man on entering a place of death and crime.

It was Coralie once again who gave the signal for action:

"Come," she said.

Patrice did not know how they would make their way into the lodge, for all its doors and windows had appeared to them to be shut. But, as they approached, they saw that the back door opening on the yard was wide open, and they at once thought that Siméon was waiting for them inside.

It was exactly ten o'clock when they crossed the threshold of the lodge. A little hall led to a kitchen on one side and a bedroom on the other. The principal room must be that opposite. The door stood ajar.

"That's where it must have happened... long ago," said Coralie, in a frightened whisper.

"Yes," said Patrice, "we shall find Siméon there. But, if your courage fails you, Coralie, we had better give it up."

An unquestioning force of will supported her. Nothing now would have induced her to stop. She walked on.

Though large, the room gave an impression of cosiness, owing to the way in which it was furnished. The sofas, armchairs, carpet and hangings all tended to add to its comfort; and its appearance might well have remained unchanged since the tragic death of the two who used to occupy it. This appearance was rather that of a studio, because of a skylight which filled the middle of the high ceiling, where the belvedere was. The light came from here. There were two other windows, but these were hidden by curtains.

"Siméon is not here," said Patrice.

Coralie did not reply. She was examining the things around her with an emotion which was reflected in every feature. There were books, all of them going back to the last century. Some of them were signed "Coralie" in pencil on their blue or yellow wrappers. There were pieces of unfinished needlework, an embroidery-frame, a piece of tapestry with a needle hanging to it by a thread of wool. And there were also books signed "Patrice" and a box of cigars and a blotting-pad and an inkstand and penholders. And there were two small framed photographs, those of two children, Patrice and Coralie. And thus the life of long ago went on, not only the life of two lovers who loved each other with a violent and fleeting passion, but of two beings who dwell together in the calm assurance of a long existence spent in common.

"Oh, my darling, darling mother!" Coralie whispered.

Her emotion increased with each new memory. She leant trembling on Patrice's shoulder.

"Let's go," he said.

"Yes, dear, yes, we had better. We will come back again... We will come back to them... We will revive the life of love that was cut short by their death. Let us go for today; I have no strength left."

But they had taken only a few steps when they stopped dismayed.

The door was closed.

Their eyes met, filled with uneasiness.

"We didn't close it, did we?" he asked.

"No," she said, "we didn't close it."

He went to open it and perceived that it had neither handle nor lock.

It was a single door, of massive wood that looked hard and substantial. It might well have been made of one piece, taken from the very heart of an oak. There was no paint or varnish on it. Here and there were scratches, as if someone had been rapping at it with a tool. And then... and then, on the right, were these few words in pencil:

Patrice and Coralie, 14 April, 1895
God will avenge us

Below this was a cross and, below the cross, another date, but in a different and more recent handwriting:

14 April, 1915

"This is terrible, this is terrible," said Patrice. "Today's date! Who can have written that? It has only just been written. Oh, it's terrible!... Come, come, after all, we can't..."

He rushed to one of the windows, tore back the curtain that veiled it and pulled upon the casement. A cry escaped him. The window was walled up, walled up with building-stones that filled the space between the glass and the shutters.

He ran to the other window and found the same obstacle.

There were two doors, leading probably to the bedroom on the right and to a room next to the kitchen on the left. He opened them quickly. Both doors were walled up.

He ran in every direction, during the first moment of terror, and then hurled himself against the first of the three doors and tried to break it down. It did not move. It might have been an immovable block.

Then, once again, they looked at each other with eyes of fear; and the same terrible thought came over them both. The thing that had happened before was being repeated! The tragedy was being played a second time. After the mother and the father, it was the turn of the daughter and the son. Like the lovers of yesteryear, those of today were prisoners. The enemy held them in his powerful grip; and they would doubtless soon know how their parents had died by seeing how they themselves would die... 14 April, 1895... 14 April, 1915...

12

IN THE ABYSS

"No, no, no!" cried Patrice. "I won't stand this!"

He flung himself against the windows and doors, took up an iron dog from the fender and banged it against the wooden doors and the stone walls. Barren efforts! They were the same which his father had made before him; and they could only result in the same mockery of impotent scratches on the wood and the stone.

"Oh, Coralie, Coralie!" he cried in his despair. "It's I who have brought you to this! What an abyss I've dragged you into! It was madness to try to fight this out by myself! I ought to have called in those who understand, who are accustomed to it!... No, I was going to be so clever!... Forgive me, Coralie."

She had sunk into a chair. He, almost on his knees beside her, threw his arms around her, imploring her pardon.

She smiled, to calm him:

"Come, dear," she said, gently, "don't lose courage. Perhaps we are mistaken... After all, there's nothing to show that it is not all an accident."

"The date!" he said. "The date of this year, of this day, written in another hand! It was your mother and my father who wrote the first... but this one, Coralie, this one proves premeditation, and an implacable determination to do away with us."

She shuddered. Still she persisted in trying to comfort him:

"It may be. But yet it is not so bad as all that. We have enemies, but we have friends also. They will look for us."

"They will look for us, but how can they ever find us, Coralie? We took steps to prevent them from guessing where we were going; and not one of them knows this house."

"Old Siméon does."

"Siméon came and placed his wreath, but someone else came with him, someone who rules him and who has perhaps already got rid of him, now that Siméon has played his part."

"And what then, Patrice?"

He felt that she was overcome and began to be ashamed of his own weakness:

"Well," he said, mastering himself, "we must just wait. After all, the attack may not materialize. The fact of our being locked in does not mean that we are lost. And, even so, we shall make a fight for it, shall we not? You need not think that I am at the end of my strength or my resources. Let us wait, Coralie, and act."

The main thing was to find out whether there was any entrance to the house which could allow of an unforeseen attack. After an hour's search they took up the carpet and found tiles which showed nothing unusual. There was certainly nothing except the door, and, as they could not prevent this from being opened, since it opened outwards, they heaped up most of the furniture in front of it, thus forming a barricade which would protect them against a surprise.

Then Patrice cocked his two revolvers and placed them beside him, in full sight.

"This will make us easy in our minds," he said. "Any enemy who appears is a dead man."

But the memory of the past bore down upon them with all its awful weight. All their words and all their actions others before them had spoken and performed, under similar conditions, with the same thoughts and the same forebodings. Patrice's father must have prepared his weapons. Coralie's mother must have folded her hands and prayed. Together they had barricaded the door and together sounded the walls and taken up the carpet. What an anguish was this, doubled as it was by a like anguish!

To dispel the horror of the idea, they turned the pages of the books, works of fiction and others, which their parents had read. On certain pages, at the end of a chapter or volume, were lines constituting notes which Patrice's father and Coralie's mother used to write each other.

"Darling Patrice,

"I ran in this morning to recreate our life of yesterday and to dream of our life this afternoon. As you will arrive before me, you will read these lines. You will read that I love you..."

And, in another book:

"My own Coralie,

"You have this minute gone; I shall not see you until tomorrow and I do not want to leave this haven where our love has tasted such delights without once more telling you..."

They looked through most of the books in this way, finding, however, instead of the clues for which they hoped, nothing but expressions of love and affection. And they spent more than two hours waiting and dreading what might happen.

"There will be nothing," said Patrice. "And perhaps that is the most awful part of it, for, if nothing occurs, it will mean that we are doomed not to leave this room. And, in that case..."

Patrice did not finish the sentence. Coralie understood. And together they received a vision of the death by starvation that seemed to threaten them. But Patrice exclaimed:

"No, no, we have not that to fear. No. For people of our age to die of hunger takes several days, three or four days or more. And we shall be rescued before then."

"How?" asked Coralie.

"How? Why, by our soldiers, by Ya-Bon, by M. Masseron! They will be uneasy if we do not come home tonight."

"You yourself said, Patrice, that they cannot know where we are."

"They'll find out. It's quite simple. There is only the lane between the two gardens. Besides, everything we do is set down in my diary, which is in the desk in my room. Ya-Bon knows of its existence. He is bound to speak of it to M. Masseron. And then... and then there is Siméon. What will have become of him? Surely they will notice his movements? And won't he give a warning of some kind?"

But words were powerless to comfort them. If they were not to die of hunger, then the enemy must have contrived another form of torture. Their inability to do anything kept them on the rack. Patrice began his investigations again. A curious accident turned them in a new direction. On opening one of the books through which they had not yet looked, a book published in 1895, Patrice saw two pages turned down together. He separated them and read a letter addressed to him by his father:

"Patrice, my dear Son,

"If ever chance places this note before your eyes, it will prove that I have met with a violent death which has prevented my destroying it. In that case, Patrice, look for the truth concerning my death on the wall of the studio, between the two windows. I shall perhaps have time to write it down."

The two victims had therefore at that time foreseen the tragic fate in store for them; and Patrice's father and Coralie's mother knew the danger which they ran in coming to the lodge. It remained to be seen whether Patrice's father had been able to carry out his intention.

Between the two windows, as all around the room, was a wainscoting of varnished wood, topped at a height of six feet by a cornice. Above the cornice was the plain plastered wall. Patrice and Coralie had already observed, without paying particular attention to it, that the wainscoting seemed to have been renewed in this part, because the varnish of the boards did not have the same uniform colour. Using one of the iron dogs as a chisel, Patrice broke down the cornice and lifted the first board. It broke easily. Under this plank, on the plaster of the wall, were lines of writing.

"It's the same method," he said, "as that which old Siméon has since employed. First write on the walls, then cover it up with wood or plaster."

He broke off the top of the other boards and in this way brought several complete lines into view, hurried lines, written in pencil and slightly worn by time. Patrice deciphered them with the greatest emotion. His father had written them at a moment when death was stalking at hand. A few hours later he had ceased to live. They were the evidence of his death-agony and perhaps too an imprecation against the enemy who was killing him and the woman he loved.

Patrice read, in an undertone:

"I am writing this in order that the scoundrel's plot may not be achieved to the end and in order to ensure his punishment. Coralie and I are no doubt going to perish, but at least we shall not die without revealing the cause of our death.

"A few days ago, he said to Coralie, 'You spurn my love, you load me with your hatred. So be it. But I shall kill you both, your lover and you, in such a manner that I can never be accused of the death, which will look like suicide. Everything is ready. Beware, Coralie.'

"Everything was, in fact, ready. He did not know me, but he must have known that Coralie used to meet somebody here daily; and it was in this lodge that he prepared our tomb.

"What manner of death ours will be we do not know. Lack of food, no doubt. It is four hours since we were imprisoned. The door closed upon us, a heavy door which he must have placed there last night. All the other openings, doors and windows alike, are stopped up with blocks of stone laid and cemented since our last meeting. Escape is impossible. What is to become of us?"

The uncovered portion stopped here. Patrice said:

"You see, Coralie, they went through the same horrors as ourselves. They too dreaded starvation. They too passed through long hours of waiting, when inaction is so painful; and it was more or less to distract their thoughts that they wrote those lines."

He went on, after examining the spot:

"They counted, most likely, on what happened, that the man who was killing them would not read this document. Look, one long curtain was hung over these two windows and the wall between them, one curtain, as is proved by the single rod covering the whole distance. After our parents' death no one thought of drawing it, and the truth remained concealed until the day when Siméon discovered it and, by way of precaution, hid it again under a wooden panel and hung up two curtains in the place of one. In this way everything seemed normal."

Patrice set to work again. A few more lines made their appearance:

"Oh, if I were the only one to suffer, the only one to die! But the horror of it all is that I am dragging my dear Coralie with me. She fainted and is lying down now, prostrate by the fears which she tries so hard to overcome. My poor darling! I seem already to see the pallor of death on her sweet face. Forgive me, dearest, forgive me!"

Patrice and Coralie exchanged glances. Here were the same sentiments which they themselves felt, the same scruples, the same delicacy, the same effacement of self in the presence of the other's grief.

"He loved your mother," Patrice murmured, "as I love you. I also am not afraid of death. I have faced it too often, with a smile! But you, Coralie, you, for whose sake I would undergo any sort of torture...!"

He began to walk up and down, once more yielding to his anger:

"I shall save you, Coralie, I swear it. And what a delight it will then be to take our revenge! He shall have the same fate which he was devising for us. Do you understand, Coralie? He shall die here, here in this room. Oh, how my hatred will spur me to bring that about!"

He tore down more pieces of boarding, in the hope of learning something that might be useful to him, since the struggle was being renewed under exactly similar conditions. But the sentences that followed, like those which Patrice had just uttered, were oaths of vengeance:

"Coralie, he shall be punished, if not by us, then by the hand of God. No, his infernal scheme will not succeed. No, it will never be believed that we had recourse to suicide to relieve ourselves of an existence that was built up of happiness and joy. No, his crime will be known. Hour by hour I shall here set down the undeniable proofs..."

"Words, words!" cried Patrice, in a tone of exasperation. "Words of vengeance and sorrow, but never a fact to guide us. Father, will you tell us nothing to save your Coralie's daughter? If your Coralie succumbed, let mine escape the disaster, thanks to your aid, father! Help me! Counsel me!"

But the father answered the son with nothing but more words of challenge and despair:

"Who can rescue us? We are walled up in this tomb, buried alive and condemned to torture without being able to defend ourselves. My revolver lies there, upon the table. What is the use of it? The enemy does not attack us. He has time on his side, unrelenting time which kills of its own strength, by the mere fact that it is time. Who can rescue us? Who will save my darling Coralie?"

The position was terrible, and they felt all its tragic horror. It seemed to them as though they were already dead, once they were enduring the same trial endured by others and that they were still enduring it under the same conditions. There was nothing to enable them to escape any of the phases through which the other two, his father and her mother, had passed. The similarity between their own and their parents' fate was so striking that they seemed to be suffering two deaths, and the second agony was now commencing.

Coralie gave way and began to cry. Moved by her tears, Patrice attacked the wainscoting with new fury, but its boards, strengthened by cross-laths, resisted his efforts:

At last he read:

"What is happening? We had an impression that someone was walking outside, in the garden. Yes, when we put our ears to the stone wall built in the embrasure of the window, we thought we heard footsteps. Is it possible? Oh, if it only were! It would mean the struggle, at last. Anything rather than the maddening silence and endless uncertainty!

"That's it!... That's it!... The sound is becoming more distinct... It is a different sound, like that which you make when you dig the ground with a pick-axe. Someone is digging the ground, not in front of the house, but on the right, near the kitchen..."

Patrice redoubled his efforts. Coralie came and helped him. This time he felt that a corner of the veil was being lifted. The writing went on:

"Another hour, with alternate spells of sound and silence: the same sound of digging and the same silence which suggests work that is being continued.

"And then someone entered the hall, one person; he, evidently. We recognized his step... He walks without attempting to deaden it... Then he went to the kitchen, where he worked the same way as before, with a pick-axe, but on the stones this time. We also heard the noise of a pane of glass breaking.

"And now he has gone outside again and there is a new sort of sound, against the house, a sound that seems to travel up the house as though the wretch had to climb to a height in order to carry out his plan..."

Patrice stopped reading and looked at Coralie. Both of them were listening.

"Hark!" he said, in a low voice.

"Yes, yes," she answered, "I hear... Steps outside the house... in the garden..."

They went to one of the windows, where they had left the casement open behind the wall of building-stones, and listened. There was really someone walking; and the knowledge that the enemy was approaching gave them the same sense of relief that their parents had experienced.

Someone walked thrice round the house. But they did not, like their parents, recognize the sound of the footsteps. They were those of a stranger, or else steps that had changed their tread. Then, for a few minutes, they heard nothing more. And suddenly another sound arose; and, though in their innermost selves they were expecting it, they were nevertheless stupefied at hearing it. And Patrice, in a hollow voice, laying stress upon each syllable, uttered the sentence which his father had written twenty years before:

"It's the sound which you make when you dig the ground with a pick-axe."

Yes, it must be that. Someone was digging the ground, not in front of the house, but on the right, near the kitchen.

And so the abominable miracle of the revived tragedy was continuing. Here again the former act was repeated, a simple enough act in itself, but one which became sinister because it was one of those which had already been performed and because it was announcing and preparing the death once before announced and prepared.

An hour passed. The work went on, paused and went on again. It was like the sound of a spade at work in a courtyard, when the grave-digger is in no hurry and takes a rest and then resumes his work.

Patrice and Coralie stood listening side by side, their eyes in each other's eyes, their hands in each other's hands.

"He's stopping," whispered Patrice.

"Yes," said Coralie; "only I think..."

"Yes, Coralie, there's someone in the hall... Oh, we need not trouble to listen! We have only to remember. There: 'He goes to the kitchen and digs as he did just now, but on the stones this time.'... And then... and then... oh, Coralie, the same sound of broken glass!"

It was memories mingling with the grewsome reality. The present and the past formed but one. They foresaw events at the very instant when these took place.

The enemy went outside again; and, forthwith, the sound seemed "to travel up the house as though the wretch had to climb to a height in order to carry out his plans."

And then... and then what would happen next? They no longer thought of consulting the inscription on the wall, or perhaps they did not dare. Their attention was concentrated on the invisible and sometimes imperceptible deeds that were being accomplished against them outside, an uninterrupted stealthy effort, a mysterious twenty-year-old plan whereof each slightest detail was settled as by clockwork!

The enemy entered the house and they heard a rustling at the bottom of the door, a rustling of soft things apparently being heaped or pushed against the wood. Next came other vague noises in the two adjoining rooms, against the walled doors, and similar noises outside, between the stones of the windows and the open shutters. And then they heard someone on the roof.

They raised their eyes. This time they felt certain that the last act was at hand, or at least one of the scenes of the last act. The roof to them was the framed skylight which occupied the centre of the ceiling and admitted the only daylight that entered the room. And still the same agonizing question rose to their minds: what was going to happen? Would the enemy show his face outside the skylight and reveal himself at last?

This work on the roof continued for a considerable time. Footsteps shook the zinc sheets that covered it, moving between the right-hand side of the house and the edge of the skylight. And suddenly this skylight, or rather a part of it, a square containing four panes, was lifted, a very little way, by a hand which inserted a stick to keep it open.

And the enemy again walked across the roof and went down the side of the house.

They were almost disappointed and felt such a craving to know the truth that Patrice once more fell to breaking the boards of the wainscoting, removing the last pieces, which covered the end of the inscription. And what they read made them live the last few minutes all over again. The enemy's return, the rustle against the walls and the walled windows, the noise on the roof, the opening of the skylight, the method of supporting it: all this had happened in the same order and, so to speak, within the same limit of time. Patrice's father and Coralie's mother had undergone the same impressions. Destiny seemed bent on following the same paths and making the same movements in seeking the same object.

And the writing went on:

"He is going up again, he is going up again... There's his footsteps on the roof... He is near the skylight... Will he look through?... Shall we see his hated face?..."

"He is going up again, he is going up again," gasped Coralie, nestling against Patrice.

The enemy's footsteps were pounding over the zinc.

"Yes," said Patrice, "he is going up as before, without departing from the procedure followed by the other. Only we do not know whose face will appear to us. Our parents knew their enemy."

She shuddered at her image of the man who had killed her mother; and she asked:

"It was he, was it not?"

"Yes, it was he. There is his name, written by my father."

Patrice had almost entirely uncovered the inscription. Bending low, he pointed with his finger:

"Look. Read the name: Essarès. You can see it down there: it was one of the last words my father wrote."

And Coralie read:

"The skylight rose higher, a hand lifted it and we saw... we saw, laughing as he looked down on us—oh, the scoundrel—Essarès!... Essarès!... And then he passed something through the opening, something that came down, that unrolled itself in the middle of the room, over our heads: a ladder, a rope-ladder.

"We did not understand. It was swinging in front of us. And then, in the end, I saw a sheet of paper rolled round the bottom rung and pinned to it. On the paper, in Essarès' handwriting, are the words, 'Send Coralie up by herself. Her life shall be saved. I give her ten minutes to accept. If not...'"

"Ah," said Patrice, rising from his stooping posture, "will this also be repeated? What about the ladder, the rope-ladder, which I found in old Siméon's cupboard?"

Coralie kept her eyes fixed on the skylight, for the footsteps were moving around it. Then they stopped. Patrice and Coralie had not a doubt that the moment had come and that they also were about to see their enemy. And Patrice said huskily, in a choking voice:

"Who will it be? There are three men who could have played this sinister part as it was played before. Two are dead, Essarès and my father. And Siméon, the third, is mad. Is it he, in his madness, who has set the machine working again? But how are we to imagine that he could have done it with such precision? No, no, it is the other one, the one who directs him and who till now has remained in the background."

He felt Coralie's fingers clutching his arm.

"Hush," she said, "here he is!"

"No, no."

"Yes, I'm sure of it."

Her imagination had foretold what was preparing; and in fact, as once before, the skylight was raised higher. A hand lifted it. And suddenly they saw a head slipping under the open framework.

It was the head of old Siméon.

"The madman!" Patrice whispered, in dismay. "The madman!"

"But perhaps he isn't mad," she said. "He can't be mad."

She could not check the trembling that shook her.

The man overhead looked down upon them, hidden behind his spectacles, which allowed no expression of satisfied hatred or joy to show on his impassive features.

"Coralie," said Patrice, in a low voice, "do what I say... Come..."

He pushed her gently along, as though he were supporting her and leading her to a chair. In reality he had but one thought, to reach the table on which he had placed his revolvers, take one of them and fire.

Siméon remained motionless, like some evil genius come to unloose the tempest... Coralie could not rid herself of that glance which weighted upon her.

"No," she murmured, resisting Patrice, as though she feared that his intention would precipitate the dreaded catastrophe, "no, you mustn't..."

But Patrice, displaying greater determination, was near his object. One more effort and his hand would hold the revolver.

He quickly made up his mind, took rapid aim and fired a shot.

The head disappeared from sight.

"Oh," said Coralie, "you were wrong, Patrice! He will take his revenge on us..."

"No, perhaps not," said Patrice, still holding his revolver. "I may very well have hit him. The bullet struck the frame of the skylight. But it may have glanced off, in which case..."

They waited hand in hand, with a gleam of hope, which did not last long, however.

The noise on the roof began again. And then, as before—and this they really had the impression of not seeing for the first time—as before, something passed through the opening, something that came down, that unrolled itself in the middle of the room, a ladder, a rope-ladder, the very one which Patrice had seen in old Siméon's cupboard.

As before, they looked at it; and they knew so well that everything was being done over again, that the facts were inexorably, pitilessly linked together, they were so certain of it that their eyes at once sought the sheet of paper which must inevitably be pinned to the bottom rung.

It was there, forming a little scroll, dry and discoloured and tom at the edges. It was the sheet of twenty years ago, written by Essarès and now serving, as before, to convey the same temptation and the same threat:

"Send Coralie up by herself. Her life shall be saved. I give her ten minutes to accept. If not..."

13

THE NAILS IN THE COFFIN

"If not..."

Patrice repeated the words mechanically, several times over, while their formidable significance became apparent to both him and Coralie. The words meant that, if Coralie did not obey and did not deliver herself to the enemy, if she did not flee from prison to go with the man who held the keys of the prison, the alternative was death.

At that moment neither of them was thinking what end was in store for them nor even of that death itself. They thought only of the command to separate which the enemy had issued against them. One was to go and the other to die.

Coralie was promised her life if she would sacrifice Patrice. But what was the price of the promise? And what would be the form of the sacrifice demanded?

There was a long silence, full of uncertainty and anguish between the two lovers. They were coming to grips with something; and the drama was no longer taking place absolutely outside them, without their playing any other part than that of helpless victims. It was being enacted within themselves; and they had the power to alter its ending. It was a terrible problem. It had already been set to the earlier Coralie; and she had solved it as a lover would, for she was dead. And now it was being set again.

Patrice read the inscription; and the rapidly scrawled words became less distinct:

"I have begged and entreated Coralie... She flung herself on her knees before me. She wants to die with me..."

Patrice looked at Coralie. He had read the words in a very low voice; and she had not heard them. Then, in a burst of passion, he drew her eagerly to him and exclaimed:

"You must go, Coralie! You can understand that my not saying so at once was not due to hesitation. No, only... I was thinking of that man's offer... and I am frightened for your sake... What he asks, Coralie, is terrible. His reason for promising to save your life is that he loves you. And so you understand... But still, Coralie, you must obey... you must go on living... Go! It is no use waiting for the ten minutes to pass. He might change his mind and condemn you to death as well. No, Coralie, you must go, you must go at once!"

"I shall stay," she replied, simply.

He gave a start:

"But this is madness! Why make a useless sacrifice? Are you afraid of what might happen if you obeyed him?"

"No."

"Then go."

"I shall stay."

"But why? Why this obstinacy? It can do no good. Then why stay?"

"Because I love you, Patrice."

He stood dumfounded. He knew that she loved him and he had already told her so. But that she loved him to the extent of preferring to die in his company, this was an unexpected, exquisite and at the same time terrible delight.

"Ah," he said, "you love me, Coralie! You love me!"

"I love you, my own Patrice."

She put her arms around his neck; and he felt that hers was an embrace too strong to be sundered. Nevertheless, he was resolved to save her; and he refused to yield:

"If you love me," he said, "you must obey me and save your life. Believe me, it is a hundred times more painful for me to die with you than to die alone. If I know that you are free and alive, death will be sweet to me."

She did not listen and continued her confession, happy in making it, happy in uttering words which she had kept to herself so long:

"I have loved you, Patrice, from the first day I saw you. I knew it without your telling me; and my only reason for not telling you earlier was that I was waiting for a solemn occasion, for a time when it would be a glory to tell you so, while I looked into the depths of your eyes and offered myself to you entirely. As I have had to speak on the brink of the grave, listen to me and do not force upon me a separation which would be worse than death."

"No, no," he said, striving to release himself, "it is your duty to go."

He made another effort and caught hold of her hands:

"It is your duty to go," he whispered, "and, when you are free, to do all that you can to save me."

"What are you saying, Patrice?"

"Yes," he repeated, "to save me. There is no reason why you should not escape from that scoundrel's clutches, report him, seek assistance, warn our friends. You can call out, you can play some trick..."

She looked at him with so sad a smile and such a doubting expression that he stopped speaking.

"You are trying to mislead me, my poor darling," she said, "but you are no more taken in by what you say than I am. No, Patrice, you well know that, if I surrender myself to that man, he will reduce me to silence or imprison me in some hiding-place, bound hand and foot, until you have drawn your last breath."

"You really think that?"

"Just as you do, Patrice. Just as you are sure of what will happen afterwards."

"Well, what will happen?"

"Ah, Patrice, if that man saves my life, it will not be out of generosity. Don't you see what his plan is, his abominable plan, once I am his prisoner? And don't you also see what my only means of escape will be? Therefore, Patrice, if I am to die in a few hours, why not die now, in your arms... at the same time as yourself, with my lips to yours? Is that dying? Is it not rather living, in one instant, the most wonderful of lives?"

He resisted her embrace. He knew that the first kiss of her proffered lips would deprive him of all his power of will.

"This is terrible," he muttered. "How can you expect me to accept your sacrifice, you, so young, with years of happiness before you?"

"Years of mourning and despair, if you are gone."

"You must live, Coralie. I entreat you to, with all my soul."

"I cannot live without you, Patrice. You are my only happiness. I have no reason for existence except to love you. You have taught me to love. I love you!"

Oh, those heavenly words! For the second time they rang between the four walls of that room. The same words, spoken by the daughter, which the mother had spoken with the same passion and the same glad acceptance of her fate! The same words made twice holy by the recollection of death past and the thought of death to come!

Coralie uttered them without alarm. All her fears seemed to disappear in her love; and it was love alone that shook her voice and dimmed the brightness of her eyes.

Patrice contemplated her with a rapt look. He too was beginning to think that minutes such as these were worth dying for. Nevertheless, he made a last effort:

"And if I ordered you to go, Coralie?"

"That is to say," she murmured, "if you ordered me to go to that man and surrender myself to him? Is that what you wish, Patrice?"

The thought was too much for him.

"Oh, the horror of it! That man... that man... you, my Coralie, so stainless and undefiled!..."

Neither he nor she pictured the man in the exact image of Siméon. To both of them, notwithstanding the hideous vision perceived above, the enemy retained a mysterious character. It was perhaps Siméon. It was perhaps another, of whom Siméon was but the instrument. Assuredly it was the enemy, the evil genius crouching above their heads, preparing their death-throes while he pursued Coralie with his foul desire.

Patrice asked one more question:

"Did you ever notice that Siméon sought your company?"

"No, never. If anything, he rather avoided me."

"Then it's because he's mad..."

"I don't think he is mad: he is revenging himself."

"Impossible. He was my father's friend. All his life long he worked to bring us together: surely he would not kill us deliberately?"

"I don't know, Patrice, I don't understand..."

They discussed it no further. It was of no importance whether their death was caused by this one or that one. It was death itself that they had to fight, without troubling who had set it loose against them. And what could they do to ward it off?

"You agree, do you not?" asked Coralie, in a low voice.

He made no answer.

"I shall not go," she went on, "but I want you to be of one mind with me. I entreat you. It tortures me to think that you are suffering more than I do. You must let me bear my share. Tell me that you agree."

"Yes," he said, "I agree."

"My own Patrice! Now give me your two hands, look right into my eyes and smile."

Mad with love and longing they plunged themselves for an instant into a sort of ecstasy. Then she asked:

"What is it, Patrice? You seem distraught again."

He gave a hoarse cry:

"Look!... Look..."

This time he was certain of what he had seen. The ladder was going up. The ten minutes were over.

He rushed forward and caught hold of one of the rungs. The ladder no longer moved.

He did not know exactly what he intended to do. The ladder afforded Coralie's only chance of safety. Could he abandon that hope and resign himself to the inevitable?

One or two minutes passed. The ladder must have been hooked fast again, for Patrice felt a firm resistance up above.

Coralie was entreating him:

"Patrice," she asked, "Patrice, what are you hoping for?"

He looked around and above him, as though seeking an idea, and he seemed also to look inside himself, as though he were seeking that idea amid all the memories which he had accumulated at the moment when his father also held the ladder, in a last effort of will. And suddenly, throwing up his leg, he placed his left foot on the fifth rung of the ladder and began to raise himself by the uprights.

It was an absurd attempt to scale the ladder, to reach the skylight, to lay hold of the enemy and thus save himself and Coralie. If his father had failed before him, how could he hope to succeed?

It was all over in less than three seconds. The ladder was at once unfastened from the hook that kept it hanging from the skylight; and Patrice and the ladder came to the ground together. At the same time a strident laugh rang out above, followed the next moment by the sound of the skylight closing.

Patrice picked himself up in a fury, hurled insults at the enemy and, as his rage increased, fired two revolver shots, which broke two of the panes. He next attacked the doors and windows, banging at them with the iron dog which he had taken from the fender. He hit the walls, he hit the floor, he shook his fist at the invisible enemy who was mocking him. But suddenly, after a few blows struck at space, he was compelled to stop. Something like a thick veil had glided overhead. They were in the dark.

He understood what had happened. The enemy had lowered a shutter upon the skylight, covering it entirely.

"Patrice! Patrice!" cried Coralie, maddened by the blotting out of the light and losing all her strength of mind. "Patrice! Where are you, Patrice? Oh, I'm frightened! Where are you?"

They began to grope for each other, like blind people, and nothing that had gone before seemed to them more horrible than to be lost in this pitiless blackness.

"Patrice! Oh, Patrice! Where are you?"

Their hands touched, Coralie's poor little frozen fingers and Patrice's hands that burned with fever, and they pressed each other and twined together and clutched each other as though to assure themselves that they were still living.

"Oh, don't leave me, Patrice!" Coralie implored.

"I am here," he replied. "Have no fear: they can't separate us."

"You are right," she panted, "they can't separate us. We are in our grave."

The word was so terrible and Coralie uttered it so mournfully that a reaction overtook Patrice.

"No! What are you talking about?" he exclaimed. "We must not despair. There is hope of safety until the last moment."

Releasing one of his hands, he took aim with his revolver. A few faint rays trickled through the chinks around the skylight. He fired three times. They heard the crack of the wood-work and the chuckle of the enemy. But the shutter must have been lined with metal, for no split appeared.

Besides, the chinks were forthwith stopped up; and they became aware that the enemy was engaged in the same work that he had performed around the doors and windows. It was obviously very thorough and took a long time in the doing. Next came another work, completing the first. The enėmy was nailing the shutter to the frame of the skylight.

It was an awful sound! Swift and light as were the taps of the hammer, they seemed to drive deep into the brain of those who heard them. It was their coffin that was being nailed down, their great coffin with a lid hermetically sealed that now bore heavy upon them. There was no hope left, not a possible chance of escape. Each tap of the hammer strengthened their dark prison, making yet more impregnable the walls that stood between them and the outer world and bade defiance to the most resolute assault:

"Patrice," stammered Coralie, "I'm frightened... That tapping hurts me so!"...

She sank back in his arms. Patrice felt tears coursing down her cheeks.

Meanwhile the work overhead was being completed. They underwent the terrible experience which condemned men must feel on the morning of their last day, when from their cells they hear the preparations: the engine of death that is being set up, or the electric batteries that are being tested. They hear men striving to have everything ready, so that not one propitious chance may remain and so that destiny may be fulfilled. Death had entered the enemy's service and was working hand in hand with him. He was death itself, acting, contriving and fighting against those whom he had resolved to destroy.

"Don't leave me," sobbed Coralie, "don't leave me!..."

"Only for a second or two," he said. "We must be avenged later."

"What is the use, Patrice? What can it matter to us?"

He had a box containing a few matches. Lighting them one after the other, he led Coralie to the panel with the inscription.

"What are you going to do?" she asked.

"I will not have our death put down to suicide. I want to do what our parents did before us and to prepare for the future. Someone will read what I am going to write and will avenge us."

He took a pencil from his pocket and bent down. There was a free space, right at the bottom of the panel. He wrote:

"Patrice Belval and Coralie, his betrothed, die the same death, murdered by Siméon Diodokis, 14 April, 1915."

But, as he finished writing, he noticed a few words of the former inscription which he had not yet read, because they were placed outside it, so to speak, and did not appear to form part of it.

"One more match," he said. "Did you see? There are some words there, the last, no doubt, that my father wrote."

She struck a match. By the flickering light they made out a certain number of misshapen letters, obviously written in a hurry and forming two words:

"*Asphyxiated... Oxide...*"

The match went out. They rose in silence. Asphyxiated! They understood. That was how their parents had perished and how they themselves would perish. But they did not yet fully realize how the thing would happen. The lack of air would never be great enough to suffocate them in this large room, which contained enough to last them for many days.

"Unless," muttered Patrice, "unless the quality of the air can be impaired and therefore..."

He stopped. Then he went on:

"Yes, that's it. I remember."

He told Coralie what he suspected, or rather what conformed so well with the reality as to leave no room for doubt. He had seen in old Siméon's cupboard not only the rope-ladder which the madman had brought with him, but also a coil of lead pipes. And now Siméon's behaviour from the moment when they were locked in, his movements to and fro around the lodge, the care with which he had stopped up every crevice, his labours along the wall and on the roof: all this was explained in the most definite fashion. Old Siméon had simply fitted to a gas-meter, probably in the kitchen, the pipe which he had next laid along the wall and on the roof. This therefore was the way in which they were about to die, as their parents had died before them, stifled by ordinary gas.

Panic-stricken, they began to run aimlessly about the room, holding hands, while their disordered brains, bereft of thought or will, seemed like tiny things shaken by the fiercest gale. Coralie uttered incoherent words. Patrice, while imploring her to keep calm, was himself carried away by the storm and powerless to resist the terrible agony of the darkness wherein death lay waiting. At such times a man tries to flee, to escape the icy breath that is already chilling his marrow. He must flee, but where? Which way? The walls are insurmountable and the darkness is even harder than the walls.

They stopped, exhausted. A low hiss was heard somewhere in the room, the faint hiss that issues from a badly-closed gas-jet. They listened and perceived that it came from above. The torture was beginning.

"It will last half an hour, or an hour at most," Patrice whispered.

Coralie had recovered her self-consciousness:

"We shall be brave," she said.

"Oh, if I were alone! But you, you, my poor Coralie!"

"It is painless," she murmured.

"You are bound to suffer, you, so weak!"

"One suffers less, the weaker one is. Besides, I know that we sha'n't suffer, Patrice."

She suddenly appeared so placid that he on his side was filled with a great peace. Seated on a sofa, their fingers still entwined, they silently steeped themselves in the mighty calm which comes when we think that events have run their course. This calm is resignation, submission to superior forces. Natures such as theirs cease to rebel when destiny has manifested its orders and when nothing remains but acquiescence and prayer.

She put her arm round Patrice's neck:

"I am your bride in the eyes of God," she said. "May He receive us as He would receive a husband and wife."

Her gentle resignation brought tears to his eyes. She dried them with her kisses, and, of her own seeking, offered him her lips.

They sat wrapped in an infinite silence. They perceived the first smell of gas descending around them, but they felt no fear.

"Everything will happen as it did before, Coralie," whispered Patrice, "down to the very last second. Your mother and my father, who loved each other as we do, also died in each other's arms, with their lips joined together. They had decided to unite us and they have united us."

"Our grave will be near theirs," she murmured.

Little by little their ideas became confused and they began to think much as a man sees through a rising mist. They had had nothing to eat; and hunger now added its discomfort to the vertigo in which their minds were imperceptibly sinking. As it increased, their uneasiness and anxiety left them, to be followed by a sense of ecstasy, then lassitude, extinction, repose. The dread of the coming annihilation faded out of their thoughts.

Coralie, the first to be affected, began to utter delirious words which astonished Patrice at first:

"Dearest, there are flowers falling, roses all around us. How delightful!"

Presently he himself grew conscious of the same blissful exaltation, expressing itself in tenderness and joyful emotion. With no sort of dismay he felt her gradually yielding in his arms and abandoning herself; and he had the impression that he was following her down a measureless abyss, all bathed with light, where they floated, he and she, descending slowly and without effort towards a happy valley.

Minutes or perhaps hours passed. They were still descending, he supporting her by the waist, she with her head thrown back a little way, her eyes closed and a smile upon her lips. He remembered pictures showing gods thus gliding through the blue of heaven; and, drunk with pure, radiant light and air, he continued to circle above the happy valley.

But, as he approached it, he felt himself grow weary. Coralie weighed heavily on his bent arm. The descent increased in speed. The waves of light turned to darkness. A thick cloud came, followed by others that formed a whirl of gloom.

And suddenly, worn out, his forehead bathed in sweat and his body shaking with fever, he pitched forward into a great black pit...

14

A STRANGE CHARACTER

It was not yet exactly death. In his present condition of agony, what lingered of Patrice's consciousness mingled, as in a nightmare, the life which he knew with the imaginary world in which he now found himself, the world which was that of death.

In this world Coralie no longer existed; and her loss distracted him with grief. But he seemed to hear and see somebody whose presence was revealed by a shadow passing before his closed eyelids. This somebody he pictured to himself, though without reason, under the aspect of Siméon, who came to verify the death of his victims, began by carrying Coralie away, then came back to Patrice and carried him away also and laid him down somewhere. And all this was so well-defined that Patrice wondered whether he had not woke up.

Next hours passed... or seconds. In the end Patrice had a feeling that he was falling asleep, but as a man sleeps in hell, suffering the moral and physical tortures of the damned. He was back at the bottom of the black pit, which he was making desperate efforts to leave, like a man who has fallen into the sea and is trying to reach the surface. In this way, with the greatest difficulty, he passed through one waste of water after another, the weight of which stifled him. He had to scale them, gripping with his hands and feet to things that slipped, to rope-ladders which, possessing no points of support, gave way beneath him.

Meanwhile the darkness became less intense. A little muffled daylight mingled with it. Patrice felt less greatly oppressed. He half-opened his eyes, drew a breath or two and, looking round, beheld a sight that surprised him, the embrasure of an open door, near which he was lying in the air, on a sofa. Beside him he saw Coralie, on another sofa. She moved restlessly and seemed to be in great discomfort.

"She is climbing out of the black pit," he thought to himself. "Like me, she is struggling. My poor Coralie!"

There was a small table between them, with two glasses of water on it. Parched with thirst, he took one of them in his hand. But he dared not drink.

At that moment someone came through the open door, which Patrice perceived to be the door of the lodge; and he observed that it was not old Siméon, as he had thought, but a stranger whom he had never seen before.

"I am not asleep," he said to himself. "I am sure that I am not asleep and that this stranger is a friend."

And he tried to say it aloud, to make certainty doubly sure. But he had not the strength.

The stranger, however, came up to him and, in a gentle voice, said:

"Don't tire yourself, captain. You're all right now. Allow me. Have some water."

The stranger handed him one of the two glasses; Patrice emptied it at a draught, without any feeling of distrust, and was glad to see Coralie also drinking.

"Yes, I'm all right now," he said. "Heavens, how good it is to be alive! Coralie is really alive, isn't she?"

He did not hear the answer and dropped into a welcome sleep.

When he woke up, the crisis was over, though he still felt a buzzing in his head and a difficulty in drawing a deep breath. He stood up, however, and realized that all these sensations were not fanciful, that he was really outside the door of the lodge and that Coralie had drunk the glass of water and was peacefully sleeping.

"How good it is to be alive!" he repeated.

He now felt a need for action, but dared not go into the lodge, notwithstanding the open door. He moved away from it, skirting the cloisters containing the graves, and then, with no exact object, for he did not yet grasp the reason of his own actions, did not understand what had happened to him and was simply walking at random, he came back towards the lodge, on the other front, the one overlooking the garden.

Suddenly he stopped. A few yards from the house, at the foot of a tree standing beside the slanting path, a man lay back in a wicker long-chair, with his face in the shade and his legs in the sun. He was sleeping, with his head fallen forward and an open book upon his knees.

Then and not till then did Patrice clearly understand that he and Coralie had escaped being killed, that they were both really alive and that they owed their safety to this man whose sleep suggested a state of absolute security and satisfied conscience.

Patrice studied the stranger's appearance. He was slim of figure, but broad-shouldered, with a sallow complexion, a slight moustache on his lips and hair beginning to turn grey at the temples. His age was probably fifty at most. The cut of his clothes pointed to dandyism. Patrice leant forward and read the title of the book; *The Memoirs of Benjamin Franklin. He* also read the initials inside a hat lying on the grass: "L. P."

"It was he who saved me," said Patrice to himself, "I recognize him. He carried us both out of the studio and looked after us. But how was the miracle brought about? Who sent him?"

He tapped him on the shoulder. The man was on his feet at once, his face lit up with a smile:

"Pardon me, captain, but my life is so much taken up that, when I have a few minutes to myself, I use them for sleeping, wherever I may be... like Napoleon, eh? Well, I don't object to the comparison... But enough about myself. How are you feeling now? And madame—'Little Mother Coralie'—is she better? I saw no use in waking you, after I had opened the doors and taken you outside. I had done what was necessary and felt quite easy. You were both breathing. So I left the rest to the good pure air."

He broke off, at the sight of Patrice's disconcerted attitude; and his smile made way for a merry laugh:

"Oh, I was forgetting: you don't know me! Of course, it's true, the letter I sent you was intercepted. Let me introduce myself. Don Luis Perenna,* a member of an old Spanish family, genuine patent of nobility, papers all in order... But I can see that all this tells you nothing," he went on, laughing still more gaily. "No doubt Ya-Bon described me differently when he wrote my name on that street-wall, one evening a fortnight ago. Aha, you're beginning to understand!... Yes, I'm the man you sent for to help you. Shall I mention the name, just bluntly? Well, here goes, captain!... Arsene Lupin, at your service."

Patrice was stupefied. He had utterly forgotten Ya-Bon's proposal and the unthinking permission which he had given him to call in the famous adventurer. And here was Arsene Lupin standing in front of him, Arsene Lupin, who, by a sheer effort of will that resembled an incredible miracle, had dragged him and Coralie out of their hermetically-sealed coffin.

He held out his hand and said:

"Thank you!"

* The Teeth of the Tiger. By Maurice Leblanc. "Luis Perenna" is one of several anagrams of "Arsene Lupin."

"Tut!" said Don Luis, playfully. "No thanks! Just a good handshake, that's all. And I'm a man you can shake hands with, captain, believe me. I may have a few peccadilloes on my conscience, but on the other hand I have committed a certain number of good actions which should win me the esteem of decent folk... beginning with my own. And so..."

He interrupted himself again, seemed to reflect and, taking Patrice by a button of his jacket, said:

"Don't move. We are being watched."

"By whom?"

"Someone on the quay, right at the end of the garden. The wall is not high. There's a grating on the top of it. They're looking through the bars and trying to see us."

"How do you know? You have your back turned to the quay; and then there are the trees."

"Listen."

"I don't hear anything out of the way."

"Yes, the sound of an engine... the engine of a stopping car. Now what would a car want to stop here for, on the quay, opposite a wall with no house near it?"

"Then who do you think it is?"

"Why, old Siméon, of course!"

"Old Siméon!"

"Certainly. He's looking to see whether I've really saved the two of you."

"Then he's not mad?"

"Mad? No more mad than you or I!"

"And yet..."

"What you mean is that Siméon used to protect you; that his object was to bring you two together; that he sent you the key of the garden-door; and so on and so on."

"Do you know all that?"

"Well, of course! If not, how could I have rescued you?"

"But," said Patrice, anxiously, "suppose the scoundrel returns to the attack. Ought we not to take some precautions? Let's go back to the lodge: Coralie is all alone."

"There's no danger."

"Why?"

"Because I'm here."

Patrice was more astounded than ever:

"Then Siméon knows you?" he asked. "He knows that you are here?"

"Yes, thanks to a letter which I wrote you under cover to Ya-Bon and which he intercepted. I told you that I was coming; and he hurried to get to work. Only, as my habit is on these occasions, I hastened on my arrival by a few hours, so that I caught him in the act."

"At that moment you did not know he was the enemy; you knew nothing?"

"Nothing at all."

"Was it this morning?"

"No, this afternoon, at a quarter to two."

Patrice took out his watch:

"And it's now four. So in two hours..."

"Not that. I've been here an hour."

"Did you find out from Ya-Bon?"

"Do you think I've no better use for my time? Ya-Bon simply told me that you were not there, which was enough to astonish me."

"After that?"

"I looked to see where you were."

"How?"

"I first searched your room and, doing so in my own thorough fashion, ended by discovering that there was a crack at the back of your roll-top desk and that this crack faced a hole in the wall of the next room. I was able therefore to pull out the book in which you kept your diary and acquaint myself with what was going on. This, moreover, was how Siméon became aware of your least intentions. This was how he knew of your plan to come here, on a pilgrimage, on the fourteenth of April. This was how, last night, seeing you write, he preferred, before attacking you, to know what you were writing. Knowing it and learning, from your own words, that you were on your guard, he refrained. You see how simple it all is. If M. Masseron had grown uneasy at your absence, he would have been just as successful. Only he would have been successful tomorrow."

"That is to say, too late."

"Yes, too late. This really isn't his business, however, nor that of the police. So I would rather that they didn't meddle with it. I asked your wounded soldiers to keep silent about anything that may strike them as queer. Therefore, if M. Masseron comes today, he will think that everything is in order. Well, having satisfied my mind in this respect and possessing the necessary information from your diary, I took Ya-Bon with me and walked across the lane and into the garden."

"Was the door open?"

"No, but Siméon happened to be coming out at that moment. Bad luck for him, wasn't it? I took advantage of it boldly. I put my hand on the latch and we went in, without his daring to protest. He certainly knew who I was."

"But you didn't know at that time that he was the enemy?"

"I didn't know? And what about your diary?"

"I had no notion..."

"But, captain, every page is an indictment of the man. There's not an incident in which he did not take part, not a crime which he did not prepare."

"In that case you should have collared him."

"And if I had? What good would it have done me? Should I have compelled him to speak? No, I shall hold him tightest by leaving him his liberty. That will give him rope, you know. You see already he's prowling round the house instead of clearing out. Besides, I had something better to do: I had first to rescue you two... if there was still time. Ya-Bon and I therefore rushed to the door of the lodge. It was open; but the other, the door of the studio, was locked and bolted. I drew the bolts; and to force the lock was, for me, child's play. Then the smell of gas was enough to tell me what had happened, Siméon must have fitted an old meter to some outside pipe, probably the one which supplied the lamps on the lane, and he was suffocating you. All that remained for us to do was to fetch the two of you out and give you the usual treatment: rubbing, artificial respiration and so on. You were saved."

"I suppose he removed all his murderous appliances?" asked Patrice.

"No, he evidently contemplated coming back and putting everything to rights, so that his share in the business could not be proved, so too that people might believe in your suicide, a mysterious suicide, death without apparent cause; in short, the same tragedy that happened with your father and Little Mother Coralie's mother."

"Then you know?..."

"Why, haven't I eyes to read with? What about the inscription on the wall, your father's revelations? I know as much as you do, captain... and perhaps a bit more."

"More?"

"Well, of course! Habit, you know, experience! Plenty of problems, unintelligible to others, seem to me the simplest and clearest that can be. Therefore..."

Don Luis hesitated whether to go on:

"No," he said, "it's better that I shouldn't speak. The mystery will be dispelled gradually. Let us wait. For the moment..."

He again stopped, this time to listen:

"There, he must have seen you. And now that he knows what he wants to, he's going away."

Patrice grew excited:

"He's going away! You really ought to have collared him. Shall we ever find him again, the scoundrel? Shall we ever be able to take our revenge?"

Don Luis smiled:

"There you go, calling him a scoundrel, the man who watched over you for twenty years, who brought you and Little Mother Coralie together, who was your benefactor!"

"Oh, I don't know! All this is so bewildering! I can't help hating him... The idea of his getting away maddens me... I should like to torture him and yet..."

He yielded to a feeling of despair and took his head between his two hands. Don Luis comforted him:

"Have no fear," he said. "He was never nearer his downfall than at the present moment. I hold him in my hand as I hold this leaf."

"But how?"

"The man who's driving him belongs to me."

"What's that? What do you mean?"

"I mean that I put one of my men on the driver's seat of a taxi, with instructions to hang about at the bottom of the lane, and that Siméon did not fail to take the taxi in question."

"That is to say, you suppose so," Patrice corrected him, feeling more and more astounded.

"I recognized the sound of the engine at the bottom of the garden when I told you."

"And are you sure of your man?"

"Certain."

"What's the use? Siméon can drive far out of Paris, stab the man in the back... and then when shall we get to know?"

"Do you imagine that people can get out of Paris and go running about the high-roads without a special permit? No, if Siméon leaves Paris he will have to drive to some railway station or other and we shall know of it twenty minutes after. And then we'll be off."

"How?"

"By motor."

"Then you have a pass?"

"Yes, valid for the whole of France."

"You don't mean it!"

"I do; and a genuine pass at that! Made out in the name of Don Luis Perenna, signed by the minister of the interior and countersigned..."

"By whom?"

"By the President of the Republic."

Patrice felt his bewilderment change all at once into violent excitement. Hitherto, in the terrible adventure in which he was engaged, he had undergone the enemy's implacable will and had known little besides defeat and the horrors of ever-threatening death. But now a more powerful will suddenly arose in his favour. And everything was abruptly altered. Fate seemed to be changing its course, like a ship which an unexpected fair wind brings back into harbour.

"Upon my word, captain," said Don Luis, "I thought you were going to cry like Little Mother Coralie. Your nerves are overstrung. And I daresay you're hungry. We must find you something to eat. Come along."

He led him slowly towards the lodge and, speaking in a rather serious voice:

"I must ask you," he said, "to be absolutely discreet in this whole matter. With the exception of a few old friends and of Ya-Bon, whom I met in Africa, where he saved my life, no one in France knows me by my real name. I call myself Don Luis Perenna. In Morocco, where I was soldiering, I had occasion to do a service to the very gracious sovereign of a neighbouring neutral nation, who, though obliged to conceal his true feelings, is ardently on our side. He sent for me; and, in return, I asked him to give me my credentials and to obtain a pass for me. Officially, therefore, I am on a secret mission, which expires in two days. In two days I shall go back... to whence I came, to a place where, during the war, I am serving France in my fashion: not a bad one, believe me, as people will see one day."

They came to the settee on which Coralie lay sleeping. Don Luis laid his hand on Patrice's arm:

"One word more, captain. I swore to myself and I gave my word of honour to him who trusted me that, while I was on this mission, my time should be devoted exclusively to defending the interests of my country to the best of my power. I must warn you, therefore, that, notwithstanding all my sympathy for you, I shall not be able to prolong my stay for a single minute after I have discovered the eighteen hundred bags of gold. They were the one and only reason why I came in answer to Ya-Bon's appeal. When the bags of gold are in our possession, that is to say, tomorrow evening at latest, I shall go away. However, the two quests are joined. The clearing up of the one will mean the end of the other. And now enough of words. Introduce me to Little Mother Coralie and let's get to work! Make no mystery with her, captain," he added, laughing. "Tell her my real name. I have nothing to fear: Arsene Lupin has every woman on his side."

Forty minutes later Coralie was back in her room, well cared for and well watched. Patrice had taken a substantial meal, while Don Luis walked up and down the terrace smoking cigarettes.

"Finished, captain? Then we'll make a start."

He looked at his watch:

"Half-past five. We have more than an hour of daylight left. That'll be enough."

"Enough? You surely don't pretend that you will achieve your aim in an hour?"

"My definite aim, no, but the aim which I am setting myself at the moment, yes... and even earlier. An hour? What for? To do what? Why, you'll be a good deal wiser in a few minutes!"

Don Luis asked to be taken to the cellar under the library; where Essarès Bey used to keep the bags of gold until the time had come to send them off.

"Was it through this ventilator that the bags were let down?"

"Yes."

"Is there no other outlet?"

"None except the staircase leading to the library and the other ventilator."

"Opening on the terrace?"

"Yes."

"Then that's clear. The bags used to come in by the first and go out by the second."

"But..."

"There's no but about it, captain: how else would you have it happen? You see, the mistake people always make is to go looking for difficulties where there are none."

They returned to the terrace. Don Luis took up his position near the ventilator and inspected the ground immediately around. It did not take long. Four yards away, outside the windows of the library, was the basin with the statue of a child spouting a jet of water through a shell.

Don Luis went up, examined the basin and, leaning forwards, reached the little statue, which he turned upon its axis from right to left. At the same time the pedestal described a quarter of a circle.

"That's it," he said, drawing himself up again.

"What?"

"The basin will empty itself."

He was right. The water sank very quickly and the bottom of the fountain appeared.

Don Luis stepped into it and squatted on his haunches. The inner wall was lined with a marble mosaic composing a wide red-and-white fretwork pattern. In the middle of one of the frets was a ring, which Don Luis lifted and pulled. All that portion of the wall which formed the pattern yielded to his effort and came down, leaving an opening of about twelve inches by ten.

"That's where the bags of gold went," said Don Luis. "It was the second stage. They were despatched in the same manner, on a hook sliding along a wire. Look, here is the wire, in this groove at the top."

"By Jove!" cried Captain Belval. "But you've unravelled this in a masterly fashion! What about the wire? Can't we follow it?"

"No, but it will serve our purpose if we know where it finishes. I say, captain, go to the end of the garden, by the wall, taking a line at right angles to the house. When you get there, cut off a branch of a tree, rather high up. Oh, I was forgetting! I shall have to go out by the lane. Have you the key of the door? Give it me, please."

Patrice handed him the key and then went down to the wall beside the quay.

"A little farther to the right," Don Luis instructed him. "A little more still. That's better. Now wait."

He left the garden by the lane, reached the quay and called out from the other side of the wall:

"Are you there, captain?"

"Yes."

"Fix your branch so that I can see it from here. Capital."

Patrice now joined Don Luis, who was crossing the road. All the way down the Seine are wharves, built on the bank of the river and used for loading and unloading vessels. Barges put in alongside, discharge their cargoes, take in fresh ones and often lie moored one next to the other. At the spot where Don Luis and Patrice descended by a flight of steps there was a series of yards, one of which, the one which they reached first, appeared to be abandoned, no doubt since the war. It contained, amid a quantity of useless materials, several heaps of bricks and building-stones, a hut with broken windows and the lower part of a steam-crane. A placard swinging from a post bore the inscription:

BERTHOU
WHARFINGER & BUILDER.

Don Luis walked along the foot of the embankment, ten or twelve feet high, above which the quay was suspended like a terrace. Half of it was occupied by a heap of sand; and they saw in the wall the bars of an iron grating, the lower half of which was hidden by the sand-heap shored up with planks.

Don Luis cleared the grating and said, jestingly:

"Have you noticed that the doors are never locked in this adventure? Let's hope that it's the same with this one."

His theory was confirmed, somewhat to his own surprise, and they entered one of those recesses where workmen put away their tools.

"So far, nothing out of the common," said Don Luis, switching on an electric torch. "Buckets, pick-axes, wheelbarrows, a ladder... Ah! Ah! Just as I expected: rails, a complete set of light rails!... Lend me a hand, captain. Let's clear out the back. Good, that's done it."

Level with the ground and opposite the grating was a rectangular opening exactly similar to the one in the basin. The wire was visible above, with a number of hooks hanging from it.

"So this is where the bags arrived," Don Luis explained. "They dropped, so to speak, into one of the two little trollies which you see over there, in the corner. The rails were laid across the bank, of course at night; and the trollies were pushed to a barge into which they tipped their contents."

"So that...?"

"So that the French gold went this way... anywhere you like... somewhere abroad."

"And you think that the last eighteen hundred bags have also been despatched?"

"I fear so."

"Then we are too late?"

Don Luis reflected for a while without answering. Patrice, though disappointed by a development which he had not foreseen, remained amazed at the extraordinary skill with which his companion, in so short a time, had succeeded in unravelling a portion of the tangled skein.

"It's an absolute miracle," he said, at last. "How on earth did you do it?"

Without a word, Don Luis took from his pocket the book which Patrice had seen lying on his knees, *The Memoirs of Benjamin Franklin*, and motioned to him to read some lines which he indicated with his finger. They were written towards the end of the reign of Louis XVI and ran:

"We go daily to the village of Passy adjoining my home, where you take the waters in a beautiful garden. Streams and waterfalls pour down on all sides, this way and that, in artfully levelled beds. I am known to like skilful mechanism, so I have been shown the baisin where the waters of all the rivulets meet and mingle. There stands a little marble figure in the midst; and the weight of water is strong enough to turn it a quarter circle to the left and then pour down straight to the Seine by a conduit, which opens in the ground of the basin."

Patrice closed the book; and Don Luis went on to explain:

"Things have changed since, no doubt, thanks to the energies of Essarès Bey. The water escapes some other way now; and the aqueduct was used to drain off the gold. Besides, the bed of the river has narrowed. Quays have been built, with a system of canals underneath them. You see, captain, all this was easy enough to discover, once I had the book to tell me. *Doctus cum libro.*"

"Yes, but, even so, you had to read the book."

"A pure accident. I unearthed it in Siméon's room and put it in my pocket, because I was curious to know why he was reading it."

"Why, that's just how he must have discovered Essarès Bey's secret!" cried Patrice. "He didn't know the secret. He found the book among his employer's papers and got up his facts that way. What do you think? Don't you agree? You seem not to share my opinion. Have you some other view?"

Don Luis did not reply. He stood looking at the river. Beside the wharves, at a slight distance from the yard, a barge lay moored, with apparently no one on her. But a slender thread of smoke now began to rise from a pipe that stood out above the deck.

"Let's go and have a look at her," he said.

The barge was lettered:

LAN ON CHALANTE. BEAUNE

They had to cross the space between the barge and the wharf and to step over a number of ropes and empty barrels covering the flat portions of the deck. A companion-way brought them to a sort of cabin, which did duty as a stateroom and a kitchen in one. Here they found a powerful-looking man, with broad shoulders, curly black hair and a clean-shaven face. His only clothes were a blouse and a pair of dirty, patched canvas trousers.

Don Luis offered him a twenty-franc note. The man took it eagerly.

"Just tell me something, mate. Have you seen a barge lately, lying at Berthou's Wharf?"

"Yes, a motor-barge. She left two days ago."

"What was her name?"

"The *Belle Hélène*. The people on board, two men and a woman, were foreigners talking I don't know what lingo... We didn't speak to one another."

"But Berthou's Wharf has stopped work, hasn't it?"

"Yes, the owner's joined the army... and the foremen as well. We've all got to, haven't we? I'm expecting to be called up myself... though I've got a weak heart."

"But, if the yard's stopped work, what was the boat doing here?"

"I don't know. They worked the whole of one night, however. They had laid rails along the quay. I heard the trollies; and they were loading up. What with I don't know. And then, early in the morning, they unmoored."

"Where did they go?"

"Downstream, Mantes way."

"Thanks, mate. That's what I wanted to know."

Ten minutes later, when they reached the house, Patrice and Don Luis found the driver of the cab which Siméon Diodokis had taken after meeting Don Luis. As Don Luis expected, Siméon had told the man to go to a railway-station, the Gare Saint-Lazare, and there bought his ticket.

"Where to?"

"To Mantes!"

15

THE BELLE HÉLÈNE

"There's no mistake about it," said Patrice. "The information conveyed to M. Masseron that the gold had been sent away; the speed with which the work was carried out, at night, mechanically, by the people belonging to the boat; their alien nationality; the direction which they took: it all agrees. The probability is that, between the cellar into which the gold was shot and the place where it finished its journey, there was some spot where it used to remain concealed... unless the eighteen hundred bags can have awaited their despatch, slung one behind the other, along the wire. But that doesn't matter much. The great thing is to know that the *Belle Hélène*, hiding somewhere in the outskirts, lay waiting for the favourable opportunity. In the old days Essarès Bey, by way of precaution, used to send her a signal with the aid of that shower of sparks which I saw. This time old Siméon, who is continuing Essarès' work, no doubt on his own account, gave the crew notice; and the bags of gold are on their way to Rouen and Le Havre, where some steamer will take them over and carry them... eastwards. After all, forty or fifty tons, hidden in the hold under a layer of coal, is nothing. What do you say? That's it, isn't it? I feel positive about it... Then we have Mantes, to which he took his ticket and for which the *Belle Hélène* is bound. Could anything be clearer? Mantes, where he'll pick up his cargo of gold and go on board in some seafaring disguise, unknown and unseen... Loot and looter disappearing together. It's as clear as daylight. Don't you agree?"

Once again Don Luis did not answer. However, he must have acquiesced in Patrice's theories, for, after a minute, he declared:

"Very well. I'll go to Mantes." And, turning to the chauffeur, "Hurry off to the garage," he said, "and come back in the six- cylinder. I want to be at Mantes in less than an hour. You, captain..."

"I shall come with you."

"And who will look after...?"

"Coralie? She's in no danger! Who can attack her now? Siméon has failed in his attempt and is thinking only of saving his own skin... and his bags of gold."

"You insist, do you?"

"Absolutely."

"I don't know that you're wise. However, that's your affair. Let's go. By the way, though, one precaution." He raised his voice. "Ya-Bon!"

The Senegalese came hastening up. While Ya-Bon felt for Patrice all the affection of a faithful dog, he seemed to profess towards Don Luis something more nearly approaching religious devotion. The adventurer's slightest action roused him to ecstasy. He never stopped laughing in the great chief's presence.

"Ya-Bon, are you all right now? Is your wound healed? You don't feel tired? Good. In that case, come with me."

He led him to the quay, a short distance away from Berthou's Wharf:

"At nine o'clock this evening," he said, "you're to be on guard here, on this bench. Bring your food and drink with you; and keep a particular look-out for anything that happens over there, downstream. Perhaps nothing will happen at all; but never mind: you're not to move until I come back... unless... unless something does happen, in which case you will act accordingly."

He paused and then continued:

"Above all, Ya-Bon, beware of Siméon. It was he who gave you that wound. If you catch sight of him, leap at his throat and bring him here. But mind you don't kill him! No nonsense now. I don't want you to hand me over a corpse, but a live man. Do you understand, Ya-Bon?"

Patrice began to feel uneasy:

"Do you fear anything from that side?" he asked. "Look here, it's out of the question, as Siméon has gone…"

"Captain," said Don Luis, "when a good general goes in pursuit of the enemy, that does not prevent him from consolidating his hold on the conquered ground and leaving garrisons in the fortresses. Berthou's Wharf is evidently one of our adversary's rallying-points. I'm keeping it under observation."

Don Luis also took serious precautions with regard to Coralie. She was very much overstrained and needed rest and attention. They put her into the car and, after making a dash at full speed towards the centre of Paris, so as to throw any spies off the scent, took her to the home on the Boulevard Maillot, where Patrice handed her over to the matron and recommended her to the doctor's care. The staff received strict orders to admit no strangers to see her. She was to answer no letter, unless the letter was signed "Captain Patrice."

At nine o'clock, the car sped down the Saint-Germain and Mantes road. Sitting inside with Don Luis, Patrice felt all the enthusiasm of victory and indulged freely in theories, every one of which possessed for him the value of an unimpeachable certainty. A few doubts lingered in his mind, however, points which remained obscure and on which he would have been glad to have Don Luis' opinion.

"There are two things," he said, "which I simply cannot understand. In the first place, who was the man murdered by Essarès, at nineteen minutes past seven in the morning, on the fourth of April? I heard his dying cries. Who was killed? And what became of the body?"

Don Luis was silent; and Patrice went on:

"The second point is stranger still. I mean Siméon's behaviour. Here's a man who devotes his whole life to a single object, that of revenging his friend Belval's murder and at the same time ensuring my happiness and Coralie's. This is his one aim in life; and nothing can make him swerve from his obsession. And then, on the day when his enemy, Essarès Bey, is put out of the way, suddenly he turns round completely and persecutes Coralie and me, going to the length of using against us the horrible contrivance which Essarès Bey had employed so successfully against our parents! You really must admit that it's an amazing change! Can it be the thought of the gold that has hypnotized him? Are his crimes to be explained by the huge treasure placed at his disposal on the day when he discovered the secret? Has a decent man transformed himself into a bandit to satisfy a sudden instinct? What do you think?"

Don Luis persisted in his silence. Patrice, who expected to see every riddle solved by the famous adventurer in a twinkling, felt peevish and surprised. He made a last attempt:

"And the golden triangle? Another mystery! For, after all, there's not a trace of a triangle in anything we've seen! Where is this golden triangle? Have you any idea what it means?"

Don Luis allowed a moment to pass and then said:

"Captain, I have the most thorough liking for you and I take the liveliest interest in all that concerns you, but I confess that there is one problem which excludes all others and one object towards which all my efforts are now directed. That is the pursuit of the gold of which we have been robbed; and I don't want this gold to escape us. I have succeeded on your side, but not yet on the other. You are both of you safe and sound, but I haven't the eighteen hundred bags; and I want them, I want them."

"You'll have them, since we know where they are."

"I shall have them," said Don Luis, "when they lie spread before my eyes. Until then, I can tell you nothing."

At Mantes the enquiries did not take long. They almost immediately had the satisfaction of learning that a traveller, whose description corresponded with old Siméon's, had gone to the Hotel des Trois-Empereurs and was now asleep in a room on the third floor.

Don Luis took a ground-floor room, while Patrice, who would have attracted the enemy's attention more easily, because of his lame leg, went to the Grand Hotel.

He woke late the next morning. Don Luis rang him up and told him that Siméon, after calling at the post-office, had gone down to the river and then to the station, where he met a fashionably- dressed woman, with her face hidden by a thick veil, and brought her back to the hotel. The two were lunching together in the room on the third floor.

At four o'clock Don Luis rang up again, to ask Patrice to join him at once in a little cafe at the end of the town, facing the Seine. Here Patrice saw Siméon on the quay. He was walking with his hands behind his back, like a man strolling without any definite object.

"Comforter, spectacles, the same get-up as usual," said Patrice. "Not a thing about him changed. Watch him. He's putting on an air of indifference, but you can bet that his eyes are looking up stream, in the direction from which the *Belle Hélène* is coming."

"Yes, yes," said Don Luis. "Here's the lady."

"Oh, that's the one, is it?" said Patrice. "I've met her two or three times already in the street."

A dust-cloak outlined her figure and shoulders, which were wide and rather well-developed. A veil fell around the brim of her felt hat. She gave Siméon a telegram to read. Then they talked for a moment, seemed to be taking their bearings, passed by the cafe and stopped a little lower down. Here Siméon wrote a few words on a sheet of note-paper and handed it to his companion. She left him and went back into the town. Siméon resumed his walk by the riverside.

"You must stay here, captain," said Don Luis.

"But the enemy doesn't seem to be on his guard," protested Patrice. "He's not turning round."

"It's better to be prudent, captain. What a pity that we can't have a look at what Siméon wrote down!"

"I might..."

"Go after the lady? No, no, captain. Without wishing to offend you, you're not quite cut out for it. I'm not sure that even I..."

And he walked away.

Patrice waited. A few boats moved up or down the river. Mechanically, he glanced at their names. And suddenly, half an hour after Don Luis had left him, he heard the clearly-marked rhythm, the pulsation of one of those powerful motors which, for a few years past, have been fitted to certain barges.

At the bend of the river a barge appeared. As she passed in front of him, he distinctly and with no little excitement read the name of the *Belle Hélène*!

She was gliding along at a fair pace, to the accompaniment of a regular, throbbing beat. She was big and broad in the beam, heavy and pretty deep in the water, though she appeared to carry no cargo. Patrice saw two watermen on board, sitting and smoking carelessly. A dinghy floated behind at the end of a painter.

The barge went on and passed out of sight at the turn. Patrice waited another hour before Don Luis came back.

"Well?" he asked. "Have you seen her?"

"Yes, they let go the dinghy, a mile and a half from here, and put in for Siméon."

"Then he's gone with them?"

"Yes."

"Without suspecting anything?"

"You're asking me too much, captain!"

"Never mind! We've won! We shall catch them up in the car, pass them and, at Vernon or somewhere, inform the military and civil authorities, so that they may proceed to arrest the men and seize the boat."

"We shall inform nobody, captain. We shall proceed to carry out these little operations ourselves."

"What do you mean? Surely..."

The two looked at each other. Patrice had been unable to dissemble the thought that occurred to his mind. Don Luis showed no resentment:

"You're afraid that I shall run away with the three hundred millions? By jingo, it's a largish parcel to hide in one's jacketpocket!"

"Still," said Patrice, "may I ask what you intend to do?"

"You may, captain, but allow me to postpone my reply until we've really won. For the moment, we must first find the barge again."

They went to the Hotel des Trois-Empereurs and drove off in the car towards Vernon. This time they were both silent.

The road joined the river a few miles lower down, at the bottom of the steep hill which begins at Rosny. Just as they reached Rosny the *Belle Hélène* was entering the long loop which curves out to La Roche-Guyon, turns back and joins the high-road again at Bonnierès. She would need at least three hours to cover the distance, whereas the car, climbing the hill and keeping straight ahead, arrived at Bonnierès in fifteen minutes.

They drove through the village. There was an inn a little way beyond it, on the right. Don Luis made his chauffeur stop here:

"If we are not back by twelve tonight," he said, "go home to Paris. Will you come with me, captain?"

Patrice followed him towards the right, whence a small road led them to the river-bank. They followed this for a quarter of an hour. At last Don Luis found what he appeared to be seeking, a boat fastened to a stake, not far from a villa with closed shutters. Don Luis unhooked the chain.

It was about seven o'clock in the evening. Night was falling fast, but a brilliant moonlight lit the landscape.

"First of all," said Don Luis, "a word of explanation. We're going to wait for the barge. She'll come in sight on the stroke of ten and find us lying across stream. I shall order her to heave to; and there's no doubt that, when they see your uniform by the light of the moon or of my electric lamp, they will obey. Then we shall go on board."

"Suppose they refuse?"

"If they refuse, we shall board her by force. There are three of them and two of us. So..."

"And then?"

"And then? Well, there's every reason to believe that the two men forming the crew are only extra hands, employed by Siméon, but ignorant of his actions and knowing nothing of the nature of the cargo. Once we have reduced Siméon to helplessness and paid them handsomely, they'll take the barge wherever I tell them. But, mind you—and this is what I was coming to—I mean to do with the barge exactly as I please. I shall hand over the cargo as and when I think fit. It's my booty, my prize. No one is entitled to it but myself."

The officer drew himself up:

"Oh, I can't agree to that, you know!"

"Very well, then give me your word of honour that you'll keep a secret which doesn't belong to you. After which, we'll say goodnight and go our own ways. I'll do the boarding alone and you can go back to your own business. Observe, however, that I am not insisting on an immediate reply. You have plenty of time to reflect and to take the decision which your interest, honour and conscience may dictate to you. For my part, excuse me, but you know my weakness: when circumstances give me a little spare time, I take advantage of it to go to sleep. *Carpe somnum*, as the poet says. Goodnight, captain."

And, without another word, Don Luis wrapped himself in his great-coat, sprang into the boat and lay down.

Patrice had had to make a violent effort to restrain his anger. Don Luis' calm, ironic tone and well-bred, bantering voice got on his nerves all the more because he felt the influence of that strange man and fully recognized that he was incapable of acting without his assistance. Besides, he could not forget that Don Luis had saved his life and Coralie's.

The hours slipped by. The adventurer slumbered peacefully in the cool night air. Patrice hesitated what to do, seeking for some plan of conduct which would enable him to get at Siméon and rid himself of that implacable adversary and at the same time to prevent Don Luis from laying hands on the enormous treasure. He was dismayed at the thought of being his accomplice. And yet, when the first throbs of the motor were heard in the distance and when Don Luis awoke, Patrice was by his side, ready for action.

They did not exchange a word. A village-clock struck ten. The *Belle Hélène* was coming towards them.

Patrice felt his excitement increase. The *Belle Hélène* meant Siméon's capture, the recovery of the millions, Coralie out of danger, the end of that most hideous nightmare and the total extinction of Essarès' handiwork. The engine was throbbing nearer and nearer. Its loud and regular beat sounded wide over the motionless Seine. Don Luis had taken the sculls and was pulling hard for the middle of the river. And suddenly they saw in the distance a black mass looming up in the white moonlight. Twelve or fifteen more minutes passed and the *Belle Hélène* was before them.

"Shall I lend you a hand?" whispered Patrice. "It looks as if you had the current against you and as if you had a difficulty in getting along."

"Not the least difficulty," said Don Luis; and he began to hum a tune.

"But..."

Patrice was stupefied. The boat had turned in its own length and was making for the bank.

"But, I say, I say," he said, "what's this? Are you going back? Are you giving up?... I don't understand... You're surely not afraid because they're three to our two?"

Don Luis leapt on shore at a bound and stretched out his hand to him. Patrice pushed it aside, growling:

"Will you explain what it all means?"

"Take too long," replied Don Luis. "Just one question, though. You know that book I found in old Siméon's room, *The Memoirs of Benjamin Franklin*: did you see it when you were making your search?"

"Look here, it seems to me we have other things to..."

"It's an urgent question, captain."

"Well, no, it wasn't there."

"Then that's it," said Don Luis. "We've been done brown, or rather, to be accurate, I have. Let's be off, captain, as fast as we can."

Patrice was still in the boat. He pushed off abruptly and caught up the scull, muttering:

"As I live, I believe the beggar's getting at me!"

He was ten yards from shore when he cried:

"If you're afraid, I'll go alone. Don't want any help."

"Right you are, captain!" replied Don Luis. "I'll expect you presently at the inn."

Patrice encountered no difficulties in his undertaking. At the first order, which he shouted in a tone of command, the *Belle Hélène* stopped; and he was able to board her peacefully. The two bargees were men of a certain age, natives of the Basque coast. He introduced himself as a representative of the military authorities; and they showed him over their craft. He found neither old Siméon nor the very smallest bag of gold. The hold was almost empty.

The questions and answers did not take long:

"Where are you going?"

"To Rouen. We've been requisitioned by the government for transport of supplies."

"But you picked up somebody on the way."

"Yes, at Mantes."

"His name, please?"

"Siméon Diodokis."

"Where's he got to?"

"He made us put him down a little after, to take the train."

"What did he want?"

"To pay us."

"For what?"

"For a shipload we took at Paris two days ago."

"Bags?"

"Yes."

"What of?"

"Don't know. We were well paid and asked no questions."

"And what's become of the load?"

"We transhipped it last night to a small steamer that came alongside of us below Passy."

"What's the steamer's name?"

"The *Chamois*. Crew of six."

"Where is she now?"

"Ahead of us. She was going fast. She must be at Rouen by this time. Siméon Diodokis is on his way to join her."

"How long have you known Siméon Diodokis?"

"It's the first time we saw him. But we knew that he was in M. Essarès' service."

"Oh, so you've worked for M. Essarès?"

"Yes, often... Same job and same trip."

"He called you by means of a signal, didn't he?"

"Yes, he used to light an old factory-chimney."

"Was it always bags?"

"Yes. We didn't know what was inside. He was a good payer."

Patrice asked no more questions. He hurriedly got into his boat, pulled back to shore and found Don Luis seated with a comfortable supper in front of him.

"Quick!" he said. "The cargo is on board a steamer, the *Chamois*. We can catch her up between Rouen and Le Hâvre."

Don Luis rose and handed the officer a white-paper packet:

"Here's a few sandwiches for you, captain," he said. "We've an arduous night before us. I'm very sorry that you didn't get a sleep, as I did. Let's be off, and this time I shall drive. We'll knock some pace out of her! Come and sit beside me, captain."

They both stepped into the car; the chauffeur took his seat behind them. But they had hardly started when Patrice exclaimed:

"Hi! What are you up to? Not this way! We're going back to Mantes or Paris!"

"That's what I mean to do," said Luis, with a chuckle.

"Eh, what? Paris?"

"Well, of course!"

"Oh, look here, this is a bit too thick! Didn't I tell you that the two bargees...?"

"Those bargees of yours are humbugs."

"They declared that the cargo..."

"Cargo? No go!"

"But the *Chamois*..."

"*Chamois?* Sham was! I tell you once more, we're done, captain, done brown! Old Siméon is a wonderful old hand! He's a match worth meeting. He gives you a run for your money. He laid a trap in which I've been fairly caught. It's a magnificent joke, but there's moderation in all things. We've been fooled enough to last us the rest of our lives. Let's be serious now."

"But..."

"Aren't you satisfied yet, captain? After the *Belle Hélène* do you want to attack the *Chamois?* As you please. You can get out at Mantes: Only, I warn you, Siméon is in Paris, with three or four hours' start of us."

Patrice gave a shudder. Siméon in Paris! In Paris, where Coralie was alone and unprotected! He made no further protest; and Don Luis ran on:

"Oh, the rascal! How well he played his hand! *The Memoirs of Benjamin Franklin* were a master stroke. Knowing of my arrival, he said to himself, 'Arsène Lupin is a dangerous fellow, capable of disentangling the affair and putting both me and the bags of gold in his pocket. To get rid of him, there's only one thing to be done: I must act in such a way as to make him rush along the real track at so fast a rate of speed that he does not perceive the moment when the real track becomes a false track.' That was clever of him, wasn't it? And so we have the Franklin book, held out as a bait; the page opening of itself, at the right place; my inevitable easy discovery of the conduit system; the clue of Ariadne most obligingly offered. I follow up the clue like a trusting child, led by Siméon's own hand, from the cellar down to Berthou's Wharf. So far all's well. But, from that moment, take care! There's nobody at Berthou's Wharf. On the other hand, there's a barge alongside, which means a chance of making enquiries, which means the certainty that

I shall make enquiries. And I make enquiries. And, having made enquiries, I am done for."

"But then that man...?"

"Yes, yes, yes, an accomplice of Siméon's, whom Siméon, knowing that he would be followed to the Gare Saint-Lazare, instructs in this way to direct me to Mantes for the second time. At Mantes the comedy continues. The *Belle Hélène* passes, with her double freight, Siméon and the bags of gold. We go running after the *Belle Hélène.* Of course, on the *Belle Hélène* there's nothing: no Siméon, no bags of gold. 'Run after the *Chamois.* We've transhipped it all on the *Chamois.* ' We run after the *Chamois,* to Rouen, to Le Hâvre, to the end of the world; and of course our pursuit is fruitless, for the *Chamois* does not exist. But we are convinced that she does exist and that she has escaped our search. And by this time the trick is played. The millions are gone, Siméon has disappeared and there is only one thing left for us to do, which is to resign ourselves and abandon our quest. You understand, we're to abandon our quest: that's the fellow's object. And he would have succeeded if..."

The car was traveling at full speed. From time to time Don Luis would stop her dead with extraordinary skill. Post of territorials. Pass to be produced. Then a leap onward and once more the breakneck pace.

"If what?" asked Patrice, half-convinced. "Which was the clue that put you on the track?"

"The presence of that woman at Mantes. It was a vague clue at first. But suddenly I remembered that, in the first barge, the *Nonchalante,* the person who gave us information—do you recollect?—well, that this person somehow gave me the queer impression, I can't tell you why, that I might be talking to a woman in disguise. The impression occurred to me once more. I made a mental comparison with the woman at Mantes... And then... and then it was like a flash of light..."

Don Luis paused to think and, in a lower voice, continued:

"But who the devil can this woman be?"

There was a brief silence, after which Patrice said, from instinct rather than reason:

"Grégoire, I suppose."

"Eh? What's that? Grégoire?"

"Yes. Yes, Grégoire is a woman."

"What are you talking about?"

"Well, obviously. Don't you remember? The accomplice told me so, on the day when I had them arrested outside the café."

"Why, your diary doesn't say a word about it!"

"Oh, that's true!... I forgot to put down that detail."

"A detail! He calls it a detail! Why, it's of the greatest importance, captain! If I had known, I should have guessed that that bargee was no other than Grégoire and we should not have wasted a whole night. Hang it all, captain, you really are the limit!"

But all this was unable to affect his good humour. While Patrice, overcome with presentiments, grew gloomier and gloomier, Don Luis began to sing victory in his turn:

"Thank goodness! The battle is becoming serious! Really, it was too easy before; and that was why I was sulking, I, Lupin! Do you imagine things go like that in real life? Does everything fit in so accurately? Benjamin Franklin, the uninterrupted conduit for the gold, the series of clues that reveal themselves of their own accord, the man and the bags meeting at Mantes, the *Belle Hélène:* no, it all worried me. The cat was being choked with cream! And then the gold escaping in a barge! All very well in times of peace, but not in wartime, in the face of the regulations: passes, patrol-boats, inspections and I don't know what... How could a fellow like Siméon risk a trip of that kind? No, I had my suspicions; and that was why, captain, I made Ya-Bon mount guard, on the off chance, outside Berthou's Wharf.

It was just an idea that occurred to me. The whole of this adventure seemed to centre round the wharf. Well, was I right or not? Is M. Lupin no longer able to follow a scent? Captain, I repeat, I shall go back tomorrow evening. Besides, as I told you, I've got to. Whether I win or lose, I'm going. But we shall win. Everything will be cleared up. There will be no more mysteries, not even the mystery of the golden triangle... Oh, I don't say that I shall bring you a beautiful triangle of eighteen-carat gold! We mustn't allow ourselves to be fascinated by words. It may be a geometrical arrangement of the bags of gold, a triangular pile... or else a hole in the ground dug in that shape. No matter, we shall have it! And the bags of gold shall be ours! And Patrice and Coralie shall appear before monsieur le maire and receive my blessing and live happily ever after!"

They reached the gates of Paris. Patrice was becoming more and more anxious:

"Then you think the danger's over?"

"Oh, I don't say that! The play isn't finished. After the great scene of the third act, which we will call the scene of the oxide of carbon, there will certainly be a fourth act and perhaps a fifth. The enemy has not laid down his arms, by any means."

They were skirting the quays.

"Let's get down," said Don Luis.

He gave a faint whistle and repeated it three times.

"No answer," he said. "Ya-Bon's not there. The battle has begun."

"But Coralie..."

"What are you afraid of for her? Siméon doesn't know her address."

There was nobody on Berthou's Wharf and nobody on the quay below. But by the light of the moon they saw the other barge, the *Nonchalante*.

"Let's go on board," said Don Luis. "I wonder if the lady known as Grégoire makes a practise of living here? Has she come back, believing us on our way to Le Hâvre? I hope so. In any case, Ya-Bon must have been there and no doubt left something behind to act as a signal. Will you come, captain?"

"Right you are. It's a queer thing, though: I feel frightened!"

"What of?" asked Don Luis, who was plucky enough himself to understand this presentiment.

"Of what we shall see."

"My dear sir, there may be nothing there!"

Each of them switched on his pocket-lamp and felt the handle of his revolver. They crossed the plank between the shore and the boat. A few steps downwards brought them to the cabin. The door was locked.

"Hi, mate! Open this, will you?"

There was no reply. They now set about breaking it down, which was no easy matter, for it was massive and quite unlike an ordinary cabin-door.

At last it gave way.

"By Jingo!" said Don Luis, who was the first to go in. "I didn't expect this!"

"What?"

"Look. The woman whom they called Grégoire. She seems to be dead."

She was lying back on a little iron bedstead, with her man's blouse open at the top and her chest uncovered. Her face still bore an expression of extreme terror. The disordered appearance of the cabin suggested that a furious struggle had taken place.

"I was right. Here, by her side, are the clothes she wore at Mantes. But what's the matter, captain?"

Patrice had stifled a cry:

"There... opposite... under the window..."

It was a little window overlooking the river. The panes were broken.

"Well?" asked Don Luis. "What? Yes, I believe someone's been thrown out that way."

"The veil... that blue veil," stammered Patrice, "is her nurse's veil... Coralie's..."

Don Luis grew vexed:

"Nonsense! Impossible! Nobody knew her address."

"Still..."

"Still what? You haven't written to her? You haven't telegraphed to her?"

"Yes... I telegraphed to her... from Mantes."

"What's that? Oh, but look here. This is madness! You don't mean that you really telegraphed?"

"Yes, I do."

"You telegraphed from the post-office at Mantes?"

"Yes."

"And was there anyone in the post-office?"

"Yes, a woman."

"What woman? The one who lies here, murdered?"

"Yes."

"But she didn't read what you wrote?"

"No, but I wrote the telegram twice over."

"And you threw the first draft anywhere, on the floor, so that anyone who came along... Oh, really, captain, you must confess...!"

But Patrice was running towards the car and was already out of ear-shot.

Half an hour after, he returned with two telegrams which he had found on Coralie's table. The first, the one which he had sent, said:

"All well. Be easy and stay indoors. Fondest love.

"Captain Patrice."

The second, which had evidently been despatched by Siméon, ran as follows:

"Events taking serious turn. Plans changed. Coming back. Expect you nine o'clock this evening at the small door of your garden.

"Captain Patrice."

This second telegram was delivered to Coralie at eight o'clock; and she had left the home immediately afterwards.

16

THE FOURTH ACT

"Captain," said Don Luis, "you've scored two fine blunders. The first was your not telling me that Grégoire was a woman. The second..."

But Don Luis saw that the officer was too much dejected for him to care about completing his charge. He put his hand on Patrice Belval's shoulder:

"Come," he said, "don't upset yourself. The position's not as bad as you think."

"Coralie jumped out of the window to escape that man," Patrice muttered.

"Your Coralie is alive," said Don Luis, shrugging his shoulders. "In Siméon's hands, but alive."

"Why, what do you know about it? Anyway, if she's in that monster's hands, might she not as well be dead? Doesn't it mean all the horrors of death? Where's the difference?"

"It means a danger of death, but it means life if we come in time; and we shall."

"Have you a clue?"

"Do you imagine that I have sat twiddling my thumbs and that an old hand like myself hasn't had time in half an hour to unravel the mysteries which this cabin presents?"

"Then let's go," cried Patrice, already eager for the fray. "Let's have at the enemy."

"Not yet," said Don Luis, who was still hunting around him. "Listen to me. I'll tell you what I know, captain, and I'll tell it you straight out, without trying to dazzle you by a parade of reasoning and without even telling you of the tiny trifles that serve me as proofs. The bare facts, that's all. Well, then..."

"Yes?"

"Little Mother Coralie kept the appointment at nine o'clock. Siméon was there with his female accomplice. Between them they bound and gagged her and brought her here. Observe that, in their eyes, it was a safe spot for the job, because they knew for certain that you and I had not discovered the trap. Nevertheless, we may assume that it was a provisional base of operations, adopted for part of the night only, and that Siméon reckoned on leaving Little Mother Coralie in the hands of his accomplice and setting out in search of a definite place of confinement, a permanent prison. But luckily—and I'm rather proud of this—Ya-Bon was on the spot. Ya-Bon was watching on his bench, in the dark. He must have seen them cross the embankment and no doubt recognized Siméon's walk in the distance. We'll take it that he gave chase at once, jumped on to the deck of the barge and arrived here at the same time as the enemy, before they had time to lock themselves in. Four people in this narrow space, in pitch darkness, must have meant a frightful upheaval. I know my Ya-Bon. He's terrible at such times. Unfortunately, it was not Siméon whom he caught by the neck with that merciless hand of his, but... the woman. Siméon took advantage of this. He had not let go of Little Mother Coralie. He picked her up in his arms and went up the companionway, flung her on the deck and then came back to lock the door on the two as they struggled."

"Do you think so? Do you think it was Ya-Bon and not Siméon who killed the woman?"

"I'm sure of it. If there were no other proof, there is this particular fracture of the wind-pipe, which is Ya-Bon's special mark. What I do not understand is why, when he had settled his adversary, Ya-Bon didn't break down the door with a push of his shoulder and go after Siméon. I presume that he was wounded and that he had not the strength to make the necessary effort. I presume also that the woman did not die at once and that she spoke, saying things against Siméon, who had abandoned her instead of defending her. This much is certain, that Ya-Bon broke the window-panes..."

"To jump into the Seine, wounded as he was, with his one arm?" said Patrice.

"Not at all. There's a ledge running along the window. He could set his feet on it and get off that way."

"Very well. But he was quite ten or twenty minutes behind Siméon?"

"That didn't matter, if the woman had time, before dying, to tell him where Siméon was taking refuge."

"How can we get to know?"

"I've been trying to find out all the time that we've been chatting... and I've just discovered the way."

"Here?"

"This minute; and I expected no less from Ya-Bon. The woman told him of a place in the cabin—look, that open drawer, probably—in which there was a visiting-card with an address on it. Ya-Bon took it and, in order to let me know, pinned the card to the curtain over there. I had seen it already; but it was only this moment that I noticed the pin that fixed it, a gold pin with which I myself fastened the Morocco Cross to Ya-Bon's breast."

"What is the address?"

"Amédée Vacherot, 18, Rue Guimard. The Rue Guimard is close to this, which makes me quite sure of the road they took."

The two men at once went away, leaving the woman's dead body behind. As Don Luis said, the police must make what they could of it.

As they crossed Berthou's Wharf they glanced at the recess and Don Luis remarked:

"There's a ladder missing. We must remember that detail. Siméon has been in there. He's beginning to make blunders too."

The car took them to the Rue Guimard, a small street in Passy. No. 18 was a large house let out in flats, of fairly ancient construction. It was two o'clock in the morning when they rang.

A long time elapsed before the door opened; and, as they passed through the carriage-entrance, the porter put his head out of his lodge:

"Who's there?" he asked.

"We want to see M. Amédée Vacherot on urgent business."

"That's myself."

"You?"

"Yes, I, the porter. But by what right...?"

"Orders of the Prefect of police," said Don Luis, displaying a badge.

They entered the lodge. Amédée Vacherot was a little, respectable-looking old man, with white whiskers. He might have been a beadle.

"Answer my questions plainly," Don Luis ordered, in a rough voice, "and don't try to prevaricate. We are looking for a man called Siméon Diodokis."

The porter took fright at once:

"To do him harm?" he exclaimed. "If it's to do him harm, it's no use asking me any questions. I would rather die by slow tortures than injure that kind M. Siméon."

Don Luis assumed a gentler tone:

"Do him harm? On the contrary, we are looking for him to do him a service, to save him from a great danger."

"A great danger?" cried M. Vacherot. "Oh, I'm not at all surprised! I never saw him in such a state of excitement."

"Then he's been here?"

"Yes, since midnight."

"Is he here now?"

"No, he went away again."

Patrice made a despairing gesture and asked:

"Perhaps he left someone behind?"

"No, but he intended to bring someone."

"A lady?"

M. Vacherot hesitated.

"We know," Don Luis resumed, "that Siméon Diodokis was trying to find a place of safety in which to shelter a lady for whom he entertained the deepest respect."

"Can you tell me the lady's name?" asked the porter, still on his guard.

"Certainly, Mme. Essarès, the widow of the banker to whom Siméon used to act as secretary. Mme. Essarès is a victim of persecution; he is defending her against her enemies; and, as we ourselves want to help the two of them and to take this criminal business in hand, we must insist that you..."

"Oh, well!" said M. Vacherot, now fully reassured. "I have known Siméon Diodokis for ever so many years. He was very good to me at the time when I was working for an undertaker; he lent me money; he got me my present job; and he used often to come and sit in my lodge and talk about heaps of things..."

"Such as relations with Essarès Bey?" asked Don Luis, carelessly. "Or his plans concerning Patrice Belval?"

"Heaps of things," said the porter, after a further hesitation. "He is one of the best of men, does a lot of good and used to employ me in distributing his local charity. And just now again he was risking his life for Mme. Essarès."

"One more word. Had you seen him since Essarès Bey's death?"

"No, it was the first time. He arrived a little before one o'clock. He was out of breath and spoke in a low voice, listening to the sounds of the street outside: 'I've been followed,' said he; 'I've been followed. I could swear it.' 'By whom?' said I. 'You don't know him,' said he. 'He has only one hand, but he wrings your neck for you. ' And then he stopped. And then he began again, in a whisper, so that I could hardly hear: 'Listen to me, you're coming with me. We're going to fetch a lady, Mme. Essarès. They want to kill her. I've hidden her all right, but she's fainted: we shall have to carry her... Or no, I'll go alone. I'll manage. But I want to know, is my room still free?' I must tell you, he has a little lodging here, since the day when he too had to hide himself. He used to come to it sometimes and he kept it on in case he might want it, for it's a detached lodging, away from the other tenants."

"What did he do after that?" asked Patrice, anxiously.

"After that, he went away."

"But why isn't he back yet?"

"I admit that it's alarming. Perhaps the man who was following him has attacked him. Or perhaps something has happened to the lady."

"What do you mean, something happened to the lady?"

"I'm afraid something may have. When he first showed me the way we should have to go to fetch her, he said, 'Quick, we must hurry. To save her life, I had to put her in a hole. That's all very well for two or three hours. But, if she's left longer, she will suffocate. The want of air..."

Patrice had leapt upon the old man. He was beside himself, maddened at the thought that Coralie, ill and worn-out as she was, might be at the point of death in some unknown place, a prey to terror and suffering.

"You shall speak," he cried, "and this very minute! You shall tell us where she is! Oh, don't imagine that you can fool us any longer! Where is she? You know! He told you!"

He was shaking M. Vacherot by the shoulders and hurling his rage into the old man's face with unspeakable violence.

Don Luis, on the other hand, stood chuckling.

"Splendid, captain," he said, "splendid! My best compliments! You're making real progress since I joined forces with you. M. Vacherot will go through fire and water for us now."

"Well, you see if I don't make the fellow speak," shouted Patrice.

"It's no use, sir," declared the porter, very firmly and calmly. "You have deceived me. You are enemies of M. Siméon's. I shall not say another word that can give you any information."

"You refuse to speak, do you? You refuse to speak?"

In his exasperation Patrice drew his revolver and aimed it at the man:

"I'm going to count three. If, by that time, you don't make up your mind to speak, you shall see the sort of man that Captain Belval is!"

The porter gave a start:

"Captain Belval, did you say? Are you Captain Belval?"

"Ah, old fellow, that seems to give you food for thought!"

"Are you Captain Belval? Patrice Belval?"

"At your service; and, if in two seconds from this you haven't told me..."

"Patrice Belval! And you are M. Siméon's enemy? And you want to...?"

"I want to do him up like the cur he is, your blackguard of a Siméon... and you, his accomplice, with him. A nice pair of rascals!... Well, have you made up your mind?"

"Unhappy man!" gasped the porter. "Unhappy man! You don't know what you're doing. Kill M. Siméon! You? You? Why, you're the last man who could commit a crime like that!"

"What about it? Speak, will you, you old numskull!"

"You, kill M. Siméon? You, Patrice? You, Captain Belval? You?"

"And why not? Speak, damn it! Why not?"

"You are his son."

All Patrice's fury, all his anguish at the thought that Coralie was in Siméon's power or else lying in some pit, all his agonized grief, all his alarm: all this gave way, for a moment, to a terrible fit of merriment, which revealed itself in a long burst of laughter.

"Siméon's son! What the devil are you talking about? Oh, this beats everything! Upon my word, you're full of ideas, when you're trying to save him! You old ruffian! Of course, it's most convenient: don't kill that man, he's your father. He my father, that putrid Siméon! Siméon Diodokis, Patrice Belval's father! Oh, it's enough to make a chap split his sides!"

Don Luis had listened in silence. He made a sign to Patrice:

"Will you allow me to clear up this business, captain? It won't take me more than a few minutes; and that certainly won't delay us." And, without waiting for the officer's reply, he turned to the old man and said slowly, "Let's have this out, M. Vacherot. It's of the highest importance. The great thing is to speak plainly and not to lose yourself in superfluous words. Besides, you have said too much not to finish your revelation. Siméon Diodokis is not your benefactor's real name, is it?"

"No, that's so."

"He is Armand Belval; and the woman who loved him used to call him Patrice?"

"Yes, his son's name."

"Nevertheless, this Armand Belval was a victim of the same murderous attempt as the woman he loved, who was Coralie Essarès' mother?"

"Yes, but Coralie Essarès' mother died; and he did not."

"That was on the fourteenth of April, 1895."

"The fourteenth of April, 1895."

Patrice caught hold of Don Luis' arm:

"Come," he spluttered, "Coralie's at death's door. The monster has buried her. That's the only thing that matters."

"Then you don't believe that monster to be your father?" asked Don Luis.

"You're mad!"

"For all that, captain, you're trembling!..."

"I dare say, I dare say, but it's because of Coralie... I can't even hear what the man's saying!... Oh, it's a nightmare, every word of it! Make him stop! Make him shut up! Why didn't I wring his neck?"

He sank into a chair, with his elbows on the table and his head in his hands. It was really a horrible moment; and no catastrophe would have overwhelmed a man more utterly.

Don Luis looked at him with feeling and then turned to the porter:

"Explain yourself, M. Vacherot," he said. "As briefly as possible, won't you? No details. We can go into them later. We were saying, on the fourteenth of April, 1895..."

"On the fourteenth of April, 1895, a solicitor's clerk, accompanied by the commissary of police, came to my governor's, close by here, and ordered two coffins for immediate delivery. The whole shop got to work. At ten o'clock in the evening, the governor, one of my mates and I went to the Rue Raynouard, to a sort of pavilion or lodge, standing in a garden."

"I know. Go on."

"There were two bodies. We wrapped them in winding-sheets and put them into the coffins. At eleven o'clock my governor and my fellow-workmen went away and left me alone with a sister of mercy. There was nothing more to do except to nail the coffins down. Well, just then, the nun, who had been watching and praying, fell asleep and something happened... Oh, an awful thing! It made my hair stand on end, sir. I shall never forget it as long as I live. My knees gave way beneath me,

I shook with fright... Sir, the man's body had moved. The man was alive!"

"Then you didn't know of the murder at that time?" asked Don Luis. "You hadn't heard of the attempt?"

"No, we were told that they had both suffocated themselves with gas... It was many hours before the man recovered consciousness entirely. He was in some way poisoned."

"But why didn't you inform the nun?"

"I couldn't say. I was simply stunned. I looked at the man as he slowly came back to life and ended by opening his eyes. His first words were, 'She's dead, I suppose?' And then at once he said, 'Not a word about all this. Let them think me dead: that will be better.' And I can't tell you why, but I consented. The miracle had deprived me of all power of will. I obeyed like a child... He ended by getting up. He leant over the other coffin, drew aside the sheet and kissed the dead woman's face over and over again, whispering, 'I will avenge you. All my life shall be devoted to avenging you and also, as you wished, to uniting our children. If I don't kill myself, it will be for Patrice and Coralie's sake. Goodbye.' Then he told me to help him. Between us, we lifted the woman out of the coffin and carried it into the little bedroom next door. Then we went into the garden, took some big stones and put them into the coffins where the two bodies had been. When this was done, I nailed the coffins down, woke the good sister and went away. The man had locked himself into the bedroom with the dead woman. Next morning the undertaker's men came and fetched away the two coffins."

Patrice had unclasped his hands and thrust his distorted features between Don Luis and the porter. Fixing his haggard eyes upon the latter, he asked, struggling with his words:

"But the graves? The inscription saying that the remains of both lie there, near the lodge where the murder was committed? The cemetery?"

"Armand Belval wished it so. At that time I was living in a garret in this house. I took a lodging for him where he came and lived by stealth, under the name of Siméon Diodokis, since Armand Belval was dead, and where he stayed for several months without going out. Then, in his new name and through me, he bought his lodge. And, bit by bit, we dug the graves. Coralie's and his. His because, I repeat, he wished it so. Patrice and Coralie were both dead. It seemed to him, in this way, that he was not leaving her. Perhaps also, I confess, despair had upset his balance a little, just a very little, only in what concerned his memory of the woman who died on the fourteenth of April, 1895, and his devotion for her. He wrote her name and his own everywhere: on the grave and also on the walls, on the trees and in the very borders of the flower-beds. They were Coralie Essarès' name and yours... And for this, for all that had to do with his revenge upon the murderer and with his son and with the dead woman's daughter, oh, for these matters he had all his wits about him, believe me, sir!"

Patrice stretched his clutching hands and his distraught face towards the porter:

"Proofs, proofs, proofs!" he insisted, in a stifled voice. "Give me proofs at once! There's someone dying at this moment by that scoundrel's criminal intentions, there's a woman at the point of death. Give me proofs!"

"You need have no fear," said M. Vacherot. "My friend has only one thought, that of saving the woman, not killing her..."

"He lured her and me into the lodge to kill us, as our parents were killed before us."

"He is trying only to unite you."

"Yes, in death."

"No, in life. You are his dearly-loved son. He always spoke of you with pride."

"He is a ruffian, a monster!" shouted the officer.

"He is the very best man living, sir, and he is your father."

Patrice started, stung by the insult:

"Proofs," he roared, "proofs! I forbid you to speak another word until you have proved the truth in a manner admitting of no doubt."

Without moving from his seat, the old man put out his arm towards an old mahogany escritoire, lowered the lid and, pressing a spring, pulled out one of the drawers. Then he held out a bundle of papers:

"You know your father's handwriting, don't you, captain?" he said. "You must have kept letters from him, since the time when you were at school in England. Well, read the letters which he wrote to me. You will see your name repeated a hundred times, the name of his son; and you will see the name of the Coralie whom he meant you to marry. Your whole life—your studies, your journeys, your work—is described in these letters. And you will also find your photographs, which he had taken by various correspondents, and photographs of Coralie, whom he had visited at Salonica. And you will see above all his hatred for Essarès Bey, whose secretary he had become, and his plans of revenge, his patience, his tenacity. And you will also see his despair when he heard of the marriage between Essarès and Coralie and, immediately afterwards, his joy at the thought that his revenge would be more cruel when he succeeded in uniting his son Patrice with Essarès' wife."

As the old fellow spoke, he placed the letters one by one under the eyes of Patrice, who had at once recognized his father's hand and sat greedily devouring sentences in which his own name was constantly repeated. M. Vacherot watched him.

"Have you any more doubts, captain?" he asked, at last.

The officer again pressed his clenched fists to his temples:

"I saw his face," he said, "above the skylight, in the lodge into which he had locked us... It was gloating over our death, it was a face mad with hatred... He hated us even more than Essarès did..."

"A mistake! Pure imagination!" the old man protested.

"Or madness," muttered Patrice.

Then he struck the table violently, in a fit of revulsion:

"It's not true, it's not true!" he exclaimed. "That man is not my father. What, a scoundrel like that!..."

He took a few steps round the little room and, stopping in front of Don Luis, jerked out:

"Let's go. Else I shall go mad too. It's a nightmare, there's no other word for it, a nightmare in which things turn upside down until the brain itself capsizes. Let's go. Coralie is in danger. That's the only thing that matters."

The old man shook his head:

"I'm very much afraid..."

"What are *you* afraid of?" bellowed the officer.

"I'm afraid that my poor friend has been caught up by the person who was following him... and then how can he have saved Mme. Essarès? The poor thing was hardly able to breathe, he told me."

Hanging on to Don Luis' arm, Patrice staggered out of the porter's lodge like a drunken man:

"She's done for, she must be!" he cried.

"Not at all," said Don Luis. "Siméon is as feverishly active as yourself. He is nearing the catastrophe. He is quaking with fear and not in a condition to weigh his words. Believe me, your Coralie is in no immediate danger. We have some hours before us."

"But Ya-Bon? Suppose Ya-Bon has laid hands upon him?"

"I gave Ya-Bon orders not to kill him. Therefore, whatever happens, Siméon is alive. That's the great thing. So long as

Siméon is alive, there is nothing to fear. He won't let your Coralie die."

"Why not, seeing that he hates her? Why not? What is there in that man's heart? He devotes all his existence to a work of love on our behalf; and, from one minute to the next, that love turns to execration."

He pressed Don Luis' arm and, in a hollow voice, asked:

"Do you believe that he is my father?"

"Siméon Diodokis is your father, captain," replied Don Luis.

"Ah, don't, don't! It's too horrible! God, but we are in the valley of the shadow!"

"On the contrary," said Don Luis, "the shadow is lifting slightly; and I confess that our talk with M. Vacherot has given me a little light."

"Do you mean it?"

But, in Patrice Belval's fevered brain, one idea jostled another. He suddenly stopped:

"Siméon may have gone back to the porter's lodge!... And we sha'n't be there!... Perhaps he will bring Coralie back!"

"No," Don Luis declared, "he would have done that before now, if it could be done. No, it's for us to go to him."

"But where?"

"Well, of course, where all the fighting has been... where the gold lies. All the enemy's operations are centred in that gold; and you may be sure that, even in retreat, he can't get away from it. Besides, we know that he is not far from Berthou's Wharf."

Patrice allowed himself to be led along without a word. But suddenly Don Luis cried:

"Did you hear?"

"Yes, a shot."

At that moment they were on the point of turning into the Rue Raynouard. The height of the houses prevented them from perceiving the exact spot from which the shot had been fired, but it came approximately from the Essarès house or the immediate precincts. Patrice was filled with alarm:

"Can it be Ya-Bon?"

"I'm afraid so," said Don Luis, "and, as Ya-Bon wouldn't fire, someone must have fired a shot at him... Oh, by Jove, if my poor Ya-Bon were to be killed...!"

"And suppose it was at her, at Coralie?" whispered Patrice.

Don Luis began to laugh:

"Oh, my dear captain, I'm almost sorry that I ever mixed myself up in this business! You were much cleverer before I came and a good deal clearer-sighted. Why the devil should Siméon attack your Coralie, considering that she's already in his power?"

They hurried their steps. As they passed the Essarès house they saw that everything was quiet and they went on until they came to the lane, down which they turned.

Patrice had the key, but the little door which opened on to the garden of the lodge was bolted inside.

"Aha!" said Don Luis. "That shows that we're warm. Meet me on the quay, captain. I shall run down to Berthou's Wharf to have a look round."

During the past few minutes a pale dawn had begun to mingle with the shades of night. The embankment was still deserted, however.

Don Luis observed nothing in particular at Berthou's Wharf; but, when he returned to the quay above, Patrice showed him a ladder lying right at the end of the pavement which skirted the garden of the lodge; and Don Luis recognized the ladder as the one whose absence he had noticed from the recess in the yard. With that quick vision which was one of his greatest assets, he at once furnished the explanation:

"As Siméon had the key of the garden, it was obviously Ya-Bon who used the ladder to make his way in. Therefore he saw Siméon take refuge there on returning from his visit to old Vacherot and after coming to fetch Coralie. Now the question is, did Siméon succeed in fetching Little Mother Coralie, or did he run away before fetching her? That I can't say. But, in any case..."

Bending low down, he examined the pavement and continued:

"In any case, what is certain is that Ya-Bon knows the hiding--place where the bags of gold are stacked and that it is there most likely that your Coralie was and perhaps still is, worse luck, if the enemy, giving his first thought to his personal safety, has not had time to remove her."

"Are you sure?"

"Look here, captain, Ya-Bon always carries a piece of chalk in his pocket. As he doesn't know how to write, except just the letters forming my name, he has drawn these two straight lines which, with the line of the wall, make a triangle... the golden triangle."

Don Luis drew himself up:

"The clue is rather meagre. But Ya-Bon looks upon me as a wizard. He never doubted that I should manage to find this spot and that those three lines would be enough for me. Poor Ya-Bon!"

"But," objected Patrice, "all this, according to you, took place before our return to Paris, between twelve and one o'clock, therefore."

"Yes."

"Then what about the shot which we have just heard, four or five hours later?"

"As to that I'm not so positive. We may assume that Siméon squatted somewhere in the dark. Possibly at the first break of day, feeling easier and hearing nothing of Ya-Bon, he risked taking a step or two. Then Ya-Bon, keeping watch in silence, would have leaped upon him."

"So you think..."

"I think that there was a struggle, that Ya-Bon was wounded and that Siméon..."

"That Siméon escaped?"

"Or else was killed. However, we shall know all about it in a few minutes."

He set the ladder against the railing at the top of the wall. Patrice climbed over with Don Luis' assistance. Then, stepping over the railing in his turn, Don Luis drew up the ladder, threw it into the garden and made a careful examination. Finally, they turned their steps, through the tall grasses and bushy shrubs, towards the lodge.

The daylight was increasing rapidly and the outlines of everything were becoming clearer. The two men walked round the lodge, Don Luis leading the way. When he came in sight of the yard, on the street side, he turned and said: "I was right."

And he ran forward.

Outside the hall-door lay the bodies of the two adversaries, clutching each other in a confused heap. Ya-Bon had a horrible wound in the head, from which the blood was flowing all over his face. With his right hand he held Siméon by the throat.

Don Luis at once perceived that Ya-Bon was dead and Siméon Diodokis alive.

17

SIMÉON GIVES BATTLE

It took them some time to loosen Ya-Bon's grip. Even in death the Senegalese did not let go his prey; and his fingers, hard as iron and armed with nails piercing as a tiger's claws, dug into the neck of the enemy, who lay gurgling, deprived of consciousness and strength.

Don Luis caught sight of Siméon's revolver on the cobbles of the yard:

"It was lucky for you, you old ruffian," he said, in a low voice, "that Ya-Bon did not have time to squeeze the breath out of you before you fired that shot. But I wouldn't chortle overmuch, if I were you. He might perhaps have spared you, whereas, now that Ya-Bon's dead, you can write to your family and book your seat below. *De profundis*, Diodokis!" And, giving way to his grief, he added, "Poor Ya-Bon! He saved me from a horrible death one day in Africa... and today he dies by my orders, so to speak. My poor Ya-Bon!"

Assisted by Patrice, he carried the negro's corpse into the little bedroom next to the studio.

"We'll inform the police this evening, captain, when the drama is finished. For the moment, it's a matter of avenging him and the others."

He thereupon applied himself to making a minute inspection of the scene of the struggle, after which he went back to Ya-Bon and then to Siméon, whose clothes and shoes he examined closely.

Patrice was face to face with his terrible enemy, whom he had propped against the wall of the lodge and was contemplating in silence, with a fixed stare of hatred. Siméon! Siméon Diodokis, the execrable demon who, two days before, had hatched the terrible plot and, bending over the skylight, had laughed as he watched their awful agony! Siméon Diodokis, who, like a wild beast, had hidden Coralie in some hole, so that he might go back and torture her at his ease!

He seemed to be in pain and to breathe with great difficulty. His wind-pipe had no doubt been injured by Ya-Bon's clutch. His yellow spectacles had fallen off during the fight. A pair of thick, grizzled eyebrows lowered about his heavy lids.

"Search him, captain," said Don Luis.

But, as Patrice seemed to shrink from the task, he himself felt in Siméon's jacket and produced a pocketbook, which he handed to the officer.

It contained first of all a registration-card, in the name of Siméon Diodokis, Greek subject, with his photograph gummed to it. The photograph was a recent one, taken with the spectacles, the comforter and the long hair, and bore a police-stamp dated December, 1914. There was a collection of business documents, invoices and memoranda, addressed to Siméon as Essarès Bey's secretary, and, among these papers, a letter from Amédée Vacherot, running as follows:

"Dear M. Siméon,

"I have succeeded. A young friend of mine has taken a snapshot of Mme. Essarès and Patrice at the hospital, at a moment when they were talking together. I am so glad to be able to gratify you. But when will you tell your dear son the truth? How delighted he will be when he hears it!"

At the foot of the letter were a few words in Siméon's hand, a sort of personal note:

"Once more I solemnly pledge myself not to reveal anything to my dearly-beloved son until Coralie, my bride, is avenged and until Patrice and Coralie Essarès are free to love each other and to marry."

"That's your father's writing, is it not?" asked Don Luis.

"Yes," said Patrice, in bewilderment. "And it is also the writing of the letters which he addressed to his friend Vacherot. Oh, it's too hideous to be true! What a man! What a scoundrel!"

Siméon moved. His eyes opened and closed repeatedly. Then, coming to himself entirely, he looked at Patrice, who at once, in a stifled voice, asked:

"Where's Coralie?"

And, as Siméon, still dazed, seemed not to understand and sat gazing at him stupidly, he repeated, in a harsher tone:

"Where's Coralie? What have you done with her? Where have you put her? She must be dying!"

Siméon was gradually recovering life and consciousness. He mumbled:

"Patrice... Patrice..."

He looked around him, saw Don Luis, no doubt remembered his fight to the death with Ya-Bon and closed his eyes again. But Patrice's rage increased:

"Will you attend?" he shouted. "I won't wait any longer! It'll cost you your life if you don't answer!"

The man's eyes opened again, red-rimmed, bloodshot eyes. He pointed to his throat to indicate his difficulty in speaking. At last, with a visible effort, he repeated:

"Patrice! Is it you?... I have been waiting for this moment so long!... And now we are meeting as enemies!..."

"As mortal enemies," said Patrice, with emphasis. "Death stands between us: Ya-Bon's death, Coralie's perhaps... Where is she? You must speak, or..."

"Patrice, is it really you?" the man repeated, in a whisper.

The familiarity exasperated the officer. He caught his adversary by the lapel of his jacket and shook him. But Siméon had seen the pocketbook which he held in his other hand and, without resisting Patrice's roughness, whined:

"You wouldn't hurt me, Patrice. You must have found some letters; and you now know the link that binds us together. Oh, how happy I should have been...!"

Patrice had released his hold and stood staring at him in horror. Sinking his voice in his turn, he said:

"Don't dare to speak of that: I won't, I won't believe it!"

"It's the truth, Patrice."

"You lie! You lie!" cried the officer, unable to restrain himself any longer, while his grief distorted his face out of all recognition.

"Ah, I see you have guessed it! Then I need not explain..."

"You lie! You're just a common scoundrel!... If what you say is true, why did you plot against Coralie and me? Why did you try to murder the two of us?"

"I was mad, Patrice. Yes, I go mad at times. All these tragedies have turned my head. My own Coralie's death... and then my life in Essarès' shadow... and then... and then, above all, the gold!... Did I really try to kill you both? I no longer remember. Or at least I remember a dream I had: it happened in the lodge, didn't it, as before? Oh, madness! What a torture! I'm like a man in the galleys. I have to do things against my will!... Then it was in the lodge, was it, as before? And in the same manner? With the same implements?... Yes, in my dream, I went through all my agony over again... and that of my darling... But, instead of being tortured, I was the torturer... What a torment!"

He spoke low, inside himself, with hesitations and intervals and an unspeakable air of suffering. Don Luis kept his eyes fixed on him, as though trying to discover what he was aiming at. And Siméon continued:

"My poor Patrice!... I was so fond of you!... And now you are my worst enemy!... How indeed could it be otherwise?... How could you forget?... Oh, why didn't they lock me up after Essarès' death? It was then that I felt my brain going..."

"So it was you who killed him?" asked Patrice.

"No, no, that's just it: somebody else robbed me of my revenge."

"Who?"

"I don't know... The whole business is incomprehensible to me... Don't speak of it... It all pains me... I have suffered so since Coralie's death!"

"Coralie!" exclaimed Patrice.

"Yes, the woman I loved... As for little Coralie, I've suffered also on her account... She ought not to have married Essarès."

"Where is she?" asked Patrice, in agony.

"I can't tell you."

"Oh," cried Patrice, shaking with rage, "you mean she's dead!"

"No, she's alive, I swear it."

"Then where is she? That's the only thing that matters. All the rest belongs to the past. But this thing, a woman's life, Coralie's life..."

"Listen."

Siméon stopped and gave a glance at Don Luis;

"Tell him to go away," he said.

Don Luis laughed:

"Of course! Little Mother Coralie is hidden in the same place as the bags of gold. To save her means surrendering the bags of gold."

"Well?" said Patrice, in an almost aggressive tone.

"Well, captain," replied Don Luis, not without a certain touch of banter in his voice, "if this honourable gentleman suggested that you should release him on parole so that he might go and fetch your Coralie, I don't suppose you'd accept?"

"No."

"You haven't the least confidence in him, have you? And you're right. The honourable gentleman, mad though he may be, gave such proofs of mental superiority and balance, when he sent us trundling down the road to Mantes, that it would be dangerous to attach the least credit to his promises. The consequence is..."

"Well?"

"This, captain, that the honourable gentleman means to propose a bargain to you, which may be couched thus: 'You can have Coralie, but I'll keep the gold.'"

"And then?"

"And then? It would be a capital notion, if you were alone with the honourable gentleman. The bargain would soon be concluded. But I'm here... by Jupiter!"

Patrice had drawn himself up. He stepped towards Don Luis and said, in a voice which became openly hostile:

"I presume that you won't raise any opposition. It's a matter of a woman's life."

"No doubt. But, on the other hand, it's a matter of three hundred million francs."

"Then you refuse?"

"Refuse? I should think so!"

"You refuse when that woman is at her last gasp? You would rather she died?... Look here, you seem to forget that this is my affair, that... that..."

The two men were standing close together. Don Luis retained that chaffing calmness, that air of knowing more than he chose to say, which irritated Patrice. At heart Patrice, while yielding to Don Luis' mastery, resented it and felt a certain embarrassment at accepting the services of a man with whose past he was so well acquainted.

"Then you actually refuse?" he rapped out, clenching his fists.

"Yes," said Don Luis, preserving his coolness. "Yes, Captain Belval, I refuse this bargain, which I consider absurd. Why, it's the confidence-trick! By Jingo! Three hundred millions! Give up a windfall like that? Never. But I haven't the least objection to leaving you alone with the honourable gentleman. That's what he wants, isn't it?"

"Yes."

"Well, talk it over between yourselves. Sign the compact. The honourable gentleman, who, for his part, has every confidence in his son, will tell you the whereabouts of the hiding-place; and you shall release your Coralie."

"And you? What about you?" snarled Patrice, angrily.

"I? I'm going to complete my little enquiry into the present and the past by revisiting the room where you nearly met your death. See you later, captain. And, whatever you do, insist on guarantees."

Switching on his pocket-lamp, Don Luis entered the lodge and walked straight to the studio. Patrice saw the electric rays playing on the panels between the walled-up windows. He went back to where Siméon sat:

"Now then," he said, in a voice of authority. "Be quick about it."

"Are you sure he's not listening?"

"Quite sure."

"Be careful with him, Patrice. He means to take the gold and keep it."

"Don't waste time," said Patrice, impatiently. "Get to Coralie."

"I've told you Coralie was alive."

"She was alive when you left her; but since then..."

"Yes, since then..."

"Since then, what? You seem to have your doubts."

"It was last night, five or six hours ago, and I am afraid..."

Patrice felt a cold shudder run down his back. He would have given anything for a decisive word; and at the same time he was almost strangling the old man to punish him. He mastered himself, however:

"Don't let's waste time," he repeated. "Tell me where to go."

"No, we'll go together."

"You haven't the strength."

"Yes, yes, I can manage... it's not far. Only, only, listen to me..."

The old man seemed utterly exhausted. From time to time his breathing was interrupted, as though Ya-Bon's hand were still clutching him by the throat, and he sank into a heap, moaning.

Patrice stooped over him:

"I'm listening," he said. "But, for God's sake, hurry!"

"All right," said Siméon. "All right. She'll be free in a few minutes. But on one condition, just one... Patrice, you must swear to me on Coralie's head that you will not touch the gold and that no one shall know..."

"I swear it on her head."

"You swear it, yes; but the other one, your damned companion, he'll follow us, he'll see."

"No, he won't."

"Yes, he will, unless you consent..."

"To what? Oh, in Heaven's name, speak!"

"I'll tell you. Listen. But remember, we must go to Coralie's assistance... and that quickly... otherwise..."

Patrice hesitated, bending one leg, almost on his knees:

"Then come, do!" he said, modifying his tone. "Please come, because Coralie..."

"Yes, but that man..."

"Oh, Coralie first!"

"What do you mean? Suppose he sees us? Suppose he takes the gold from us?"

"What does that matter!"

"Oh, don't say that, Patrice!... The gold! That's the one thing! Since that gold has been mine, my life is changed. The past no longer counts... nor does hatred... nor love... There's only the gold, the bags of gold... I'd rather die... and let Coralie die... and see the whole world disappear..."

"But, look here, what is it you want? What is it you demand?"

Patrice had taken the two arms of this man who was his father and whom he had never detested with greater vehemence. He was imploring him with all the strength of his being. He would have shed tears had he thought that the old man would allow himself to be moved by tears.

"What is it?"

"I'll tell you. Listen. He's there, isn't he?"

"Yes."

"In the studio?"

"Yes."

"In that case... he mustn't come out..."

"How do you mean?"

"No, he must stay there until we've done."

"But..."

"It's quite easy. Listen carefully. You've only to make a movement, to shut the door on him. The lock has been forced, but there are the two bolts; and those will do. Do you consent?"

Patrice rebelled:

"But you're mad! *I* consent, *I*?... Why, the man saved my life!... He saved Coralie!"

"But he's doing for her now. Think a moment: if he were not there, if he were not interfering, Coralie would be free. Do you accept?"

"No."

"Why not? Do you know what that man is? A highway robber... a wretch who has only one thought, to get hold of the millions. And you have scruples! Come, it's absurd, isn't it?... Do you accept?"

"No and again no!"

"Then so much the worse for Coralie... Oh, yes, I see you don't realize the position exactly! It's time you did, Patrice. Perhaps it's even too late."

"Oh, don't say that!"

"Yes, yes, you must learn the facts and take your share of the responsibility. When that damned negro was chasing me, I got rid of Coralie as best I could, intending to release her in an hour or two. And then... and then you know what happened... It was eleven o'clock at night... nearly eight hours ago... So work it out for yourself..."

Patrice wrung his hands. Never had he imagined that a man could be tortured to such a degree. And Siméon continued, unrelentingly.

"She can't breathe, on my soul she can't!... Perhaps just a very little air reaches her, but that is all... Then again I can't tell that all that covers and protects her hasn't given way. If it has, she's suffocating... while you stand here arguing... Look here, can it matter to you to lock up that man for ten minutes?... Only ten minutes, you know. And you still hesitate! Then it's you who are killing her, Patrice. Think... buried alive!"

Patrice drew himself up. His resolve was taken. At that moment he would have shrunk from no act, however painful. And what Siméon asked was so little.

"What do you want me to do?" he asked. "Give your orders."

"You know what I want," said the other. "It's quite simple. Go to the door, bolt it and come back again."

The officer entered the lodge with a firm step and walked through the hall. The light was dancing up and down at the far end of the studio.

Without a word, without a moment's hesitation, he slammed the door, shot both the bolts and hastened back. He felt relieved. The action was a base one, but he never doubted that he had fulfilled an imperative duty.

"That's it," he said, "Let's hurry."

"Help me up," said the old man. "I can't manage by myself."

Patrice took him under the armpits and lifted him to his feet. But he had to support him, for the old man's legs were swaying beneath him.

"Oh, curse it!" blurted Siméon. "That blasted nigger has done for me. I'm suffocating too, I can't walk."

Patrice almost carried him, while Siméon, in the last stage of weakness, stammered:

"This way... Now straight ahead..."

They passed the corner of the lodge and turned their steps towards the graves.

"You're quite sure you fastened the door?" the old man continued. "Yes, I heard it slam. Oh, he's a terrible fellow, that! You have to be on your guard with him! But you swore not to say anything, didn't you? Swear it again, by your mother's memory... no, better, swear it by Coralie... May she die on the spot if you betray your oath!"

He stopped. A spasm prevented his going any further until he had drawn a little air into his lungs. Nevertheless he went on talking:

"I needn't worry, need I? Besides, you don't care about gold. That being so, why should you speak? Never mind, swear that you will be silent. Or, look here, give me your word of honour. That's best. Your word, eh?"

Patrice was still holding him round the waist. It was a terrible, long agony for the officer, this slow crawl and this sort of embrace which he was compelled to adopt in order to effect Coralie's release. As he felt the contact of the detested man's body, he was more inclined to squeeze the life out of it. And yet a vile phrase kept recurring deep down within him:

"I am his son, I am his son..."

"It's here," said the old man.

"Here? But these are the graves."

"Coralie's grave and mine. It's what we were making for."

He turned round in alarm:

"I say, the footprints! You'll get rid of them on the way back, won't you? For he would find our tracks otherwise and he would know that this is the place..."

"Let's hurry... So Coralie is here? Down there? Buried? Oh, how horrible!"

It seemed to Patrice as if each minute that passed meant more than an hour's delay and as if Coralie's safety might be jeopardized by a moment's hesitation or a single false step.

He took every oath that was demanded of him. He swore upon Coralie's head. He pledged his word of honour. At that moment there was not an action which he would not have been ready to perform.

Siméon knelt down on the grass, under the little temple, pointing with his finger:

"It's there," he repeated. "Underneath that."

"Under the tombstone?"

"Yes."

"Then the stone lifts?" asked Patrice, anxiously. "I can't lift it by myself. It can't be done. It would take three men to lift that."

"No," said the old man, "the stone swings on a pivot. You'll manage quite easily. All you have to do is to pull at one end... this one, on the right."

Patrice came and caught hold of the great stone slab, with its inscription, "Here lie Patrice and Coralie," and pulled.

The stone rose at the first endeavour, as if a counterweight had forced the other end down.

"Wait," said the old man. "We must hold it in position, or it will fall down again. You'll find an iron bar at the bottom of the second step."

There were three steps running into a small cavity, barely large enough to contain a man stooping. Patrice saw the iron bar and, propping up the stone with his shoulder, took the bar and set it up.

"Good," said Siméon. "That will keep it steady. What you must now do is to lie down in the hollow. This was where my coffin was to have been and where I often used to come and lie beside my dear Coralie. I would remain for hours, flat on the ground, speaking to her... We both talked... Yes, I assure you, we used to talk... Oh, Patrice!..."

Patrice had bent his tall figure in the narrow space where he was hardly able to move.

"What am I to do?" he asked.

"Don't you hear your Coralie? There's only a partition-wall between you: a few bricks hidden under a thin layer of earth. And a door. The other vault, Coralie's, is behind it. And behind that there's a third, with the bags of gold."

The old man was bending over and directing the search as he knelt on the grass:

"The door's on the left. Farther than that. Can't you find it? That's odd. You mustn't be too slow about it, though. Ah, have you got it now? No? Oh, if I could only go down too! But there's not room for more than one."

There was a brief silence. Then he began again:

"Stretch a bit farther. Good. Can you move?"

"Yes," said Patrice.

"Then go on moving, my lad!" cried the old man, with a yell of laughter.

And, stepping back briskly, he snatched away the iron bar. The enormous block of stone came down heavily, slowly, because of the counterweight, but with irresistible force.

Though floundering in the newly-turned earth, Patrice tried to rise, at the sight of his danger. Siméon had taken up the iron bar and now struck him a blow on the head with it. Patrice gave a cry and moved no more. The stone covered him up. The whole incident had lasted but a few seconds.

Siméon did not lose an instant. He knew that Patrice, wounded as he was bound to be and weakened by the posture to which he was condemned, was incapable of making the necessary effort to lift the lid of his tomb. On that side, therefore, there was no danger.

He went back to the lodge and, though he walked with some difficulty, he had no doubt exaggerated his injuries, for he did not stop until he reached the door. He even scorned to obliterate his footprints and went straight ahead.

On entering the hall he listened. Don Luis was tapping against the walls and the partition inside the studio and the bedroom.

"Capital!" said Siméon, with a grin. "His turn now."

It did not take long. He walked to the kitchen on the right, opened the door of the meter and, turning the key, released the gas, thus beginning again with Don Luis what he had failed to achieve with Patrice and Coralie.

Not till then did he yield to the immense weariness with which he was overcome and allow himself to lie back in a chair for two or three minutes.

His most terrible enemy also was now out of the way. But it was still necessary for him to act and ensure his personal safety. He walked round the lodge, looked for his yellow spectacles and put them on, went through the garden, opened the door and closed it behind him. Then he turned down the lane to the quay.

Once more stopping, in front of the parapet above Berthou's Wharf, he seemed to hesitate what to do. But the sight of people passing, carmen, market-gardeners and others, put an end to his indecision. He hailed a taxi and drove to the Rue Guimard.

His friend Vacherot was standing at the door of his lodge.

"Oh, is that you, M. Siméon?" cried the porter. "But what a state you're in!"

"Hush, no names!" he whispered, entering the lodge. "Has anyone seen me?"

"No. It's only half-past seven and the house is hardly awake. But, Lord forgive us, what have the scoundrels done to you? You look as if you had no breath left in your body!"

"Yes, that nigger who came after me..."

"But the others?"

"What others?"

"The two who were here? Patrice?"

"Eh? Has Patrice been?" asked Siméon, still speaking in a whisper.

"Yes, last night, after you left."

"And you told him?"

"That he was your son."

"Then that," mumbled the old man, "is why he did not seem surprised at what I said."

"Where are they now?"

"With Coralie. I was able to save her. I've handed her over to them. But it's not a question of her. Quick, I must see a doctor; there's no time to lose."

"We have one in the house."

"No, that's no use. Have you a telephone-directory?"

"Here you are."

"Turn up Dr Géradec."

"What? You can't mean that?"

"Why not? He has a private hospital quite close, on the Boulevard de Montmorency, with no other house near it."

"That's so, but haven't you heard? There are all sorts of rumours about him afloat: something to do with passports and forged certificates."

"Never mind that."

M. Vacherot hunted out the number in the directory and rang up the exchange. The line was engaged; and he wrote down the number on the margin of a newspaper. Then he telephoned again. The answer was that the doctor had gone out and would be back at ten.

"It's just as well," said Siméon. "I'm not feeling strong enough yet. Say that I'll call at ten o'clock."

"Shall I give your name as Siméon?"

"No, my real name, Armand Belval. Say it's urgent, say it's a surgical case."

The porter did so and hung up the instrument, with a moan:

"Oh, my poor M. Siméon! A man like you, so good and kind to everybody! Tell me what happened?"

"Don't worry about that. Is my place ready?"

"To be sure it is."

"Take me there without anyone seeing us."

"As usual."

"Be quick. Put your revolver in your pocket. What about your lodge? Can you leave it?"

"Five minutes won't hurt."

The lodge opened at the back on a small courtyard, which communicated with a long corridor. At the end of this passage was another yard, in which stood a little house consisting of a ground-floor and an attic.

They went in. There was an entrance-hall followed by three rooms, leading one into the other. Only the second room was furnished. The third had a door opening straight on a street that ran parallel with the Rue Guimard.

They stopped in the second room.

"Did you shut the hall-door after you?"

"Yes, M. Siméon."

"No one saw us come in, I suppose?"

"Not a soul."

"No one suspects that you're here?"

"No."

"Give me your revolver."

"Here it is."

"Do you think, if I fired it off, anyone would hear?"

"No, certainly not. Who is there to hear? But..."

"But what?"

"You're surely not going to fire?"

"Yes, I am."

"At yourself, M. Siméon, at yourself? Are you going to kill yourself?"

"Don't be an ass."

"Well, who then?"

"You, of course!" chuckled Siméon.

Pressing the trigger, he blew out the luckless man's brains. His victim fell in a heap, stone dead. Siméon flung aside the revolver and remained impassive, a little undecided as to his next step. He opened out his fingers, one by one, up to six, apparently counting the six persons of whom he had got rid in a few hours: Grégoire, Coralie, Ya-Bon, Patrice, Don Luis, old Vacherot!

His mouth gave a grin of satisfaction. One more endeavour; and his flight and safety were assured.

For the moment he was incapable of making the endeavour. His head whirled. His arms struck out at space. He fell into a faint, with a gurgle in his throat, his chest crushed under an unbearable weight.

But, at a quarter to ten, with an effort of will, he picked himself up and, mastering himself and disregarding the pain, he went out by the other door of the house.

At ten o'clock, after twice changing his taxi, he arrived at the Boulevard Montmorency, just at the moment when Dr Géradec was alighting from his car and mounting the steps of the handsome villa in which his private hospital had been installed since the beginning of the war.

18

SIMÉON'S LAST VICTIM

Dr Géradec's hospital had several annexes, each of which served a specific purpose, grouped around it in a fine garden. The villa itself was used for the big operations. The doctor had his consulting-room here also; and it was to this room that Siméon Diodokis was first shown. But, after answering a few questions put to him by a male nurse, Siméon was taken to another room in a separate wing.

Here he was received by the doctor, a man of about sixty, still young in his movements, clean-shaven and wearing a glass screwed into his right eye, which contracted his features into a constant grimace. He was wrapped from the shoulders to the feet in a large white operating-apron.

Siméon explained his case with great difficulty, for he could hardly speak. A footpad had attacked him the night before, taken him by the throat and robbed him, leaving him half-dead in the road.

"You have had time to send for a doctor since," said Dr Géradec, fixing him with a glance.

Siméon did not reply; and the doctor added:

"However, it's nothing much. The fact that you are alive shows that there's no fracture. It reduces itself therefore to a contraction of the larynx, which we shall easily get rid of by tubing."

He gave his assistant some instructions. A long aluminum tube was inserted in the patient's wind-pipe. The doctor, who had absented himself meanwhile, returned and, after removing the tube, examined the patient, who was already beginning to breathe with greater ease.

"That's over," said Dr Géradec, "and much quicker than I expected. There was evidently in your case an inhibition which caused the throat to shrink. Go home now; and, when you've had a rest, you'll forget all about it."

Siméon asked what the fee was and paid it. But, as the doctor was seeing him to the door, he stopped and, without further preface, said:

"I am a friend of Mme. Albonin's."

The doctor did not seem to understand what he meant.

"Perhaps you don't recognize the name," Siméon insisted. "When I tell you, however, that it conceals the identity of Mme. Mosgranem, I have no doubt that we shall be able to arrange something."

"What about?" asked the doctor, while his face displayed still greater astonishment.

"Come, doctor, there's no need to be on your guard. We are alone. You have sound-proof, double doors. Sit down and let's talk."

He took a chair. The doctor sat down opposite him, looking more and more surprised. And Siméon proceeded with his statement:

"I am a Greek subject. Greece is a neutral; indeed, I may say, a friendly country; and I can easily obtain a passport and leave France. But, for personal reasons, I want the passport made out not in my own name but in some other, which you and I will decide upon together and which will enable me, with your assistance, to go away without any danger."

The doctor rose to his feet indignantly.

Siméon persisted:

"Oh, please don't be theatrical! It's a question of price, is it not? My mind is made up. How much do you want?"

The doctor pointed to the door.

Siméon raised no protest. He put on his hat. But, on reaching the door, he said:

"Twenty thousand francs? Is that enough?"

"Do you want me to ring?" asked the doctor, "and have you turned out?"

Siméon laughed and quietly, with a pause after each figure:

"Thirty thousand?" he asked. "Forty?... Fifty?... Oh, I see, we're playing a great game, we want a round sum... All right. Only, you know, everything must be included in the price we settle. You must not only fix me up a passport so genuine that it can't be disputed, but you must guarantee me the means of leaving France, as you did for Mme. Mosgranem, on terms not half so handsome, by Jove! However, I'm not haggling. I need your assistance. Is it a bargain? A hundred thousand francs?"

Dr Géradec bolted the door, came back, sat down at his desk and said, simply:

"We'll talk about it."

"I repeat the question," said Siméon, coming closer. "Are we agreed at a hundred thousand?"

"We are agreed," said the doctor, "unless any complications appear later."

"What do you mean?"

"I mean that the figure of a hundred thousand francs forms a suitable basis for discussion, that's all."

Siméon hesitated a second. The man struck him as rather greedy. However, he sat down once more; and the doctor at once resumed the conversation:

"Your real name, please."

"You mustn't ask me that. I tell you, there are reasons..."

"Then it will be two hundred thousand francs."

"Eh?" said Siméon, with a start. "I say, that's a bit steep! I never heard of such a price."

"You're not obliged to accept," replied Géradec, calmly. "We are discussing a bargain. You are free to do as you please."

"But, look here, once you agree to fix me up a false passport, what can it matter to you whether you know my name or not?"

"It matters a great deal. I run an infinitely greater risk in assisting the escape—for that's the only word—of a spy than I do in assisting the escape of a respectable man."

"I'm not a spy."

"How do I know? Look here, you come to me to propose a shady transaction. You conceal your name and your identity; and you're in such a hurry to disappear from sight that you're prepared to pay me a hundred thousand francs to help you. And, in the face of that, you lay claim to being a respectable man! Come, come! It's absurd! A respectable man does not behave like a burglar or a murderer."

Old Siméon did not wince. He slowly wiped his forehead with his handkerchief. He was evidently thinking that Géradec was a hardy antagonist and that he would perhaps have done better not to go to him. But, after all, the contract was a conditional one. There would always be time enough to break it off.

"I say, I say!" he said, with an attempt at a laugh. "You are using big words!"

"They're only words," said the doctor. "I am stating no hypothesis. I am content to sum up the position and to justify my demands."

"You're quite right."

"Then we're agreed?"

"Yes. Perhaps, however—and this is the last observation I propose to make—you might let me off more cheaply, considering that I'm a friend of Mme. Mosgranem's."

"What do you suggest by that?" asked the doctor.

"Mme. Mosgranem herself told me that you charged her nothing."

"That's true, I charged her nothing," replied the doctor, with a fatuous smile, "but perhaps she presented me with a good deal. Mme. Mosgranem was one of those attractive women whose favours command their own price."

There was a silence. Old Siméon seemed to feel more and more uncomfortable in his interlocutor's presence. At last the doctor sighed:

"Poor Mme. Mosgranem!"

"What makes you speak like that?" asked Siméon.

"What! Haven't you heard?"

"I have had no letters from her since she left."

"I see. I had one last night; and I was greatly surprised to learn that she was back in France."

"In France! Mme. Mosgranem!"

"Yes. And she even gave me an appointment for this morning, a very strange appointment."

"Where?" asked Siméon, with visible concern.

"You'll never guess. On a barge, yes, called the *Nonchalante*, moored at the Quai de Passy, alongside Berthou's Wharf."

"Is it possible?" said Siméon.

"It's as I tell you. And do you know how the letter was signed? It was signed Grégoire."

"Grégoire? A man's name?" muttered the old man, almost with a groan.

"Yes, a man's name. Look, I have the letter on me. She tells me that she is leading a very dangerous life, that she distrusts the man with whom her fortunes are bound up and that she would like to ask my advice."

"Then... then you went?"

"Yes, I was there this morning, while you were ringing up here. Unfortunately..."

"Well?"

"I arrived too late. Grégoire, or rather Mme. Mosgranem, was dead. She had been strangled."

"So you know nothing more than that?" asked Siméon, who seemed unable to get his words out.

"Nothing more about what?"

"About the man whom she mentioned."

"Yes, I do, for she told me his name in the letter. He's a Greek, who calls himself Siméon Diodokis. She even gave me a description of him. I haven't read it very carefully."

He unfolded the letter and ran his eyes down the second page, mumbling:

"A broken-down old man... Passes himself off as mad... Always goes about in a comforter and a pair of large yellow spectacles..."

Dr Géradec ceased reading and looked at Siméon with an air of amazement. Both of them sat for a moment without speaking. Then the doctor said:

"You are Siméon Diodokis."

The other did not protest. All these incidents were so strangely and, at the same time, so naturally interlinked as to persuade him that lying was useless.

"This alters the situation," declared the doctor. "The time for trifling is past. It's a most serious and terribly dangerous matter for me, I can tell you! You'll have to make it a million."

"Oh, no!" cried Siméon, excitedly. "Certainly not! Besides, I never touched Mme. Mosgranem. I was myself attacked by the man who strangled her, the same man—a negro called Ya-Bon—who caught me up and took me by the throat."

"Ya-Bon? Did you say Ya-Bon?"

"Yes, a one-armed Senegalese."

"And did you two fight?"

"Yes."

"And did you kill him?"

"Well..."

The doctor shrugged his shoulders with a smile:

"Listen, sir, to a curious coincidence. When I left the barge, I met half-a-dozen wounded soldiers. They spoke to me and said that they were looking for a comrade, this very Ya-Bon, and also for their captain, Captain Belval, and a friend of this officer's and a lady, the lady they were staying with. All these people had disappeared; and they accused a certain person... wait, they told me his name... Oh, but this is more and more curious! The man's name was Siméon Diodokis. It was you they accused!... Isn't it odd? But, on the other hand, you must confess that all this constitutes fresh facts and therefore..."

There was a pause. Then the doctor formulated his demand in plain tones:

"I shall want two millions."

This time Siméon remained impassive. He felt that he was in the man's clutches, like a mouse clawed by a cat. The doctor was playing with him, letting him go and catching him again, without giving him the least hope of escaping from this grim sport.

"This is blackmail," he said, quietly.

The doctor nodded:

"There's no other word for it," he admitted. "It's blackmail. Moreover, it's a case of blackmail in which I have not the excuse of creating the opportunity that gives me my advantage. A wonderful chance comes within reach of my hand. I grab at it, as you would do in my place. What else is possible? I have had a few differences, which you know of, with the police. We've signed a peace, the police and I. But my professional position has been so much injured that I cannot afford to reject with scorn what you so kindly bring me."

"Suppose I refuse to submit?"

"Then I shall telephone to the headquarters of police, with whom I stand in great favour at present, as I am able to do them a good turn now and again."

Siméon glanced at the window and at the door. The doctor had his hand on the receiver of the telephone. There was no way out of it.

"Very well," he declared. "After all, it's better so. You know me; and I know you. We can come to terms."

"On the basis suggested?"

"Yes. Tell me your plan."

"No, it's not worthwhile. I have my methods; and there's no object in revealing them beforehand. The point is to secure your escape and to put an end to your present danger. I'll answer for all that."

"What guarantee have I...?"

"You will pay me half the money now and the other half when the business is done. There remains the matter of the passport, a secondary matter for me. Still, we shall have to make one out. In what name is it to be?"

"Any name you like."

The doctor took a sheet of paper and wrote down the description, looking at Siméon between the phrases and muttering:

"Grey hair... Clean-shaven... Yellow spectacles..."

Then he stopped and asked:

"But how do I know that I shall be paid the money? That's essential, you know. I want bank-notes, real ones."

"You shall have them."

"Where are they?"

"In a hiding-place that can't be got at."

"Tell me where."

"I have no objection. Even if I give you a clue to the general position, you'll never find it."

"Well, go on."

"Grégoire had the money in her keeping, four million francs. It's on board the barge. We'll go there together and I'll count you out the first million."

"You say those millions are on board the barge?"

"Yes."

"And there are four of those millions?"

"Yes."

"I won't accept any of them in payment."

"Why not? You must be mad!"

"Why not? Because you can't pay a man with what already belongs to him."

"What's that you're saying?" cried Siméon, in dismay.

"Those four millions belong to me, so you can't offer them to me."

Siméon shrugged his shoulders:

"You're talking nonsense. For the money to belong to you, it must first be in your possession."

"Certainly."

"And is it?"

"It is."

"Explain yourself, explain yourself at once!" snarled Siméon, beside himself with anger and alarm.

"I will explain myself. The hiding-place that couldn't be got at consisted of four old books, back numbers of Bottin's directory for Paris and the provinces, each in two volumes. The four volumes were hollow inside, as though they had been scooped out; and there was a million francs in each of them."

"You lie! You lie!"

"They were on a shelf, in a little lumber-room next to the cabin."

"Well, what then?"

"What then? They're here."

"Here?"

"Yes, here, on that bookshelf, in front of your nose. So, in the circumstances, you see, as I am already the lawful owner, I can't accept..."

"You thief! You thief!" shouted Siméon, shaking with rage and clenching his fist. "You're nothing but a thief; and I'll make you disgorge. Oh, you dirty thief!"

Dr Géradec smiled very calmly and raised his hand in protest:

"This is strong language and quite unjustified! Quite unjustified! Let me remind you that Mme. Mosgranem honoured me with her affection. One day, or rather one morning, after a moment of expansiveness, 'My dear friend,' she said—she used to call me her dear friend—'my dear friend, when I die'—she was given to those gloomy forebodings—'when I die, I bequeath to you the contents of my home! ' Her home, at that moment, was the barge. Do you suggest that I should insult her memory by refusing to obey so sacred a wish?"

Old Siméon was not listening. An infernal thought was awakening in him; and he turned to the doctor with a movement of affrighted attention.

"We are wasting precious time, my dear sir," said the doctor. "What have you decided to do?"

He was playing with the sheet of paper on which he had written the particulars required for the passport. Siméon came up to him without a word. At last the old man whispered:

"Give me that sheet of paper... I want to see..."

He took the paper out of the doctor's hand, ran his eyes down it and suddenly leapt backwards:

"What name have you put? What name have you put? What right have you to give me that name? Why did you do it?"

"You told me to put any name I pleased, you know."

"But why this one? Why this one?"

"Can it be your own?"

The old man started with terror and, bending lower and lower over the doctor, said, in a trembling voice:

"One man alone, one man alone was capable of guessing..."

There was a long pause. Then the doctor gave a little chuckle:

"I know that only one man was capable of it. So let's take it that I'm the man."

"One man alone," continued the other, while his breath once again seemed to fail him, "one man alone could find the hiding-place of the four millions in a few seconds."

The doctor did not answer. He smiled; and his features gradually relaxed.

In a sort of terror-stricken tone Siméon hissed out:

"Arsène Lupin!... Arsène Lupin!..."

"You've hit it in one," exclaimed the doctor, rising.

He dropped his eye-glass, took from his pocket a little pot of grease, smeared his face with it, washed it off in a basin in a recess and reappeared with a clear skin, a smiling, bantering face and an easy carriage.

"Arsène Lupin!" repeated Siméon, petrified. "Arsène Lupin! I'm in for it!"

"Up to the neck, you old fool! And what a silly fool you must be! Why, you know me by reputation, you feel for me the intense and wholesome awe with which a decent man of my stamp is bound to inspire an old rascal like you... and you go and imagine that I should be ass enough to let myself be bottled up in that lethal chamber of yours! Mind you, at that very moment I could have taken you by the hair of the head and gone straight on to the great scene in the fifth act, which we are now playing. Only my fifth act would have been a bit short, you see; and I'm a born actor-manager. As it is, observe how well the interest is sustained! And what fun it was seeing the thought of it take birth in your old Turkish noddle! And what a lark to go into the studio, fasten my electric lamp to a bit of string, make poor, dear Patrice believe that I was there and go out and hear Patrice denying me three times and carefully bolting the door on... what? My electric lamp! That was all first-class work, don't you think? What do you say to it? I can feel that you're speechless with admiration... And, ten minutes after, when you came back, the same scene in the wings and with the same success. Of course, you old Siméon, I was banging at the walled-up door, between the studio and the bedroom on the left. Only I wasn't in the studio: I was in the bedroom; and you went away quietly, like a good kind landlord. As for me, I had no need to hurry. I was as certain as that twice two is four that you would go to your friend M. Amédée Vacherot, the porter. And here, I may say, old Siméon, you committed a nice piece of imprudence, which got me out of my difficulty. No one in the porter's lodge: that couldn't be helped; but what I did find was a telephone-number on a scrap of newspaper. I did not hesitate for a moment. I rang up the number, coolly: 'Monsieur, it was I who telephoned to you just now. Only I've got your number, but not your address.' Back came the answer: 'Dr Géradec, Boulevard de Montmorency. ' Then I understood. Dr Géradec? You would want your throat tubed for a bit, then the all-essential passport; and I came off here, without troubling about your poor friend M. Vacherot, whom you murdered in some corner or other to escape a possible give away on his side. And I saw Dr Géradec, a charming man, whose worries have made him very wise and submissive and who... lent me his place for the morning. I had still two hours before me. I went to the barge, took the millions, cleared up a few odds and ends and here I am!"

He came and stood in front of the old man:

"Well, are you ready?" he asked.

Siméon, who seemed absorbed in thought, gave a start.

"Ready for what?" said Don Luis, replying to his unspoken question. "Why, for the great journey, of course! Your passport is in order. Your ticket's taken: Paris to Hell, single. Non-stop hearse. Sleeping-coffin. Step in, sir!"

The old man, tottering on his legs, made an effort and stammered:

"And Patrice?"

"What about him?"

"I offer you his life in exchange for my own."

Don Luis folded his arms across his chest:

"Well, of all the cheek! Patrice is a friend; and you think me capable of abandoning him like that? Do you see me, Lupin, making more or less witty jokes upon your imminent death while my friend Patrice is in danger? Old Siméon, you're getting played out. It's time you went and rested in a better world."

He lifted a hanging, opened a door and called out:

"Well, captain, how are you getting on? Ah, I see you've recovered consciousness! Are you surprised to see me? No, no thanks, but please come in here. Our old Siméon's asking for you."

Then, turning to the old man, he said:

"Here's your son, you unnatural father!"

Patrice entered the room with his head bandaged, for the blow which Siméon had struck him and the weight of the tombstone had opened his old wounds. He was very pale and seemed to be in great pain.

At the sight of Siméon Diodokis he gave signs of terrible anger. He controlled himself, however. The two men stood facing each other, without stirring, and Don Luis, rubbing his hands, said, in an undertone:

"What a scene! What a splendid scene? Isn't it well-arranged? The father and the son! The murderer and his victim! Listen to the orchestra!... A slight tremolo... What are they going to do? Will the son kill his father or the father kill his son? A thrilling moment... And the mighty silence! Only the call of the blood is heard... and in what terms! Now we're off! The call of the blood has sounded; and they are going to throw themselves into each other's arms, the better to strangle the life out of each other!"

Patrice had taken two steps forward; and the movement suggested by Don Luis was about to be performed. Already the officer's arms were flung wide for the fight. But suddenly Siméon, weakened by pain and dominated by a stronger will than his own, let himself go and implored his adversary:

"Patrice!" he entreated. "Patrice! What are you thinking of doing?"

Stretching out his hands, he threw himself upon the other's pity; and Patrice, arrested in his onrush, stood perplexed, staring at the man to whom he was bound by so mysterious and strange a tie:

"Coralie," he said, without lowering his hands, "Coralie... tell me where she is and I'll spare your life."

The old man started. His evil nature was stimulated by the remembrance of Coralie; and he recovered a part of his energy at the possibility of wrong-doing. He gave a cruel laugh:

"No, no," he answered. "Coralie in one scale and I in the other? I'd rather die. Besides, Coralie's hiding-place is where the gold is. No, never! I may just as well die."

"Kill him then, captain," said Don Luis, intervening. "Kill him, since he prefers it."

Once more the thought of immediate murder and revenge sent the red blood rushing to the officer's face. But the same hesitation unnerved him.

"No, no," he said, in a low voice, "I can't do it."

"Why not?" Don Luis insisted. "It's so easy. Come along! Wring his neck, like a chicken's, and have done with it!"

"I can't."

"But why? Do you dislike the thought of strangling him? Does it repel you? And yet, if it were a Boche, on the battlefield..."

"Yes... but this man...

"Is it your hands that refuse? The idea of taking hold of the flesh and squeezing?... Here, captain, take my revolver and blow out his brains."

Patrice accepted the weapon eagerly and aimed it at old Siméon. The silence was appalling. Old Siméon's eyes had closed and drops of sweat were streaming down his livid cheeks.

At last the officer lowered his arm:

"I can't do it," he said.

"Nonsense," said Don Luis. "Get on with the work."

"No... No..."

"But, in Heaven's name, why not?"

"I can't."

"You can't? Shall I tell you the reason? You are thinking of that man as if he were your father."

"Perhaps it's that," said the officer, speaking very low. "There's a chance of it, you know."

"What does it matter, if he's a beast and a blackguard?"

"No, no, I haven't the right. Let him die by all means, but not by my hand. I haven't the right."

"You have the right."

"No, it would be abominable! It would be monstrous!"

Don Luis went up to him and, tapping him on the shoulder, said, gravely:

"You surely don't believe that I should stand here, urging you to kill that man, if he were your father?"

Patrice looked at him wildly:

"Do you know something? Do you know something for certain? Oh, for Heaven's sake...!"

Don Luis continued:

"Do you believe that I would even encourage you to hate him, if he were your father?"

"Oh!" exclaimed Patrice. "Do you mean that he's not my father?"

"Of course he's not!" cried Don Luis, with irresistible conviction and increasing eagerness. "Your father indeed! Why, look at him! Look at that scoundrelly head. Every sort of vice and violence is written on the brute's face. Throughout this adventure, from the first day to the last, there was not a crime committed but was his handiwork: not one, do you follow me? There were not two criminals, as we thought, not Essarès, to begin the hellish business, and old Siméon, to finish it. There was only one criminal, one, do you understand, Patrice? Before killing Coralie and Ya-Bon and Vacherot the porter and the woman who was his own accomplice, he killed others! He killed one other in particular, one whose flesh and blood you are, the man whose dying cries you heard over the telephone, the man who called you Patrice and who only lived for you! He killed that man; and that man was your father, Patrice; he was Armand Belval! Now do you understand?"

Patrice did not understand. Don Luis' words fell uncomprehended; not one of them lit up the darkness of Patrice's brain. However, one thought insistently possessed him; and he stammered:

"*That* was my father? I heard his voice, you say? Then it was *he* who called to me?"

"Yes, Patrice, your father."

"And the man who killed him...?"

"Was this one," said Don Luis, pointing to Siméon.

The old man remained motionless, wild-eyed, like a felon awaiting sentence of death. Patrice, quivering with rage, stared at him fixedly:

"Who are you? Who are you?" he asked. And, turning to Don Luis, "Tell me his name, I beseech you. I want to know his name, before I destroy him."

"His name? Haven't you guessed it yet? Why, from the very first day, I took it for granted! After all, it was the only possible theory."

"But what theory? What was it you took for granted?" cried Patrice, impatiently.

"Do you really want to know?"

"Oh, please! I'm longing to kill him, but I must first know his name."

"Well, then..."

There was a long silence between the two men, as they stood close together, looking into each other's eyes. Then Lupin let fall these four syllables:

"Essarès Bey."

Patrice felt a shock that ran through him from head to foot. Not for a second did he try to understand by what prodigy this revelation came to be merely an expression of the truth. He instantly accepted this truth, as though it were undeniable and proved by the most evident facts. The man was Essarès Bey and had killed his father. He had killed him, so to speak, twice over: first years ago, in the lodge in the garden, taking from him all the light of life and any reason for living; and again the other day, in the library, when Armand Belval had telephoned to his son.

This time Patrice was determined to do the deed. His eyes expressed an indomitable resolution. His father's murderer, Coralie's murderer, must die then and there. His duty was clear and precise. The terrible Essarès was doomed to die by the hand of the son and the bridegroom.

"Say your prayers," said Patrice, coldly. "In ten seconds you will be a dead man."

He counted out the seconds and, at the tenth, was about to fire, when his enemy, in an access of mad energy proving that, under the outward appearance of old Siméon, there was hidden a man still young and vigorous, shouted with a violence so extraordinary that it made Patrice hesitate:

"Very well, kill me!... Yes, let it be finished!... I am beaten: I accept defeat. But it is a victory all the same, because Coralie is dead and my gold is saved!... I shall die, but nobody shall have either one or the other, the woman whom I love or the gold that was my life. Ah, Patrice, Patrice, the woman whom we both loved to distraction is no longer alive... or else she is dying without a possibility of saving her now. If I cannot have her, you shall not have her either, Patrice. My revenge has done its work. Coralie is lost!"

He had recovered a fierce energy and was shouting and stammering at the same time. Patrice stood opposite him, holding him covered with the revolver, ready to act, but still waiting to hear the terrible words that tortured him.

"She is lost, Patrice!" Siméon continued, raising his voice still louder. "Lost! There's nothing to be done! And you will not find even her body in the bowels of the earth, where I buried her with the bags of gold. Under the tombstone? No, not such a fool! No, Patrice, you will never find her. The gold is stifling her. She's dead! Coralie is dead! Oh, the delight of throwing that in your face! The anguish you must be feeling! Coralie is dead! Coralie is dead!"

"Don't shout so, you'll wake her," said Don Luis, calmly.

The brief sentence was followed by a sort of stupor which paralyzed the two adversaries. Patrice's arms dropped to his sides. Siméon turned giddy and sank into a chair. Both of them, knowing the things of which Don Luis was capable, knew what he meant.

But Patrice wanted something more than a vague sentence that might just as easily be taken as a jest. He wanted a certainty.

"Wake her?" he asked, in a broken voice.

"Well, of course!" said Don Luis. "When you shout too loud, you wake people up."

"Then she's alive?"

"You can't wake the dead, whatever people may say. You can only wake the living."

"Coralie is alive! Coralie is alive!" Patrice repeated, in a sort of rapture that transfigured his features. "Can it be possible? But then she must be here! Oh, I beg of you, say you're in earnest, give me your word!... Or no, it's not true, is it? I can't believe it... you must be joking..."

"Let me answer you, captain, as I answered that wretch just now. You are admitting that it is possible for me to abandon my work before completing it. How little you know me! What I undertake to do I do. It's one of my habits and a good one at that. That's why I cling to it. Now watch me."

He turned to one side of the room. Opposite the hanging that covered the door by which Patrice had entered was a second curtain, concealing another door. He lifted the curtain.

"No, no, she's not there," said Patrice, in an almost inaudible voice. "I dare not believe it. The disappointment would be too great. Swear to me..."

"I swear nothing, captain. You have only to open your eyes. By Jove, for a French officer, you're cutting a pretty figure! Why, you're as white as a sheet! Of course it's she! It's Little Mother Coralie! Look, she's in bed asleep, with two nurses to watch her. But there's no danger; she's not wounded. A bit of a temperature, that's all, and extreme weakness. Poor Little Mother Coralie! I never could have imagined her in such a state of exhaustion and coma."

Patrice had stepped forward, brimming over with joy. Don Luis stopped him:

"That will do, captain. Don't go any nearer. I brought her here, instead of taking her home, because I thought a change of scene and atmosphere essential. But she must have no excitement. She's had her share of that; and you might spoil everything by showing yourself."

"You're right," said Patrice. "But are you quite sure...?"

"That she's alive?" asked Don Luis, laughing. "She's as much alive as you or I and quite ready to give you the happiness you deserve and to change her name to Mme. Patrice Belval. You must have just a little patience, that's all. And there is yet one obstacle to overcome, captain, for remember she's a married woman!"

He closed the door and led Patrice back to Essarès Bey:

"There's the obstacle, captain. Is your mind made up now? This wretch still stands between you and your Coralie."

Essarès had not even glanced into the next room, as though he knew that there could be no doubt about Don Luis' word. He sat shivering in his chair, cowering, weak and helpless.

"You don't seem comfortable," said Don Luis. "What's worrying you? You're frightened, perhaps? What for? I promise you that we will do nothing except by mutual consent and until we are all of the same opinion. That ought to cheer you up. We'll be your judges, the three of us, here and now. Captain Patrice Belval, Arsène Lupin and old Siméon will form the court. Let the trial begin. Does anyone wish to speak in defence of the prisoner at the bar, Essarès Bey? No one. The prisoner at the bar is sentenced to death. Extenuating circumstances? No notice of appeal? No. Commutation of sentence? No. Reprieve? No. Immediate execution? Yes. You see, there's no delay. What about the means of death? A revolver-shot? That will do. It's clean, quick work. Captain Belval, your bird. The gun's loaded. Here you are."

Patrice did not move. He stood gazing at the foul brute who had done him so many injuries. His whole being seethed with hatred. Nevertheless, he replied:

"I will not kill that man."

"I agree, captain. Your scruples do you honour. You have not the right to kill a man whom you know to be the husband of the woman you love. It is not for you to remove the obstacle. Besides, you hate taking life. So do I. This animal is too filthy for words. And so, my good man, there's no one left but yourself to help us out of this delicate position."

Don Luis ceased speaking for a moment and leant over Essarès. Had the wretched man heard? Was he even alive? He looked as if he were in a faint, deprived of consciousness.

Don Luis shook him by the shoulder.

"The gold," moaned Essarès, "the bags of gold..."

"Oh, you're thinking of that, you old scoundrel, are you? You're still interested? The bags of gold are in my pocket... if a pocket can contain eighteen hundred bags of gold."

"The hiding-place?"

"Your hiding-place? It doesn't exist, so far as I'm concerned. I needn't prove it to you, need I, since Coralie's here? As Coralie was buried among the bags of gold, you can draw your own conclusion. So you're nicely done. The woman you wanted is free and, what is worse still, free by the side of the man whom she adores and whom she will never leave. And, on the other hand, your treasure is discovered. So it's all finished, eh? We are agreed? Come, here's the toy that will release you."

He handed him the revolver. Essarès took it mechanically and pointed it at Don Luis; but his arm lacked the strength to take aim and fell by his side.

"Capital!" said Don Luis. "We understand each other; and the action which you are about to perform will atone for your evil life, you old blackguard. When a man's last hope is dispelled, there's nothing for it but death. That's the final refuge."

He took hold of the other's hand and, bending Essarès' nerveless fingers round the revolver, forced him to point it towards his own face.

"Come," said he, "just a little pluck. What you've resolved to do is a very good thing. As Captain Belval and I refuse to disgrace ourselves by killing you, you've decided to do the job yourself. We are touched; and we congratulate you. But you must behave with courage. No resistance, come! That's right, that's much more like it. Once more, my compliments. It's very smart, your manner of getting out of it. You perceive that there's no room for you on earth, that you're standing in the way of Patrice and Coralie and that the best thing you can do is to retire. And you're jolly well right! No love and no gold! No gold, Siméon! The beautiful shiny coins which you coveted, with which you would have managed to secure a nice, comfortable existence, all fled, vanished! You may just as well vanish yourself, what?"

Whether because he felt himself to be helpless or because he really understood that Don Luis was right and that his life was no longer worth living, Siméon offered hardly any resistance. The revolver rose to his forehead. The barrel touched his temple.

At the touch of the cold steel he gave a moan:

"Mercy!"

"No, no, no!" said Don Luis. "You mustn't show yourself any mercy. And I won't help you either. Perhaps, if you hadn't killed my poor Ya-Bon, we might have put our heads together and sought for another ending. But, honestly, you inspire me with no more pity than you feel for yourself. You want to die and you are right. I won't prevent you. Besides, your passport is made out; you've got your ticket in your pocket. They are expecting you down below. And, you know, you need have no fear of being bored. Have you ever seen a picture of Hell? Everyone has a huge stone over his tomb; and everyone is lifting the stone and supporting it with his back, in order to escape the flames bursting forth beneath him. You see, there's plenty of fun. Well, your grave is reserved. Bath's ready, sir!"

Slowly and patiently he had succeeded in slipping the wretched man's fore-finger under the handle, so as to bring it against the trigger. Essarès was letting himself go. He was little more than a limp rag. Death had already cast its shadow upon him.

"Mind you," said Don Luis, "you're perfectly free. You can pull the trigger if you feel like it. It's not my business. I'm not here to compel you to commit suicide, but only to advise you and to lend you a hand."

He had in fact let go the fore-finger and was holding only the arm. But he was bearing upon Essarès with all his extraordinary power of will, the will to seek destruction, the will to seek annihilation, an indomitable will which Essarès was unable to resist. Every second death sank a little deeper into that invertebrate body, breaking up instinct, obscuring thought and bringing an immense craving for rest and inaction.

"You see how easy it is. The intoxication is flying to your brain. It's an almost voluptuous feeling, isn't it? What a riddance! To cease living! To cease suffering! To cease thinking of that gold which you no longer possess and can never possess again, of that woman who belongs to another and offers him her lips and all her entrancing self!... You couldn't live, could you, with that thought on you? Then come on!..."

Seized with cowardice, the wretch was yielding by slow degrees. He found himself face to face with one of those crushing forces, one of nature's forces, powerful as fate, which a man must needs accept. His head turned giddy and swam. He was descending into the abyss.

"Come along now, show yourself a man. Don't forget either that you are dead already. Remember, you can't appear in this world again without falling into the hands of the police. And, of course, I'm there to inform them in case of need. That means prison and the scaffold. The scaffold, my poor fellow, the icy dawn, the knife..."

It was over. Essarès was sinking into the depths of darkness. Everything whirled around him. Don Luis' will penetrated him and annihilated his own.

For one moment he turned to Patrice and tried to implore his aid. But Patrice persisted in his impassive attitude. Standing with his arms folded, he gazed with eyes devoid of pity upon his father's murderer. The punishment was well-deserved. Fate must be allowed to take its course. Patrice did not interfere.

And Don Luis continued, unrelentingly and without intermission:

"Come along, come along!... It's a mere nothing and it means eternal rest!... How good it feels, already! To forget! To cease fighting!... Think of the gold which you have lost... Three hundred millions gone for ever!... And Coralie lost as well. Mother and daughter: you can't have either. In that case, life is nothing but a snare and a delusion. You may as well leave it. Come, one little effort, one little movement..."

That little movement the miscreant made. Hardly knowing what he did, he pulled the trigger. The shot rang through the room; and Essarès fell forward, with his knees on the floor. Don Luis had to spring to one side to escape being splashed by the blood that trickled from the man's shattered head.

"By Jove!" he cried. "The blood of vermin like that would have brought me ill-luck. And, Lord, what crawling vermin it is!... Upon my word, I believe that this makes one more good action I've done in my life and that this suicide entitles me to a little seat in Paradise. What say you, captain?"

19

FIAT LUX!

On the evening of the same day, Patrice was pacing up and down the Quai de Passy. It was nearly six o'clock. From time to time, a tram-car passed, or some motor-lorry. There were very few people about on foot. Patrice had the pavement almost to himself.

He had not seen Don Luis Perenna since the morning, had merely received a line in which Don Luis asked him to have Ya-Bon's body moved into the Essarès' house and afterwards to meet him on the quay above Berthou's Wharf. The time appointed for the meeting was near at hand and Patrice was looking forward to this interview in which the truth would be revealed to him at last. He partly guessed the truth, but no little darkness and any number of unsolved problems remained. The tragedy was played out. The curtain had fallen on the villain's death. All was well: there was nothing more to fear, no more pitfalls in store for them. The formidable enemy was laid low. But Patrice's anxiety was intense as he waited for the moment when light would be cast freely and fully upon the tragedy.

"A few words," he said to himself, "a few words from that incredible person known as Arsène Lupin, will clear up the mystery. It will not take him long. He will be gone in an hour. Will he take the secret of the gold with him, I wonder? Will he solve the secret of the golden triangle for me? And how will he keep the gold for himself? How will he take it away?"

A motor-car arrived from the direction of the Trocadéro. It slowed down and stopped beside the pavement. It must be Don Luis, thought Patrice. But, to his great surprise, he recognized M. Masseron, who opened the door and came towards him with outstretched hand:

"Well, captain, how are you? I'm punctual for the appointment, am I not? But, I say, have you been wounded in the head again?"

"Yes, an accident of no importance," replied Patrice. "But what appointment are you speaking of?"

"Why, the one you gave me, of course!"

"I gave you no appointment."

"Oh, I say!" said M. Masseron. "What does this mean? Why, here's the note they brought me at the police-office: 'Captain Belval's compliments to M. Masseron. The problem of the golden triangle is solved. The eighteen hundred bags are at his disposal. Will he please come to the Quai de Passy, at six o'clock, with full powers from the government to accept the conditions of delivery. It would be well if he brought with him twenty powerful detectives, of whom half should be posted a hundred yards on one side of Essarès' property and the other half on the other.' There you are. Is it clear?"

"Perfectly clear," said Patrice, "but I never sent you that note."

"Who sent it then?"

"An extraordinary man who deciphered all those problems like so many children's riddles and who certainly will be here himself to bring you the solution."

"What's his name?"

"I sha'n't say."

"Oh, I don't know about that! Secrets are hard to keep in war time."

"Very easy, on the contrary, sir," said a voice behind M. Masseron. "All you need do is to make up your mind to it."

M. Masseron and Patrice turned round and saw a gentleman dressed in a long, black overcoat, cut like a frock-coat, and a tall collar which gave him a look of an English clergyman.

"This is the friend I was speaking of," said Patrice, though he had some difficulty in recognizing Don Luis. "He twice saved my life and also that of the lady whom I am going to marry. I will answer for him in every respect."

M. Masseron bowed; and Don Luis at once began, speaking with a slight accent:

"Sir, your time is valuable and so is mine, for I am leaving Paris tonight and France tomorrow. My explanation therefore will be brief. I will pass over the drama itself, of which you have followed the main vicissitudes so far. It came to an end this morning. Captain Belval will tell you all about it. I will merely add that our poor Ya-Bon is dead and that you will find three other bodies: that of Grégoire, whose real name was Mme. Mosgranem, in the barge over there; that of one Vacherot, a hall-porter, in some corner of a block of flats at 18, Rue Guimard; and lastly the body of Siméon Diodokis, in Dr Géradec's private hospital on the Boulevard de Montmorency."

"Old Siméon?" asked M. Masseron in great surprise.

"Old Siméon has killed himself. Captain Belval will give you every possible information about that person and his real identity; and I think you will agree with me that this business will have to be hushed up. But, as I said, we will pass over all this. There remains the question of the gold, which, if I am not mistaken, interests you more than anything else. Have you brought your men?"

"Yes, I have. But why? The hiding-place, even after you have told me where it is, will be what it was before, undiscovered by those who do not know it."

"Certainly; but, as the number of those who do know it increases, the secret may slip out. In any case that is one of my two conditions."

"As you see, it is accepted. What is the other?"

"A more serious condition, sir, so serious indeed that, whatever powers may have been conferred upon you, I doubt whether they will be sufficient."

"Let me hear; then we shall see."

"Very well."

And Don Luis, speaking in a phlegmatic tone, as though he were telling the most unimportant story, calmly set forth his incredible proposal:

"Two months ago, sir, thanks to my connection with the Near East and to my influence in certain Ottoman circles, I persuaded the clique which rules Turkey today to accept the idea of a separate peace. It was simply a question of a few hundred millions for distribution. I had the offer transmitted to the Allies, who rejected it, certainly not for financial reasons, but for reasons of policy, which it is not for me to judge. But I am not content to suffer this little diplomatic check. I failed in my first negotiation; I do not mean to fail in the second. That is why I am taking my precautions."

He paused and then resumed, while his voice took on a rather more serious tone:

"At this moment, in April, 1915, as you are well aware, conferences are in progress between the Allies and the last of the great European powers that has remained neutral. These conferences are going to succeed; and they will succeed because the future of that power demands it and because the whole nation is uplifted with enthusiasm. Among the questions raised is one which forms the object of a certain divergency of opinion. I mean the question of money. This foreign power is asking us for a loan of three hundred million francs in gold, while making it quite clear that a refusal on our part would in no way affect a decision which is already irrevocably taken. Well, I have three hundred millions in gold; I have them at my command; and I desire to place them at the disposal of our new allies. This is my second and, in reality, my only condition."

M. Masseron seemed utterly taken aback:

"But, my dear sir," he said, "these are matters quite outside our province; they must be examined and decided by others, not by us."

"Everyone has the right to dispose of his money as he pleases."

M. Masseron made a gesture of distress:

"Come, sir, think a moment. You yourself said that this power was only putting forward the question as a secondary one."

"Yes, but the mere fact that it is being discussed will delay the conclusion of the agreement for a few days."

"Well, a few days will make no difference, surely?"

"Sir, a few hours *will* make a difference."

"But why?"

"For a reason which you do not know and which nobody knows... except myself and a few people some fifteen hundred miles away."

"What reason?"

"The Russians have no munitions left."

M. Masseron shrugged his shoulders impatiently. What had all this to do with the matter?

"The Russians have no munitions left," repeated Don Luis. "Now there is a tremendous battle being fought over there, a battle which will be decided not many hours hence. The Russian front will be broken and the Russian troops will retreat and retreat... Heaven knows when they'll stop retreating! Of course, this assured, this inevitable contingency will have no influence on the wishes of the great power of which we are talking. Nevertheless, that nation has in its midst a very considerable party on the side of neutrality, a party which is held in check, but none the less violent for that. Think what a weapon you will place in its hands by postponing the agreement! Think of the difficulties which you are making for rulers preparing to go to war! It would be an unpardonable mistake, from which I wish to save my country. That is why I have laid down this condition."

M. Masseron seemed quite discomforted. Waving his hands and shaking his head, he mumbled:

"It's impossible. Such a condition as that will never be accepted. It will take time, it will need discussion..."

A hand was laid on his arm by someone who had come up a moment before and who had listened to Don Luis' little speech. Its owner had alighted from a car which was waiting some way off; and, to Patrice's great astonishment, his presence had aroused no opposition on the part of either M. Masseron or Don Luis Perenna. He was a man well-advanced in years, with a powerful, lined face.

"My dear Masseron," he said, "it seems to me that you are not looking at the question from the right point of view."

"That's what I think, monsieur le president," said Don Luis.

"Ah, do you know me, sir?"

"M. Valenglay, I believe? I had the honor of calling on you some years ago, sir, when you were president of the council."

"Yes, I thought I remembered... though I can't say exactly..."

"Please don't tax your memory, sir. The past does not concern us. What matters is that you should be of my opinion."

"I don't know that I am of your opinion. But I consider that this makes no difference. And that is what I was telling you, my dear Masseron. It's not a question of knowing whether you ought to discuss this gentleman's conditions. It's a question of accepting them or refusing them without discussion. There's no bargain to be driven in the circumstances. A bargain presupposes that each party has something to offer. Now we have no offer to make, whereas this gentleman comes with his offer in his hand and says, 'Would you like three hundred million francs in gold? In that case you must do so-and-so with it. If that doesn't suit you, good evening.' That's the position, isn't it, Masseron?"

"Yes, monsieur le president."

"Well, can you dispense with our friend here? Can you, without his assistance, find the place where the gold is hidden? Observe that he makes things very easy for you by bringing you to the place and almost pointing out the exact spot to you. Is that enough? Have you any hope of discovering the secret which you have been seeking for weeks and months?"

M. Masseron was very frank in his reply:

"No, monsieur le president," he said, plainly and without hesitation.

"Well, then..."

And, turning to Don Luis:

"And you, sir," Valenglay asked, "is it your last word?"

"My last word."

"If we refuse... good evening?"

"You have stated the case precisely, monsieur le president."

"And, if we accept, will the gold be handed over at once?"

"At once."

"We accept."

And, after a slight pause, he repeated:

"We accept. The ambassador shall receive his instructions this evening."

"Do you give me your word, sir?"

"I give you my word."

"In that case, we are agreed."

"We are agreed. Now then!..."

All these sentences were uttered rapidly. Not five minutes had elapsed since the former prime minister had appeared upon the scene. Nothing remained to do but for Don Luis to keep his promise.

It was a solemn moment. The four men were standing close together, like acquaintances who have met in the course of a walk and who stop for a minute to exchange their news. Valenglay, leaning with one arm on the parapet overlooking the lower quay, had his face turned to the river and kept raising and lowering his cane above the sand-heap. Patrice and M. Masseron stood silent, with faces a little set.

Don Luis gave a laugh:

"Don't be too sure, monsieur le president," he said, "that I shall make the gold rise from the ground with a magic wand or show you a cave in which the bags lie stacked. I always thought those words, 'the golden triangle,' misleading, because they suggest something mysterious and fabulous. Now according to me it was simply a question of the space containing the gold, which space would have the shape of a triangle. The golden triangle, that's it: bags of gold arranged in a triangle, a triangular site. The reality is much simpler, therefore; and you will perhaps be disappointed."

"I sha'n't be," said Valenglay, "if you put me with my face towards the eighteen hundred bags of gold."

"You're that now, sir."

"What do you mean?"

"Exactly what I say. Short of touching the bags of gold, it would be difficult to be nearer to them than you are."

For all his self-control, Valenglay could not conceal his surprise:

"You are not suggesting, I suppose, that I am walking on gold and that we have only to lift up the flags of the pavement or to break down this parapet?"

"That would be removing obstacles, sir, whereas there is no obstacle between you and what you are seeking."

"No obstacle!"

"None, monsieur le président, for you have only to make the least little movement in order to touch the bags."

"The least little movement!" said Valenglay, mechanically repeating Don Luis' words.

"I call a little movement what one can make without an effort, almost without stirring, such as dipping one's stick into a sheet of water, for instance, or..."

"Or what?"

"Well, or a heap of sand."

Valenglay remained silent and impassive, with at most a slight shiver passing across his shoulders. He did not make the suggested movement. He had no need to make it. He understood.

The others also did not speak a word, struck dumb by the simplicity of the amazing truth which had suddenly flashed upon them like lightning. And, amid this silence, unbroken by protest or sign of incredulity, Don Luis went on quietly talking:

"If you had the least doubt, monsieur le président—and I see that you have not—you would dig your cane, no great distance, twenty inches at most, into the sand beneath you. You would then encounter a resistance which would compel you to stop. That is the bags of gold. There ought to be eighteen hundred of them; and, as you see, they do not make an enormous heap. A kilogram of gold represents three thousand one hundred francs. Therefore, according to my calculation, a bag containing approximately fifty kilograms, or one hundred and fifty-five thousand francs done up in rouleaus of a thousand francs, is not a very large bag. Piled one against the other and one on top of the other, the bags represent a bulk of about fifteen cubic yards, no more. If you shape the mass roughly like a triangular pyramid you will have a base each of whose sides would be three yards long at most, or three yards and a half allowing for the space lost between the rouleaus of coins. The height will be that of the wall, nearly. Cover the whole with a layer of sand and you have the heap which lies before your eyes..."

Don Luis paused once more before continuing:

"And which has been there for months, monsieur le président, safe from discovery not only by those who were looking for it, but also by accident on the part of a casual passer-by. Just think, a heap of sand! Who would dream of digging a hole in it to see what is going on inside? The dogs sniff at it, the children play beside it and make mudpies, an occasional tramp lies down against it and takes a snooze. The rain softens it, the sun hardens it, the snow whitens it all over; but all this happens on the surface, in the part that shows. Inside reigns impenetrable mystery, darkness unexplored. There is not a hiding-place in the world to equal the inside of a sand heap exposed to view in a public place. The man who thought of using it to hide three hundred millions of gold, monsieur le président, knew what he was about."

The late prime minister had listened to Don Luis' explanation without interrupting him. When Don Luis had finished, Valenglay nodded his head once or twice and said:

"He did indeed. But there is one man who is cleverer still."

"I don't believe it."

"Yes, there's the man who guessed that the heap of sand concealed the three hundred million francs. That man is a master, before whom we must all bow."

Flattered by the compliment, Don Luis raised his hat. Valenglay gave him his hand:

"I can think of no reward worthy of the service which you have done the country."

"I ask for no reward," said Don Luis.

"I daresay, sir, but I should wish you at least to be thanked by voices that carry more weight than mine."

"Is it really necessary, monsieur le président?"

"I consider it essential. May I also confess that I am curious to learn how you discovered the secret? I should be glad, therefore, if you would call at my department in an hour's time."

"I am very sorry, sir, but I shall be gone in fifteen minutes."

"No, no, you can't go like this," said Valenglay, with authority.

"Why not, sir?"

"Well, because we don't know your name or anything about you."

"That makes so little difference!"

"In peacetime, perhaps. But, in wartime, it won't do at all."

"Surely, monsieur le président, you will make an exception in my case?"

"An exception, indeed? What next?"

"Suppose it's the reward which I ask, will you refuse me then?"

"It's the only one which we are obliged to refuse you. However, you won't ask for it. A good citizen like yourself understands the constraints to which everybody is bound to submit. My dear Masseron, arrange it with this gentleman. At the department in an hour from now. Goodbye till then, sir. I shall expect you."

And, after a very civil bow, he walked away to his car, twirling his stick gaily and escorted by M. Masseron.

"Well, on my soul!" chuckled Don Luis. "There's a character for you! In the twinkling of an eye, he accepts three hundred millions in gold, signs an epoch-making treaty and orders the arrest of Arsène Lupin!"

"What do you mean?" cried Patrice, startled out of his life. "Your arrest?"

"Well, he orders me to appear before him, to produce my papers and the devil knows what."

"But that's monstrous!"

"It's the law of the land, my dear captain. We must bow to it."

"But..."

"Captain, believe me when I say that a few little worries of this sort deprive me of none of the whole-hearted satisfaction which I feel at rendering this great service to my country.

I wanted, during the war, to do something for France and to make the most of the time which I was able to devote to her during my stay. I've done it. And then I have another reward: the four millions. For I think highly enough of your Coralie to believe her incapable of wishing to touch this money... which is really her property."

"I'll go bail for her over that."

"Thank you. And you may be sure that the gift will be well employed. So everything is settled. I have still a few minutes to give you. Let us turn them to good account. M. Masseron is collecting his men by now. To simplify their task and avoid a scandal, we'll go down to the lower quay, by the sand-heap. It'll be easier for him to collar me there."

"I accept your few minutes," said Patrice, as they went down the steps. "But first of all I want to apologize..."

"For what? For behaving a little treacherously and locking me into the studio of the lodge? You couldn't help yourself: you were trying to assist your Coralie. For thinking me capable of keeping the treasure on the day when I discovered it? You couldn't help that either: how could you imagine that Arsène Lupin would despise three hundred million francs?"

"Very well, no apologies," said Patrice, laughing. "But all my thanks."

"For what? For saving your life and saving Coralie's? Don't thank me. It's a hobby of mine, saving people."

Patrice took Don Luis' hand and pressed it firmly. Then, in a chaffing tone which hid his emotion, he said:

"Then I won't thank you. I won't tell you that you rid me of a hideous nightmare by letting me know that I was not that monster's son and by unveiling his real identity. I will not tell you either that I am a happy man now that life is opening radiantly before me, with Coralie free to love me. No, we won't talk of it. But shall I confess to you that my happiness is still a little—what shall I say?—a little dim, a little timid? I no longer feel any doubt; but in spite of all, I don't quite understand the truth, and, until I do understand it, the truth will cause me some anxiety. So tell me... explain to me... I want to know..."

"And yet the truth is so obvious!" cried Don Luis. "The most complex truths are always so simple! Look here, don't you understand anything? Just think of the way in which the problem is set. For sixteen or eighteen years, Siméon Diodokis behaves like a perfect friend, devoted to the pitch of self-denial, in short, like a father. He has not a thought, outside that of his revenge, but to secure your happiness and Coralie's. He wants to bring you together. He collects your photographs. He follows the whole course of your life. He almost gets into touch with you. He sends you the key of the garden and prepares a meeting. Then, suddenly, a complete change takes place. He becomes your inveterate enemy and thinks of nothing but killing the pair of you. What is there that separates those two states of mind? One fact, that's all, or rather one date, the night of the third of April and the tragedy that takes place that night and the following day at Essarès' house. Until that date, you were Siméon Diodokis' son. After that date, you were Siméon Diodokis' greatest enemy. Does that suggest nothing to you? It's really curious. As for me, all my discoveries are due to this general view of the case which I took from the beginning."

Patrice shook his head without replying. He did not understand. The riddle retained a part of its unfathomable secret.

"Sit down there," said Don Luis, "on our famous sand-heap, and listen to me. It won't take me ten minutes."

They were on Berthou's Wharf. The light was beginning to wane and the outlines on the opposite bank of the river were becoming indistinct. The barge rocked lazily at the edge of the quay.

Don Luis expressed himself in the following terms:

"On the evening when, from the inner gallery of the library, you witnessed the tragedy at Essarès' house, you saw before your eyes two men bound by their accomplices: Essarès Bey and Siméon Diodokis. They are both dead. One of them was your father. Let us speak first of the other. Essarès Bey's position was a critical one that evening. After draining our gold currency on behalf of an eastern power, he was trying to filch the remainder of the millions of francs collected. The *Belle Hélène*, summoned by the rain of sparks, was lying moored alongside Berthou's Wharf. The gold was to be shifted at night from the sand-bags to the motor-barge. All was going well, when the accomplices, warned by Siméon, broke in. Thereupon we have the blackmailing-scene, Colonel Fakhi's death and so on, with Essarès learning at one and the same time that his accomplices knew of his schemes and his plan to pilfer the gold and also that Colonel Fakhi had informed the police about him. He was cornered. What could he do? Run away? But, in wartime, running away is almost impossible. Besides, running away meant giving up the gold and likewise giving up Coralie, which would never have done. So there was only one thing, to disappear from sight. To disappear from sight and yet to remain there, on the battlefield, near the gold and near Coralie. Night came; and he employed it in carrying out his plan. So much for Essarès. We now come to Siméon Diodokis."

Don Luis stopped to take breath. Patrice had been listening eagerly, as though each word had brought its share of light into the oppressive darkness.

"The man who was known as old Siméon," continued Don Luis, "that is to say, your father, Armand Belval, a former victim, together with Coralie's mother, of Essarès Bey, had also reached a turning-point of his career. He was nearly achieving his object. He had betrayed and delivered his enemy, Essarès, into the hands of Colonel Fakhi and the accomplices. He had succeeded in bringing you and Coralie together. He had sent you the key of the lodge. He was justified in hoping that, in a few days more, everything would end according to his wishes. But, next morning, on waking, certain indications unknown to me revealed to him a threatening danger; and he no doubt foresaw the plan which Essarès was engaged in elaborating. And he too put himself the same question: What was he to do? What was there for him to do? He must warn you, warn you without delay, telephone to you at once. For time was pressing, the danger was becoming definite. Essarès was watching and hunting down the man whom he had chosen as his victim for the second time. You can picture Siméon possibly feeling himself pursued and locking himself into the library. You can picture him wondering whether he would ever be able to telephone to you and whether you would be there. He asks for you. He calls out to you. Essarès hammers away at the door. And your father, gasping for breath, shouts, 'Is that you, Patrice? Have you the key?... And the letter?... No?... But this is terrible! Then you don't know'... And then a hoarse cry, which you hear at your end of the wire, and incoherent noises, the sound of an altercation. And then the lips gluing themselves to the instrument and stammering words at random: 'Patrice, the amethyst pendant... Patrice, I should so much have liked... Patrice, Coralie!' Then a loud scream... cries that grow weaker and weaker... silence, and that is all. Your father is dead, murdered. This time, Essarès Bey, who had failed before, in the lodge, took his revenge on his old rival."

"Oh, my unhappy father!" murmured Patrice, in great distress.

"Yes, it was he. That was at nineteen minutes past seven in the morning, as you noted. A few minutes later, eager to know and understand, you yourself rang up; and it was Essarès who replied, with your father's dead body at his feet."

"Oh, the scoundrel! So that this body, which we did not find and were not able to find..."

"Was simply made up by Essarès, made up, disfigured, transformed into his own likeness. That, captain, is how—and the whole mystery lies in this—Siméon Diodokis, dead, became Essarès Bey, while Essarès Bey, transformed into Siméon Diodokis, played the part of Siméon Diodokis."

"Yes," said Patrice, "I see, I understand."

"As to the relations existing between the two men," continued Don Luis, "I am not certain. Essarès may or may not have known before that old Siméon was none other than his former rival, the lover of Coralie's mother, the man in short who had escaped death. He may or may not have known that Siméon was your father. These are points which will never be decided and which, moreover, do not matter. What I do take for granted is that this new murder was not improvised on the spot. I firmly believe that Essarès, having noticed certain similarities in height and figure, had made every preparation to take Siméon's place if circumstances obliged him to disappear. And it was easily done. Siméon Diodokis wore a wig and no beard. Essarès, on the contrary, was bald-headed and had a beard. He shaved himself, smashed Siméon's face against the grate, mingled the hairs of his own beard with the bleeding mass, dressed the body in his clothes, took his victim's clothes for himself, put on the wig, the spectacles and the comforter. The transformation was complete."

Patrice thought for a moment. Then he raised an objection:

"Yes, that's what happened at nineteen minutes past seven. But something else happened at twenty-three minutes past twelve."

"No, nothing at all."

"But that clock, which stopped at twenty-three minutes past twelve?"

"I tell you, nothing happened at all. Only, he had to put people off the scent. He had above all to avoid the inevitable accusation that would have been brought against the new Siméon."

"What accusation?"

"What accusation? Why, that he had killed Essarès Bey, of course! A dead body is discovered in the morning. Who has committed the murder? Suspicion would at once have fallen on Siméon. He would have been questioned and arrested. And Essarès would have been found under Siméon's mask. No, he needed liberty and facilities to move about as he pleased. To achieve this, he kept the murder concealed all the morning and arranged so that no one set foot in the library. He went three times and knocked at his wife's door, so that she should say that Essarès Bey was still alive during the morning. Then, when she went out, he raised his voice and ordered Siméon, in other words himself, to see her to the hospital in the Champs-Élysées. And in this way Mme. Essarès thought that she was leaving her husband behind her alive and that she was escorted by old Siméon, whereas actually she was leaving old Siméon's corpse in an empty part of the house and was escorted by her husband. Then what happened? What the rascal had planned. At one o'clock, the police, acting on the information laid by Colonel Fakhi, arrived and found themselves in the presence of a corpse. Whose corpse? There was not a shadow of hesitation on that point. The maids recognized their master; and, when Mme. Essarès returned, it was her husband whom she saw lying in front of the fireplace at which he had been tortured the night before. Old Siméon, that is to say, Essarès himself, helped to establish the identification. You yourself were taken in. The trick was played."

"Yes," said Patrice, nodding his head, "that is how things must have gone. They all fit in."

"The trick was played," Don Luis repeated, "and nobody could make out how it was done. Was there not this further proof, the letter written in Essarès' own hand and found on his desk? The letter was dated at twelve o'clock on the fourth of April, addressed to his wife, and told her that he was going away. Better still, the trick was so successfully played that the very clues which ought to have revealed the truth merely concealed it. For instance, your father used to carry a tiny album of photographs in a pocket stitched inside his under-vest. Essarès did not notice it and did not remove the vest from the body. Well, when they found the album, they at once accepted that most unlikely hypothesis: Essarès Bey carrying on his person an album filled with photographs of his wife and Captain Belval! In the same way, when they found in the dead man's hand an amethyst pendant containing your two latest photographs and when they also found a crumpled paper with something on it about the golden triangle, they at once admitted that Essarès Bey had stolen the pendant and the document and was holding them in his hand when he died! So absolutely certain were they all that it was Essarès Bey who had been murdered, that his dead body lay before their eyes and that they must not trouble about the question any longer. And in this way the new Siméon was master of the situation. Essarès Bey is dead, long live Siméon!"

Don Luis indulged in a hearty laugh. The adventure struck him as really amusing.

"Then and there," he went on, "Essarès, behind his impenetrable mask, set to work. That very day he listened to your conversation with Coralie and, overcome with fury at seeing you bend over her, fired a shot from his revolver. But, when this new attempt failed, he ran away and played an elaborate comedy near the little door in the garden, crying murder, tossing the key over the wall to lay a false scent and falling to the ground half dead, as though he had been strangled by the enemy who was supposed to have fired the shot. The comedy ended with a skilful assumption of madness."

"But what was the object of this madness?"

"What was the object? Why, to make people leave him alone and keep them from questioning him or suspecting him. Once he was looked upon as mad, he could remain silent and unobserved. Otherwise, Mme. Essarès would have recognized his voice at the first words he spoke, however cleverly he might have altered his tone. From this time onward, he is mad. He is an irresponsible being. He goes about as he pleases. He is a madman! And his madness is so thoroughly admitted that he leads you, so to speak, by the hand to his former accomplices and causes you to have them arrested, without asking yourself for an instant if this madman is not acting with the clearest possible sense of his own interest. He's a madman, a poor, harmless madman, one of those unfortunates with whom nobody dreams of interfering. Henceforth, he has only his last two adversaries to fight: Coralie and you. And this is an easy matter for him. I presume that he got hold of a diary kept by your father. At any rate, he knows every day of the one which you keep. From this he learns the whole story of the graves; and he knows that, on the fourteenth of April, Coralie and you are both going on a pilgrimage to those graves. Besides, he plans to make you go there, for his plot is laid. He prepares against the son and the daughter, against the Patrice and Coralie of today, the attempt which he once prepared against the father and the mother. The attempt succeeds at the start. It would have succeeded to the end, but for an idea that occurred to our poor Ya-Bon, thanks to which a new adversary, in the person of myself, entered the lists... But I need hardly go on. You know the rest as well as I do; and, like myself, you can judge in all his glory the inhuman villain who, in the space of those twenty-four hours, allowed his accomplice Grégoire to be strangled, buried your Coralie under the sand-heap, killed Ya-Bon, locked me in the lodge, or thought he did, buried you alive in the grave dug by your father and made away with Vacherot, the porter. And now, Captain Belval, do you think that I ought to have prevented him from committing suicide, this pretty gentleman who, in the last resort, was trying to pass himself off as your father?"

"You were right," said Patrice. "You have been right all through, from start to finish. I see it all now, as a whole and in every detail. Only one point remains: the golden triangle. How did you find out the truth? What was it that brought you to this sand-heap and enabled you to save Coralie from the most awful death?"

"Oh, that part was even simpler," replied Don Luis, "and the light came almost without my knowing it! I'll tell it you in a few words. But let us move away first. M. Masseron and his men are becoming a little troublesome."

The detectives were distributed at the two entrances to Berthou's Wharf. M. Masseron was giving them his instructions. He was obviously speaking to them of Don Luis and preparing to accost him.

"Let's get on the barge," said Don Luis. "I've left some important papers there."

Patrice followed him. Opposite the cabin containing Grégoire's body was another cabin, reached by the same companion-way. It was furnished with a table and a chair.

"Here, captain," said Don Luis, taking a letter from the drawer of the table and settling it, "is a letter which I will ask you to... but don't let us waste words. I shall hardly have time to satisfy your curiosity. Our friends are coming nearer. Well, we were saying, the golden triangle..."

He listened to what was happening outside with an attention whose real meaning Patrice was soon to understand. And, continuing to give ear, he resumed:

"The golden triangle? There are problems which we solve more or less by accident, without trying. We are guided to a right solution by external events, among which we choose unconsciously, feeling our way in the dark, examining this one, thrusting aside that one and suddenly beholding the object aimed at... Well, this morning, after taking you to the tombs and burying you under the stone, Essarès Bey came back to me. Believing me to be locked into the studio, he had the pretty thought to turn on the gas-meter and then went off to the quay above Berthou's Wharf. Here he hesitated; and his hesitation provided me with a precious clue. He was certainly then thinking of releasing Coralie. People passed and he went away. Knowing where he was going, I returned to your assistance, told your friends at Essarès' house and asked them to look after you. Then I came back here. Indeed, the whole course of events obliged me to come back. It was unlikely that the bags of gold were inside the conduit; and, as the *Belle Hélène* had not taken them off, they must be beyond the garden, outside the conduit and therefore somewhere near here. I explored the barge we are now on, not so much with the object of looking for the bags as with the hope of finding some unexpected piece of information and also, I confess, the four millions in Grégoire's possession. Well, when I start exploring a place where I fail to find what I want, I always remember that capital story of Edgar Allan Poe's, *The Purloined Letter.* Do you recollect? The stolen diplomatic document which was known to be hidden in a certain room. The police investigate every nook and corner of the room and take up all the boards of the floor, without results. But Dupin arrives and almost immediately goes to a card-rack dangling from a little brass knob on the wall and containing a solitary soiled and crumpled letter. This is the document of which he was in search. Well, I instinctively adopted the same process. I looked where no one would dream of looking, in places which do not constitute a hiding-place because it would really be too easy to discover. This gave me the idea of turning the pages of four old directories standing in a row on that shelf. The four millions were there. And I knew all that I wanted to know."

"About what?"

"About Essarès' temperament, his habits, the extent of his attainments, his notion of a good hiding-place. We had plunged on the expectation of meeting with difficulties; we ought to have looked at the outside, to have looked at the surface of things. I was assisted by two further clues. I had noticed that the uprights of the ladder which Ya-Bon must have taken from here had a few grains of sand on them. Lastly, I remembered that Ya-Bon had drawn a triangle on the pavement with a piece of chalk and that this triangle had only two sides, the third side being formed by the foot of the wall. Why this detail? Why not a third line in chalk?... To make a long story short, I lit a cigarette, sat down upstairs, on the deck of the barge, and, looking round me, said to myself, 'Lupin, my son, five minutes and no more.' When I say, 'Lupin, my son,' I simply can't resist myself. By the time I had smoked a quarter of the cigarette, I was there."

"You had found out?"

"I had found out. I can't say which of the factors at my disposal kindled the spark. No doubt it was all of them together. It's a rather complicated psychological operation, you know, like a chemical experiment. The correct idea is formed suddenly by mysterious reactions and combinations among the elements in which it existed in a potential stage. And then I was carrying within myself an intuitive principle, a very special incentive which obliged me, which inevitably compelled me, to discover the hiding-place: Little Mother Coralie was there! I knew for certain that failure on my part, prolonged weakness or hesitation would mean her destruction. There was a woman there, within a radius of a dozen yards or so. I had to find out and I found out. The spark was kindled. The elements combined. And I made straight for the sand-heap. I at once saw the marks of footsteps and, almost at the top, the signs of a slight stamping. I started digging. You can imagine my excitement when I first touched one of the bags. But I had no time for excitement. I shifted a few bags. Coralie was there, unconscious, hardly protected from the sand which was slowly stifling her, trickling through, stopping up her eyes, suffocating her. I needn't tell you more, need I? The wharf was deserted, as usual. I got her out. I hailed a taxi. I first took her home. Then I turned my attention to Essarès, to Vacherot the porter; and, when I had discovered our enemy's plans, I went and made my arrangements with Dr Géradec. Lastly, I had you moved to the private hospital on the Boulevard de Montmorency and gave orders for Coralie to be taken there too. And there you are, captain! All done in three hours. When the doctor's car brought me back to the hospital, Essarès arrived at the same time, to have his injuries seen to. I had him safe."

Don Luis ceased speaking. There were no words necessary between the two men. One had done the other the greatest services which a man has it in his power to render; and the other knew that these were services for which no thanks are adequate. And he also knew that he would never have an opportunity to prove his gratitude. Don Luis was in a manner above those proofs, owing to the mere fact that they were impossible. There was no service to be rendered to a man like him, disposing of his resources and performing miracles with the same ease with which we perform the trivial actions of everyday life.

Patrice once again pressed his hand warmly, without a word. Don Luis accepted the homage of this silent emotion and said:

"If ever people talk of Arsène Lupin before you, captain, say a good word for him, won't you? He deserves it." And he added, with a laugh, "It's funny, but, as I get on in life, I find myself caring about my reputation. The devil was old, the devil a monk would be!"

He pricked up his ears and, after a moment, said:

"Captain, it is time for us to part. Present my respects to Little Mother Coralie. I shall not have known her, so to speak, and she will not know me. It is better so. Goodbye, captain."

"Then we are taking leave of each other?"

"Yes, I hear M. Masseron. Go to him, will you, and have the kindness to bring him here?"

Patrice hesitated. Why was Don Luis sending him to meet M. Masseron? Was it so that he, Patrice, might intervene in his favour?

The idea appealed to him; and he ran up the companion-way.

Then a thing happened which Patrice was destined never to understand, something very quick and quite inexplicable. It was as though a long and gloomy adventure were to finish suddenly with melodramatic unexpectedness.

Patrice met M. Masseron on the deck of the barge.

"Is your friend here?" asked the magistrate.

"Yes. But one word first: you don't mean to...?"

"Have no fear. We shall do him no harm, on the contrary."

The answer was so definite that the officer could find nothing more to say. M. Masseron went down first, with Patrice following him.

"Hullo!" said Patrice. "I left the cabin-door open!"

He pushed the door. It opened. But Don Luis was no longer in the cabin.

Immediate enquiries showed that no one had seen him go, neither the men remaining on the wharf nor those who had already crossed the gangway.

"When you have time to examine this barge thoroughly," said Patrice, "I've no doubt you will find it pretty nicely faked."

"So your friend has probably escaped through some trap-door and swum away?" asked M. Masseron, who seemed greatly annoyed.

"I expect so," said Patrice, laughing. "Unless he's gone off on a submarine!"

"A submarine in the Seine?"

"Why not? I don't believe that there's any limit to my friend's resourcefulness and determination."

But what completely dumbfounded M. Masseron was the discovery, on the table, of a letter directed to himself, the letter which Don Luis had placed there at the beginning of his interview with Patrice.

"Then he knew that I should come here? He foresaw, even before we met, that I should ask him to fulfil certain formalities?"

The letter ran as follows:

"*Sir*,

"Forgive my departure and believe that I, on my side, quite understand the reason that brings you here. My position is not in fact regular; and you are entitled to ask me for an explanation. I will give you that explanation some day or other. You will then see that, if I serve France in a manner of my own, that manner is not a bad one and that my country will owe me some gratitude for the immense services, if I may venture to use the word, which I have done her during this war. On the day of our interview, I should like you to thank me, sir. You will then—for I know your secret ambition—be Prefect of police. Perhaps I shall even be able personally to forward a nomination which I consider well-deserved. I will exert myself in that direction without delay.

"I have the honour to be, etc."

M. Masseron remained silent for a time.

"A strange character!" he said, at last. "Had he been willing, we should have given him great things to do. That was what I was instructed to tell him."

"You may be sure, sir," said Patrice, "that the things which he is actually doing are greater still." And he added, "A strange character, as you say. And stranger still, more powerful and more extraordinary than you can imagine. If each of the allied nations had had three or four men of his stamp at its disposal, the war would have been over in six months."

"I quite agree," said M. Masseron. "Only those men are usually solitary, intractable people, who act solely upon their own judgment and refuse to accept any authority. I'll tell you what: they're something like that famous adventurer who, a few years ago, compelled the Kaiser to visit him in prison and obtain his release... and afterwards, owing to a disappointment in love, threw himself into the sea from the cliffs at Capri."

"Who was that?"

"Oh, you know the fellow's name as well as I do!... Lupin, that's it: Arsène Lupin."